Also from Ken Vanderpool

WHEN THE MUSIC DIES

FACE THE MUSIC

FACE THE MUSIC

Ken Vanderpool

Copyright © 2014 Ken Vanderpool

All rights reserved.

This book may not be reproduced or transmitted in whole or in part, through any means electronic or mechanical including photo copying or electronic transmission without prior written permission from the author, except short excerpts considered normal for review.

This story is a work of fiction. All the names, characters, places, organizations and incidents are either products of the author's imagination or are used fictitiously. Any resemblance to actual persons, living or dead, businesses, establishments, companies, events, or locales is entirely coincidental.

ISBN 978-0-9903655-0-1

Printed in the United States of America

Cover and Interior Design
By Sandra Vanderpool

Dedication

For my wife Sandra - my love and my biggest fan.

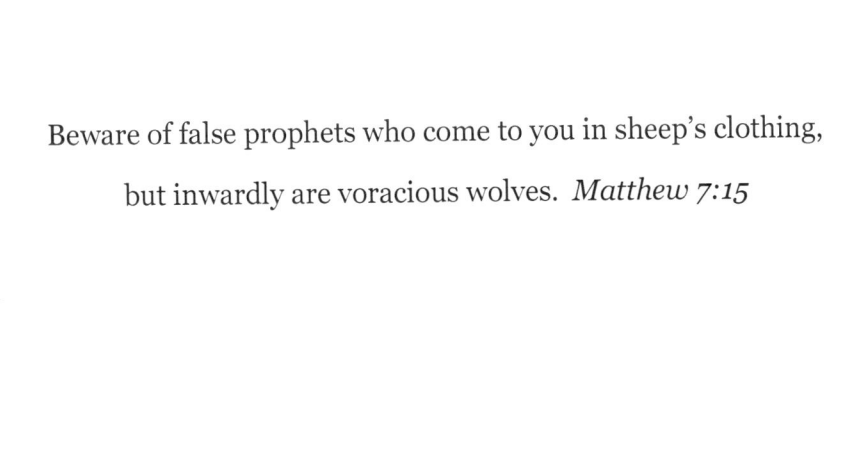

Beware of false prophets who come to you in sheep's clothing, but inwardly are voracious wolves. *Matthew 7:15*

PROLOGUE

The Bowles Estate
Belle Meade
Nashville, Tennessee
May 30, 2005

I can't believe she has the audacity to think she can seduce my father and pilfer a share of my inheritance. After the hell I've been through—there is no damn way.
 He tugged on the starched cuffs of his white shirt and straightened his suit jacket. He'd turned the oversized Natuzzi Italian leather chair away from the massive stone fireplace. It now offered him a direct line of sight to the kitchen door which opened in from her four-car garage. His pistol lay on the broad padded arm of the chair forward of his gloved right hand. After checking his wristwatch off and on for most of an hour, he heard the jolt of the garage door as it was yanked upward to allow her Silver Mercedes to enter.
 He pulled the mask down so it covered his face. Too many nights alone watching action movies convinced him the mask was a good idea.
 He wrapped his hand around the pistol's knurled grip and drew in another large breath. Beneath the mask, his untested

confidence provided him an anxious smile. He was in control and intended to remain there for however long it took.

The electric garage door began its return trip. At the same moment it met the cold concrete floor, she unlocked and pushed open the kitchen door. In the small hallway, she turned and kicked the door closed with a well-worn burgundy Prada. The scent of her Chanel preceded her. She set her purse and two plastic bags filled with groceries on the granite counter and reached for the light switch.

"Leave the light off," he said, speaking as if in casual conversation.

She shrieked at the sound of his voice and flipped up the switch.

He aimed the 9mm Smith & Wesson and pulled the trigger. The ceiling light exploded, filled the kitchen with small pieces of translucent glass, and returned the room to semi-darkness.

She screamed again, louder this time, and dropped to a squat with her hands over her ears. The thunderous report of the pistol had momentarily deafened them both.

He swallowed in an attempt to regain his hearing. "I told you to leave it off. You need to follow directions."

Meredith Bowles stood before him silent, cringing in her pink two-piece suit, her chest rising and falling with labored breaths.

"Put your hands up, where I can see them."

She made no effort to respond.

"If you don't want to be scattered across the kitchen like the light fixture," he raised his voice, "I suggest you consider doing as I tell you."

She lifted her hands and held them on either side of her pricey hairdresser's handiwork. "What do you want? I have money and jewelry—diamonds. Take them. Just don't hurt me, please."

"Don't hurt me. Seriously? Maybe you should have thought about that before *you* started hurting other people."

"I don't know what you're talking about."

"Of course, you don't. You would have to give a damn first, wouldn't you?" He stared at her through the small cut-out holes in the plastic mask.

"I—I don't understand."

He stood.

She stepped back as he approached.

"In your self-absorbed effort to catch and reel in a prosperous replacement for the late Senator Sumner Bowles, you are callously trampling on the lives of others. Your desperate search for another cash cow, or should I say *bull*, is not going unnoticed."

"I don't know what you mean."

"Bullshit!" he shouted. "Quit playing stupid."

She cringed and took another step backward.

"You know damned well what I'm talking about." He ripped off the mask.

Her apparent lack of surprise confirmed she'd already determined his identity.

"Why are you doing this?" She lowered her hands.

He extended the semi-automatic and raised his aim to just above her augmented crimson lips. "Don't." His brow rutted. "Keep your hands *up* where I can see them."

"Look. Let's talk about this. If I've hurt you in some way, I'm sorry. It was not my intent."

"I know all about your damned intent. But, I'm here to put a stop to it. You see, all the money you planned to suck up into your private account; it's not going to make the trip."

"I don't need your father's—"

"Please," he interrupted her. "Spare me the lying socialite rhetoric. It doesn't work on me. I know what you have and what you don't have. Your beloved late senator husband didn't leave you with shit except this debt-free mansion, which you've reverse mortgaged in order to support your pleasured existence. You sold off your diamonds two years ago and replaced them in the settings with fakes. '*No one will notice,*'" he mocked her. "I know your jeweler."

She offered no retort.

"You're realizing as you receive the depleting balance statements on this estate; it alone will not continue to support you and your high-living habits forever. You have to find another source of funds before you lose *it*, and your aging looks. So, you've gone on a mission to find yourself a horny surrogate with plenty of cash."

"I love your father," she said with her chin lifted in defiance.

"You love *money* and the lifestyle large amounts of it can offer you. He just happens to *own* what you love."

"That's not true."

"You'd have a hard time convincing anyone otherwise." He looked around the house and then back at her. "It's time to bring your deceitful scheme to a halt."

"If you think I'm going to stop seeing your father, you're mistaken. He loves me, and I love him too much to allow you to ruin it for us."

"You can drop the phony devotion."

"We've discussed getting married in the fall."

"You what?" He wasn't ready for this disgusting revelation.

"We've begun making plans," she announced. "Your father was going to tell you as soon as we'd set a date."

This was the kind of thing he'd hoped to prevent. He stared into her eyes, seeing in his vision the future and all that would change if this unthinkable union took place.

"Your father is happier now than he's been since before Pamela went craz—." She stopped herself.

"Since what?" His face reflected the adrenaline surge. "You have *no right* to speak my mother's name with those lying red lips." His eyes flared beneath his wrinkled brow. Her cruel words caused his entire body to stiffen.

"I'm sorry—" Her mouth flared before her self-serving apology was complete. An incredulous expression overtook her face. Gravity pulled her body to the ceramic tile floor.

He clenched his teeth as he watched the red pattern expand across her white silk blouse. He knew she was dead. He wasn't sure if he'd shot her for his mother or for himself.

"You're *what*?" He shouted as he looked down at her frozen wide-eyed stare. "You're sorry you said that about my mother? Too late—you gold-digging bitch."

He squatted and removed her jewelry, then stood and examined it in his hand. "Who wears this gaudy shit?" He looked over the rings and the huge gold pin he'd ripped from her jacket. "More fakes, no doubt." He shoved the trinkets into his pocket.

Before her arrival, he'd ransacked her closets and pulled open drawers throughout the home, stirring their contents to create the appearance of a break-in. He pocketed the jewelry he'd found in her dressing room.

He moved fast in case her distant neighbors heard the gunshots. He emptied her purse onto the granite island in the center of the kitchen. After pushing aside the makeup and the miscellaneous female junk, he gathered her money, her checkbook and her credit cards to help sell the crime scene as the result of another Belle Meade burglary turned robbery.

Satisfied, he exited the rear of the home through the sliding glass door, the same door he'd pried open after spotting the green light on the security panel by the kitchen door.

As he climbed the wooded hill at the rear of the mansion's ten acre lot, he tugged at his gloves and considered what he'd done. He'd preserved his mother's honor, and he was confident he'd protected his inheritance. His father would just have to get over it.

CHAPTER 1

Eight Years Later

East Nashville

Homicide Sergeant Mike Neal leaned closer to the small monitor. He squinted as he focused on the hazy digital video recording made by the Briarcliff Apartments spider web-covered camera. He ran the DVR playback at half speed so he wouldn't miss anything.

A young wife, Cynthia Gaston, was leaving the East Nashville apartment she shared with her husband, apparently headed to the market. It was late. Her husband worked second shift at a local book bindery. It was April 21st, their second wedding anniversary. She was preparing red velvet cake; her Bobby's all time favorite.

Mounted high beneath Building D's eight-vehicle carport, the camera's obscure video images showed twenty-six year old Cynthia, her purse in her left hand and car keys in her right, approaching the couple's six year old beige Japanese sedan from the rear. The white numerals at the bottom corner of the monitor's screen displayed the time as 22:12.

Mike slowed the recording even more on his seventh viewing. She unlocked the driver's side door with the remote keyless entry. As she pulled the door open, a stocky man with a dark complexion wearing a navy blue hooded sweatshirt rushed in from behind her. He grabbed her door with his gloved hand and slammed it hard against her body. The impact caused her head to strike the upper door frame.

The assailant snatched a hand full of her shoulder-length dark brown hair and jerked her head back, granting him control of her body. With his other hand covering her mouth, he dragged her away from the car. There was no sound with the video recording, but Mike was confident Cynthia was screaming beneath the man's hand. The car door swung closed behind them.

The attacker held his face close to Cynthia's. He appeared to be talking as he pulled her backward toward the apartment building. His head swiveled side to side, no doubt surveying the area for witnesses. It was during his scan of the parking area that the camera captured the blurred image of his face. Mike stopped the recording.

"Print me a couple of screen shots of this," he instructed the apartment manager.

"Yes sir."

From this point, Cynthia and her attacker exited the camera's field of view and nothing else was definite, except the young woman's rape and subsequent fatal stabbing.

"Can you burn two DVDs with the time from 8:00pm to 1:00am?"

"Yes sir. Is this all you need?" the apartment manager asked.

"I hope so," Mike said. "Capture them at normal speed and make sure they're as clear as you can make them."

"Yes sir. Sorry the image is cloudy."

"I've had to work with worse. Thanks." Mike yawned as he stood and stretched. He rubbed his face with both hands trying to fight off fatigue.

According to the report from the first officer on the scene, Cynthia's body was discovered at about 23:45 by her husband when he arrived home from work. The 911 call was registered at the emergency call center at 23:51.

Once Bobby Gaston recovered enough to talk with Mike, the first officer stepped outside to allow the two men some privacy. They sat across from each other at the couple's small kitchen table.

The pleasant sweet aroma of freshly baked cake remained in the air, fighting with the scent of the gruesome reality that had taken place less than fifty feet away.

While answering Mike's questions, Gaston's tear-filled gaze scanned the room where he and his bride had shared her southern cooking and their plans for the future. Appearing distracted, he stopped in the middle of an answer and stood. He walked to the kitchen counter. He stared at the three layers of dark red cake cooling on Cynthia's bakery racks. As he picked up a package of cream cheese that set opened on the counter, he broke down.

Mike walked to where the young man leaned against the counter. "What is it, Bob?"

Through his tears, Gaston seemed to struggle for his answer. "The only reason ... she could have ... for leaving the apartment that late," he paused sobbing, "was to replace the cream cheese she needed for her icing. She knew how much I loved her red velvet cake."

He watched the young man and allowed him time to collect himself.

Mike had witnessed so many distraught spouses and families as they fought to deal with the violent death of a family member. He felt their pain more than most since he too had lost family and friends to extreme violence. The horrific murder that always came to mind whenever a homicide victim was a young woman was that of his seventeen year old sister. Connie Neal was raped and brutally murdered nine years ago this month. It still hurt.

"I used that package of cream cheese last Sunday to mix a batch of dip while I watched the game. She wasn't here. I didn't know she had plans for it." He held his face in his hands. "I can't believe this," he sobbed. "It's my fault. It's all my fault."

Mike put his hand on Gaston's shoulder.

"She did it for me," he said. "She could have asked me to pick it up on the way home, but she wanted to surprise me, and I blew it. God, I want to die." Gaston struggled for breath as he spoke.

"Bob, you know Cynthia wouldn't want you thinking like this. This is not your fault."

"It's not *her* fault," Gaston said. "She was just trying to please me."

"I know. We're going to catch the bastard who did this."

Mike turned away from Gaston for a moment and punched into his cell phone the number for the police department's chaplain on call. He asked Gaston for his parents' number and gave it to the chaplain.

Mike kept Gaston's mind occupied with questions while they waited for his parents and the chaplain to arrive.

When the young man's mother and father came through the door, Mike heard Gaston moan like an injured wolf calling for his pack. The three of them met in the middle of the room and, physically leaning against each other for support, broke down and sobbed together.

"What am I gonna tell her parents, Daddy?" Gaston panted. "What am I gonna tell them?"

While the Gastons tried to comfort their son, Mike shared what he could with the chaplain so he might be better able to answer the parents' questions later.

The chaplain spoke with the senior Gaston and explained that it was best for them to take their son away from the crime scene as soon as possible.

With the Gastons on their way to the parents' home, Cynthia's body now with the Medical Examiner, and the Crime Scene Unit almost finished with their collection of evidence; Mike looked at his watch and decided he should leave before he dropped from lack of sleep.

On the slow drive to his home in the Green Hills area of Nashville, Mike recalled the night in 1994 when his father picked him up at the airport following his flight from Iraq after notification of Connie's death. He hadn't seen his little sister in almost two years, and his father asked him if he would identify her body for the police. His father's request hit him like a sucker punch. Mike hadn't considered the unbearable task. Rather than put his father through it, he conceded.

Connie's horrifying image on the stainless steel gurney was burned into his memory. He knew as dreadful as that experience was for him, Bobby Gaston's shocking discovery of his slaughtered wife in their bed had to be a hundred times worse.

"God help me find the *animal* who killed his wife," Mike prayed, "and please help Bobby Gaston get through this."

CHAPTER 2

Brentwood
South Nashville

Attorney Tyler McKinnon's secondhand Lexus descended the backside of the hill into the fifty-year-old subdivision populated with large ranch style homes. Dinner with his friend and client Al Ricks had included a few too many drinks. He was glad he was almost home.

Four bright headlights shot from the darkness as they crested the hilltop behind him. The intense blue halogen beams flooded his mirrors and blinded him.

"What the...?" He squinted in order to make out the road before him.

The car was inches from Tyler's rear bumper. He scowled at his mirror and wondered if this clown was as drunk as he was.

Tyler's windows were down to take in the cool night air in the hope it would keep him alert enough to make it home safely. He could hear the roar of the trailing car's engine swell each time it swerved into the oncoming lane. Tyler slowed to let the hostile driver pass.

As the car pulled alongside him, the driver reduced his speed to match Tyler's.

"What the hell are you waiting for?"

Tyler glanced to his left as the car's dark tinted window dropped into the passenger side door. He could barely make out the driver's silhouette. Tyler checked the roadway ahead and was about to challenge the aggressive driver's intellect when he saw the flash in his peripheral vision.

The weight of Tyler's lifeless torso tugged at the steering wheel enough to send his car plowing through the manicured lawn of his next-door neighbor, across Tyler's front lawn and directly into his favorite old oak tree in his own front yard.

CHAPTER 3

Green Hills
Nashville

Mike stepped into the small kitchen and closed the back door of his 1950s era bungalow. He slipped off his tweed sport coat and carefully draped it over the back of a kitchen chair as if it was a gentleman's valet stand. He flipped through his snail mail from the past two days and tossed it all on the kitchen counter. He blinked several times on his way to the bedroom in an attempt to clear the strain from his overworked eyes.

Home from the Gaston crime scene, he was ready for a nap and a hot shower before he returned to his escalating workload. As tired as he was, he decided to shower first.

His desire for cleansing was more psychological than physical. He'd spent so much time at last night's crime scene he felt he had a veneer of the carnage covering him.

He stepped into his bathtub and invited the shower's near-scalding water to beat his rigid neck and shoulder muscles back to normal. He relaxed for a moment. As he stepped off the edge of the tub's textured surface, his foot slipped. Suddenly wide awake, he extended his arms to catch himself between the wall and the shower curtain. He found his balance.

The near accident caused him to recall a distressing evening almost a year ago. He thought of his father.

From an active crime scene, he'd called home to check on his dad; it was something he did several times each day. He got no answer. After three successive calls, the priority of his elderly father's safety moved ahead of the current domestic homicide investigation. Mike turned the crime scene over to his partner and raced home.

He'd moved his dad in with him following the senior Neal's stroke in 2009. At seventy-six, he was still able to care for himself on most days, but Mike could see the onslaught of dementia catching up.

When he arrived home, he found his father lying in the bathtub. The shower had emptied the water heater's tank and was now running cold on the elder Neal's body. He had asked his dad not to shower when he was gone, fearing his unsteadiness. The deep but bloodless gash in his father's forehead told him his heart was no longer pumping.

With his focus back from the memory of his father's death, he finished his shower and was toweling off when his cell phone began its vibrating slow-dance across the bathroom's tile countertop. He reached for the phone and tapped a button to put the caller on the speaker. He continued drying himself.

"Mike Neal."

"Hey Mike," Sergeant Weaver said. "We've got a male, white, mid-thirties in a wrecked Lexus on the north side of Brentwood."

Mike hesitated. "And the reason you're not calling Brentwood P.D. at ..." he glanced at the phone. "05:45?"

"They called us. The victim has a bloody hole forward of his left ear. They asked for our help."

"Oh?" He stared at his hazy image in the fogged-over mirror and rubbed his hand back and forth across his short brown hair.

"And, a larger one on the right."

"Hollow point?"

"Looks to be."

"The address?" Mike filled his left hand with shave cream.

"2811 Hillside, off Franklin Road."

"We question the homeowner yet?" He patted the shaving foam across his stubble.

"Based on the car's tag," Weaver said, "it looks like the homeowner is the one whose brains are covering the expensive leather interior."

"Hmm," Mike grunted. "I'll be about forty-five minutes."

"I'll let them know."

He tapped the red button to end the call.

This new homicide was not in the area of town where folks concerned themselves with their safety on the streets. This was the *older* part of Brentwood—where the only real criminal enterprise was the over-charging of seniors for landscape services. It was the place where even if your neighbors were more prosperous than you, they still waved when you cruised past *their* mansion.

After six years with the U.S. Army Criminal Investigation Command and twelve years as a homicide detective in Nashville, Mike remained mystified by the myriad of ways people found to do away with each other.

Lately, he'd not enjoyed his normal clearance rate on his investigations. As the result of recent retirements and Nashville's continuing population growth, not only had the detective teams been inundated with cases, but some of the more senior detectives had split with their partners into single investigators in order to deal with the temporary glut.

Most of his recent cases had been devoid of indisputable evidence or repentant suspects. Mike was due for a slam dunk. The day was young, and he was already praying for a stroke of good fortune in at least one of his two freshest cases.

He'd found himself talking with God more in the months since his dad's passing. If He was willing to help uncover the truth for the homicide survivors in Nashville, Mike was willing to ask Him for it.

CHAPTER 4

Brentwood
South Nashville

As he cleared the hilltop, Mike could see an EMS ambulance, two MNPD cruisers, and a unit from the Brentwood Police Department.

The fifth vehicle in the center of the mix, a white Lexus ES350, had smacked a large oak tree near the middle of a spacious front lawn. The driver was tactfully hidden from view by a large sheet which had been draped over the left side of the wreckage.

A perimeter of yellow crime scene tape was holding back what appeared to be, based upon their casual morning attire, a small crowd of inquisitive neighbors.

"Morning, Sergeant," Officer Dodd said, as Mike approached.

"Hello, Paul. What do we have so far?" He reached into his jacket pocket for his black Nitrile gloves.

"Victim is Tyler McKinnon," Dodd read from his notepad. "According to neighbors, he lived here." Dodd gestured toward the house behind him. "Married, but separated from his wife. They say he was a lawyer."

That'll lengthen the suspect list. "I assume you checked the house?"

"Front and rear both locked; no answer. There are signs of forced entry on the rear door."

"Get the house number. Call it. Be sure there's no one inside."

"Will do."

"Do any of these homes," he scanned the neighborhood, "have outdoor cameras?"

"We asked the neighbors there," Dodd gestured toward the group behind the yellow tape on the adjoining lawn, "and we checked all the homes nearby. We didn't see any, but we'll check the rest between here and Franklin Road."

"Did the neighbors offer up any information on the *separated* status?"

"The lady next door said they've been split for a few months. Her familiarity sounds like she and the victim's wife may have been acquainted. She said the wife left him and moved in with her widowed mother in Franklin."

I guess mother and daughter now have even more in common.

Mike placed a call to request the Crime Scene Unit. He folded the sheet back onto the wrinkled roof of the car so he could snap some photos with his digital camera. When possible, Mike liked to take crime scene photos of his own prior to the arrival of the criminalists and the department's photographer. The movement of the sheet fanned the sweet smell of ethylene glycol leaking from the car's crushed radiator.

"Hey, Paul. Make sure we don't have any neighborhood pups get interested in the anti-freeze that's collecting under the car. They're drawn to it, and it'll kill them. And, be sure the ground here under the car's engine is taken up and removed when the car is towed."

"Will do."

He snapped three photographs of the deceased man as his vacant eyes stared upward.

The driver's body had been thrown back against the seat by the explosion of gas into the now deflated airbag lying in his lap. His inexpensive navy pinstripe suit was covered with a light dusting of white powder. The small amount of talcum used in the loading of the nylon airbag prevented sticking when it was time for deployment.

As he inspected the car's interior, he spotted a smart phone on the carpet still dangling from a coiled cord plugged into the dash's power outlet. He hoped it was smart enough to provide him a list of viable suspects.

He added four close-up shots of the victim's wounds, both the small entry and the nasty exit.

"Have you called the medical examiner's office?"

"About an hour ago," Dodd said. "They said they'd put us on the list. Sergeant, there was no answer inside the home; a machine picked up. Man's voice said, 'Leave a message'. I didn't."

"Thanks." Mike spent a few minutes finishing his cursory sketch of the crime scene before he approached the neighbors. The group was still watching the activities from the adjoining property.

"Morning," he said, intentionally leaving off the pleasant portion of the greeting. "I'm Sergeant Mike Neal with the Nashville Police Department."

"Arthur Metcalf. This is my wife Joan. We live here." The sixty-something man gestured toward the home on the property where they were standing.

"Ted Abernathy, sergeant." The next man offered his hand, but Mike held up his gloved hand. "I live next door to Arthur and Joan there." He pointed to the house on the other side of the Metcalf home.

"Gus Hammond. I'm across the street there," The elder man said as he hiked up his loose blue jeans beneath his wife-beater undershirt.

"Thank you. I'll try to be brief. Were you all acquainted with Mr. and Mrs. McKinnon?"

"I didn't know them; never spoke with him." Hammond pulled up his pants again.

"I waved the times I did see them," Abernathy said. "Actually —," he stopped himself, "I spoke with McKinnon a couple of weeks ago. I forgot. We were both checking our mail. I remember, he was pleasant, but didn't say much."

Mike turned toward Joan Metcalf as he continued making notes.

"I guess I knew Allison better than any of our neighbors," she said with a soft southern accent. Mrs. Metcalf looked at the others, who nodded their agreement. "She and I used to have coffee and chat rather frequently. She was not a happy lady in the months before she decided to leave."

"Thank you. I'll need to talk with you soon. I need to get in touch with Mrs. McKinnon and gain access to the home. We'll need to search for evidence."

"Evidence?" Abernathy asked.

"Yes, anything that could point us in the direction of who may have wanted Mr. McKinnon killed."

"What do you mean, Sergeant?" Abernathy asked. "What's this got to do with McKinnon's wreck?"

"Mr. McKinnon didn't die as the result of his collision with the tree. He died from a fatal gunshot wound to his head."

"Oh my God," Joan said.

"We assumed he was drunk again, Arthur said. "Are you sure? When was he shot?"

"Apparently, it happened here on your street as he was driving home early this morning."

"Oh, my. I can't believe this," Joan said, looking from her husband to Abernathy and back.

Mike looked at Mrs. Metcalf. "Is there a place where we can talk?"

CHAPTER 5

Stone Asset Management, LLC
Downtown Nashville

"Have you heard from Tyler this morning?" Al Ricks asked Shannon Richards as he pushed through the front door to the three-person office of Stone Asset Management. He rushed past his assistant's desk and aimed for his office.

"Was he supposed to call you?"

"No, but ..." He dropped his briefcase at the end of his credenza and hung his suit jacket behind his door. "I texted him and called him twice. It's not like him to not answer my calls."

"Maybe he's in an early meeting with a client."

"Last night he said he was open this morning. Is Barrett here yet?"

"Yes, he—"

The senior partner of Stone Asset Management, LLC entered the lobby and tossed some files on Shannon's desk. "What's the matter?"

"I can't find Tyler."

"This is a problem?" Barrett looked from Al to Shannon and then turned his palms up.

Without speaking again, Al stepped into Barrett's office and held the door, waiting for Barrett.

"We had dinner last night," he said softly. "We talked." He shut the door. "He's changed his mind. He's beginning to see what the consequences would be if he followed through with his warning." He looked at Barrett searching for a scrap of understanding.

"*Beginning* to see?"

He noticed Barrett's head moving, only slightly, from side to side. "Yes. I don't think he is a threat any longer."

Barrett stepped behind his desk and dropped into his chair. He leaned forward with a look that caused Al to cringe. He clasped his hands together above his monogrammed leather desk pad.

"You didn't think he was a threat when you hired him as your personal attorney ... against my advice."

"But—"

"You didn't think he was a problem," Barrett interrupted, "when, in a drunken stupor, his indiscretion almost blew us and our future out of the water the *first* time. Tell me, when is it exactly, you plan to recognize Tyler McKinnon as a threat?"

He took a breath and braced himself for another Barrett Stone tirade.

"You begged me to allow you to hire your *friend* so you could give him a break—help him back on his feet. I told you then I would continue to act as your personal attorney without a fee. You didn't want that."

"He needed my help."

"You helped him," Barrett raised his voice. "What did you accomplish?"

"He's—"

"He's been nothing but one more reason for worry since you took him under your wing. We don't need more reasons for concern at this time. He asks too many questions. His periodic presence here has given me a damned ulcer."

"Barrett—"

"Listen to me. I don't want to see him in this office going forward. Do you understand? I have no confidence in him. He's a lush with loose lips, and he cannot be trusted."

"He's my friend. His personal life has been in the shitter for a while, but he's a pretty good attorney. He just needs to get a fresh start."

"A fresh start. If he was a good attorney, he wouldn't need your help. And, he's not getting a fresh start at our expense? *We* can't afford it. He puts our entire future at risk."

Barrett stood and began his dramatic 'impress-the-jury' stroll around the office as he spoke. This display of arrogance irritated Al because Barrett had never litigated a court case in his life.

"I have spent the last several years preparing and babysitting this project, for *us*. You know, I didn't have to share it with you ... but I did."

"Barrett —"

Barrett held up his hand, turned and tilted his head.

"I shared this with you because I care about you. This plan is going to make us both multi-millionaires. It will give us the opportunity we deserve to start our lives over. We cannot *afford* high-risk friends. You do understand this, don't you?"

Al looked at the floor and nodded.

"You'll be free again, *rich* and free.

He tried to smile, not because he felt it, but because Barrett expected it.

"I feel sorry for Tyler. His life has fallen apart."

"I understand. But, *he's* the chef who cooked that dish. You tried to help him, and it didn't work. See it for what it is. You did nothing wrong. You can't jump into his muck and save him without taking yourself, *and me*, down too."

Barrett paused and gazed at Al. "We've been together for a long time."

Al acknowledged with a single nod.

"I'll have to say, you've prospered during that time, haven't you?"

He nodded again.

"I think so, too. Much of the time, you've arrived there by trusting my advice."

"Yes." As much as he wished it otherwise, Al knew this was true.

"Then how is it ... you find yourself in a position of doubting my judgment? Have I failed you in some way I don't realize? Have you lost money riding my coattails?"

"No, Barrett." He hated it when Barrett took this tone.

"My plan's working, isn't it?"

"Yes."

"Then what *is* the problem?"

Al thought for a moment. He knew no matter what he said at this point, it would carry no weight with Barrett. He knew enough about Barrett to ruin him, and he also knew enough to be suspect of anything Barrett said. He'd heard Barrett tell over a hundred people blatant lies; lies that would deceive them and, at some point, cost them much of their investment portfolio. What he was unsure of was how far Barrett was willing to go in order to protect himself, to see that no one could be a liability for him.

I know how far he'd go.

"Nothing's wrong. I'm just nervous. The idea of pulling the plug on this life and starting a new one from scratch, as exciting as it sounds ... it's drastic. I trust your planning," he lied. "I know everything will be fine. I'm just anxious." He finished with a counterfeit smile.

Barrett's brow relaxed. "It is a huge change. But, I've planned it out, and I know exactly how it all will work. Trust me."

"You know I do," he said quickly. "I've trusted you for years." He knew better than to say anything else.

"Then be patient a little longer. Soon it will be over and we'll be thousands of miles from here with new names and new identities. You'll have all you've ever wanted, and much more."

"Sounds great," he forced out the words. "I can't wait to get most of this life behind me."

Barrett watched Al walk from his office.

Al knew Barrett would be wondering what he meant by *most* of this life.

CHAPTER 6

Brentwood
South Nashville

"Cream and sugar?"

"Just a little cream. Thank you," Mike said, as he and Arthur took their seats at the oak breakfast table.

The Metcalf home with its collection of family photos looked to be one which had seen many years of family happiness. The setting reflected the age of its owners, and was salted throughout with snapshots of smiling grandchildren.

"You have a beautiful home."

"Thank you," Joan said. "It's awfully quiet now. When the kids were home, it was somewhat different."

"I'm sure. How many children do you have?"

"We were blessed with three," Arthur said. "Two boys and a girl."

"And we have seven beautiful grandchildren," Joan added as she served the coffee, and then joined the men at the table.

He readied his note pad. "You mentioned that you and Mrs. McKinnon spoke frequently?"

"Yes. Allison and I loved our flowers." She smiled. "We called them our babies. She grew the most beautiful Lantanas you have ever seen." Joan paused for a sip of coffee and a glance at her husband. "I know she must have dreaded abandoning her babies. I hated to see her leave them as much as she did."

She stared out the window for a moment as Arthur patted her hand.

"I thought about trying to care for them along with mine, so that when she returned—if she returned, they would be there for her. I realized after speaking with her a couple of times, she wasn't coming back."

"So, you stayed in contact?"

"Oh, yes. We still talk on the phone, and we've met for lunch three times since she left." Joan looked at Arthur and said, "This is still going to hurt her."

Mike made notes and then turned to Arthur.

"How well did you know Tyler McKinnon?"

"Neither of us saw Tyler much at all, especially after Allison moved out. When we did see him, it was when he was pulling into or out of the driveway. He'd only recently started driving the Lexus, maybe a month or two ago. He didn't spend a lot of time at home. He wasn't an outdoors type, so we didn't see him on the weekends. He had some local landscape service do his yard. I do my own." He turned quickly to his wife. "Sorry. We do *our* own." The seasoned couple shared a caring smile.

"What time-of-day did you usually see Tyler?"

"If I saw him leaving in the morning, it was usually around seven o'clock. That's the time I make my coffee, and while it's brewing, I step outside to pick up the newspaper. He kept his car in the garage so it was hard to know when he was and was not at home. As far as seeing him at night, I don't recall any particular time, but it must have always been late. I'd say after ten anyway. That's usually when I'm taking our little Honey here out to potty before we go to bed." He scratched the snow-white head of the couple's West Highland Terrier.

"Do you remember seeing anyone other than Tyler, or Mrs. McKinnon, at the residence lately?"

Arthur looked at Joan. "Allison hasn't been there, that's for sure, and I don't recall seeing anyone other than the landscapers, or maybe the dry cleaning van making a delivery. They hung his cleaning inside the storm door." Arthur turned to his wife. "Have you seen anyone, dear?"

"I did see a car driving slowly in front of their house the other day." Her expression communicated the challenge to her memory. "It must have been yesterday or maybe the day before. It was late morning around eleven or so. I wait for the dew to dry so I can pull the weeds without soaking my gardening gloves. I remember looking up when I saw the car drive away."

"Can you describe the car?"

"It was dark. Blue or black. I'm not sure."

"Did you notice the make or model?"

"The what?" She looked at Arthur.

"He means what kind of car it was and the year?" Arthur said.

"Oh, I don't notice that kind of thing. You men know all that nonsense. It looked like a new car to me."

"That's fine, Mrs. Metcalf."

"Could you see anyone *inside* the car?"

"No. It had dark windows." She nodded. "It was not the kind of car we normally see in our neighborhood. I know that much for sure."

Arthur nodded his agreement.

"Thanks," Mike said as he wrote more notes.

"What do you believe happened, Sergeant?" Arthur asked.

"It's too early to tell. We have a lot of investigation and interviews to conduct before we can expect to learn all we need to know. Do you know of anyone else in the area here who knew or spent any time with the McKinnons?"

"I don't think so," Joan said. "They both seemed sort of quiet. I don't know any of the other ladies on the block who talked with Allison. She was considerably younger than the rest of us."

"Yes, ma'am."

"She once told me she appreciated my willingness to talk with her about their problems. She was hesitant to discuss them with her mother. She told me she felt like a failure at her marriage, and didn't want to disappoint her mom. I feel sorry for her."

"Can you tell me how I can get in touch with Mrs. McKinnon?"

"Yes. I have her phone number and her mother's address in Franklin. I'll get it for you."

Joan Metcalf stood, caressed her husband's head in her hand and whispered in his ear before she left the room.

"Sergeant, Allison told Joan several weeks before she left, she thought Tyler might have been involved in something shady."

"Did she say what it was or how she knew about it?"

"No. She told Joan she didn't know anything definite. She just had a feeling based upon the hours he was keeping. Seems when he was home he didn't want to spend any time with her."

"Why didn't your wife mention it earlier?"

"She was uncomfortable with it. She called it women's intuition. She wasn't sure if you would consider it credible information." Arthur smiled. "So, she asked me to tell you."

"I've learned over the years to never assume anything in a homicide investigation is unimportant. I've seen dozens go to jail on evidence that was almost overlooked."

CHAPTER 7

Belle Meade
Nashville

Barrett coveted the old money that long ago paid off the ivy-cloaked mansions lining the secure avenues of Belle Meade. His attraction was born solely from self-interest.

He delighted in the drive. He aimed his make-believe finger pistol at each of the homes that belonged to individuals whose investment portfolios he'd penetrated, and in some cases, whose comfortable retirements he'd destroyed, though as yet they remained unaware.

The commotion caused by the political fundraiser produced so much congestion in front of the Blanchard mansion; it had traffic backed up for three blocks.

He checked his watch and then called Al. "Are you on schedule?"

"On schedule? I'm standing by Blanchard's pool enjoying Sevruga caviar and Cristal champagne while I wait for my dawdling partner."

"Try not to make a pig out of yourself. I'm stuck out here in this wagon train waiting for the valets to park me."

"You should do like I did," Al said, "park yourself down the street and walk."

"That's not going to happen, so chill. Keep an eye out for Blanchard and any other potential prey. I'll be in there as soon as I can."

After several more minutes of frustration, he pulled his BMW onto the circular etched concrete drive. He was met there by one of the red-vested valets.

"Good afternoon, sir. Your ticket," the boy said, offering him a small numbered tag as he exited the car.

He accepted the receipt without comment. He buttoned his jacket as he climbed the curved brick steps leading up to the home's striking entry.

"Welcome." An attractive young blond came close. His focus moved from her cleavage to her sparkling smile and back again. She grasped his lapel in her left hand and was about to stick the campaign button's pin through the fabric of his three-thousand dollar Italian suit.

He grasped her wrist as if she'd intended to strike him. "Don't do that."

"Pardon me?" The young woman froze with her mouth half open and a wrinkle in her brow.

"Don't stick the pin in my suit." He released her arm.

Her hand with the campaign button dropped to her side.

"The food and champagne are out back on the patio," she announced as she'd been taught, but without the smile she'd offered previously.

He adjusted his suit jacket and offered her a manufactured smirk. He marched through the marble foyer and the vast great room toward the rear doors which opened out onto the bright white veranda. The happy rumbling of numerous conversations and laughter greeted him as he stepped outside.

He scanned the sizeable pool patio, and surrounding well-groomed lawn. There were two to three hundred people talking, eating, and drinking. From his elevated position on the veranda, he searched the affluent crowd for Al. The considerable gathering made it difficult to single out an individual.

His phone vibrated a brief announcement that he'd received a text message. He retrieved the phone without interrupting his scan of the crowd. Al's message simply read, "2:00."

He looked up and across the pool. Slightly to his right, he saw an arm wave once.

He typed his response. "Blanchard?"

His phone pulsed again. "4:00."

He spotted Blanchard pressing the flesh with his guests. He tucked away the phone, snatched a flute of champagne from a passing server's tray and began his pursuit of the mansion's owner.

Hugh Blanchard owned three construction companies which operated globally. He'd invested in Halius Systems over fifteen years ago following Barrett Stone II's recommendation. He and Barrett's father made a sizable fortune from their support of this emerging technology company.

As Barrett made his way toward Blanchard, he spotted several of his own clients and made certain he acknowledged each one.

Blanchard was chatting as he moved through the crowd. Barrett placed himself in his path.

"Nice turnout." He lifted the champagne flute with his left hand.

"It's great isn't it?" Blanchard said.

Barrett offered his best salesman's smile.

"Hugh Blanchard." The millionaire's squint declared he was sure they'd met before, but didn't remember when.

"Barrett Stone." He grasped Blanchard's hand.

"I thought you looked familiar. I guess I haven't seen you since your father's funeral."

"It's good to see you again and under better circumstances."

"Welcome to my home. Are you a Josh Foreman supporter?"

"Absolutely. He's our only hope for correcting all the liberal blunders Logan Craft has committed over the last two years."

"I agree," Blanchard said as he waved to another guest. "I can't figure out how the tax-and-spend jackass got elected."

"Mr. Blanchard."

"Hugh, please."

He smiled. "Hugh. Is there a place where we can talk for five minutes or so?"

"I'd rather not leave my guests."

"I understand. I assure you, I'll be brief. I need to tell you something my dad wanted you to know about," he lied.

Blanchard stared at him for a moment then gestured. "The pool house."

As the two men stepped through the doorway into the twelve hundred square foot pool house, Blanchard approached the bar and asked, "Can I get you something a little more potent than Cristal?"

"I'm fine. Thanks." Never taking his gaze off Blanchard, he pulled one of the leather covered stools from under the bar and sat.

Blanchard poured himself three fingers of Jack Daniel's over a glass half-full of ice and looked at Barrett as if to say, 'the floor is yours'.

"Hugh, I know you and my dad were good friends. I remember hearing him speak well of you on several occasions, and I know the two of you made a considerable return on your common investments."

Blanchard took a sip of his whiskey and nodded.

"My dad taught me about wise investments, in addition to how best to manage my money and that of others who charged me with the responsibility. I've built Stone Asset Management with the tools and the instincts my dad gave me; the same tools he used to help *his* business flourish."

"I'm happy for you. What's this got to do with me?"

"I've taken advantage of a unique opportunity which has brought some impressive returns for me and several of my clients, some of which were my dad's former associates and friends. I wanted to speak with you about this months ago, but your work in Europe and Asia prevented me from connecting with you."

"What is it?" Blanchard swirled the ice and what was left of the whiskey in his glass.

"A roommate of mine from our years at the University of Tennessee, Phil Stafford, is an Information Technology expert. After his Masters degree, he obtained his Doctorate in IT Engineering. Some say he's the second coming of Steven Jobs. I don't know about that, but I do know he is an unrivaled innovator with one of the most creative minds out there.

"He came to me two years ago with an idea for a high-speed server intended solely to buy and sell equities. He needed capital to build it. Some college friends and I, who were in a position to help, loaned him some cash. I am so glad I was able to do so. I've already recovered my investment with a significant return."

"Again," Blanchard said, affirming his impatience, "what's this have to do with me?"

"We're about to take this venture to phase two. Phil says he can upgrade our current mainframe and construct sister computers like it to be positioned at locations in close proximity to each stock exchange's server. This will take more time out of the equation, putting us ahead of even more of the other traders. It's quite expensive to set up these servers, but we're projecting our return on investment in twelve to fourteen months."

"On the surface, no more than you've told me, it sounds unrealistic." Blanchard downed the balance of his Jack Daniel's and reached for the bottle.

"We don't think so. Worst case, we're looking at two years. The issue now is getting our hands on enough capital to build these high-speed supercomputers and construct the network that will place our transactions in front of eighty percent of all the others."

"How much capital is this *second phase* going to take?"

"Six million." He pulled the number out of his ass and watched Blanchard to see if he flinched. He didn't.

"How much time can placing computers near the exchanges be expected to save?"

"Milliseconds."

"Milliseconds?" Blanchard asked.

"Milliseconds per trade can mean millions in additional profits each year."

"Seriously?" He squinted.

"The majority of trades are no longer made by guys barking at each other across telephone lines. They're made by highly programmed computers buying and selling hundreds, sometimes thousands, of securities before you can say IBM."

"If I know the SEC," Blanchard said, "they'll be investigating the use of these computers, suspicious that people are attempting to manipulate the markets."

"I remember my dad talking about the SEC and their concern about insider trading back when I was in school. My guess is, those apprehensions will always exist. They fuel the SEC's existence. Actually, with their antiquated ways, I have my doubts they can even keep up with all the action in the markets today. New trading tools like these are being developed daily by large financial organizations all over the world. These are folks who are trading millions of shares every day. We, as investors, can decide to be a part of this acceleration, or we can sit on the sidelines and watch it happen. My father was not a spectator and I don't believe the people he chose for his friends and business associates are either. This is why I came to you." He was silent. He waited for Blanchard to chew up and swallow his bait. He'd learned that questions and expressed doubt were always the best indicators of potential interest.

"How can owning equities for a matter of seconds, much less milliseconds, generate profits sufficient to justify this kind of expense?"

"Through the use of pattern-recognition software and mathematics, sometimes seasoned with a little time critical information, all moving at light-speed, the computer is able to make decisions based on factors such as market volume, momentum and direction, and the historic pricing relationships between various stocks and asset classes. These high-velocity purchases and sales, best case, garner us pennies per share, but that's on many, many shares. Buy low—sell high. That's all we need to get in and get out with our pockets filled.

"I'm not interested in risking my money on insider information," Blanchard said.

"We aren't either. This speed trading is not illegal. Our information is not from the inside; it's available to everyone. It just comes to us much faster. We're prepared for it. We're able to react to it and *use it* sooner. Our expectation of success is based upon the knowledge that, over time, we know we can make money. Do we make money on every trade, every day? No. Sometimes we have a bad day, but not often."

"What if something goes wrong? We all know computers can act crazy sometimes," Blanchard said. "What happens then?"

He was glad Blanchard was asking all the same questions he was used to getting in response to his well-practiced pitch. He was smiling on the inside.

"Regulators have put in place circuit breakers of a sort which, by design, halt stock activity when it fluctuates more than expected within an established time parameter. We know they work. They've already been activated by algorithms that have run amuck."

Blanchard nodded.

Barrett could see the wall of resistance crumbling.

"So, what if I saw this as a potentially worthwhile place to grow some cash?"

It was time to close the sale.

"I'd say we need to spend about thirty minutes when you aren't entertaining guests and decide how much of a role you'd like to play in this project."

"You're right." Blanchard checked his Rolex. "I've got to get back to my guests. I'm leaving for Singapore tomorrow. Can we talk before then?"

"Here or at my office?"

"Here tonight at six."

Barrett pulled out his smart phone and scrolled the calendar. "I may be able to reschedule this appointment." He shook his head. "I'm not sure. This man's a demanding investor, and I can't afford to piss him off. He's already made a sizable commitment. I'll check and call you."

He offered his card and his hand. "It was good to see you again, Hugh."

"Same here," Blanchard said softly.

As Barrett weaved his way around the pool carefully dodging guests, a young lady turned abruptly and collided with him.

"Oh!" she gasped.

He caught her before she fell.

"I'm so sorry."

"No damage done. Are you okay?" He smiled at the stunning brunette. She was dressed in a thin flowing print dress that showed off her features.

"I think so," she said as she looked Barrett over with little discretion.

"Good. Let's start over. I'm Barrett Stone," he said, as he slipped his left hand inside his trousers pocket.

"I'm Samantha Rowe," she said, offering her slender hand and a bright smile.

"Rowe." His gaze was locked on her sparkling hazel eyes as he took her hand and held it momentarily. "I know that name."

"My father is Mayor Harrison Rowe."

"That would be it." He delivered his marketing smile and let his wedding band slide from his finger down into his trouser pocket.

"Are you a Josh Foreman fan?"

"Absolutely."

"You don't have a campaign button." She frowned, admonishing him, and then smiled again.

"It's in my BMW."

"Oh," she said. What model?"

"750Li."

"Nice. I have a 535i myself."

"Looks like we have some things in common, Miss Rowe. Would you have a moment to talk?"

"Why not?" she said with an alluring smile.

"I'll get us some champagne."

"Good idea."

After he joined the queue at the bar, he sensed someone close behind him. A hand reached into his jacket pocket. He grabbed the person's wrist and turned to see who was attempting to pick his pocket.

"Your father was one of my closest friends. His expertise made me millions. But, you'd better be right about that damned computer."

Blanchard turned and walked into the crowd, shaking hands and welcoming his guests.

Barrett reached into his pocket and pulled out a folded check. It was made to Stone Asset Management in the amount of five hundred thousand dollars.

He stepped forward and smiled. "Two Cristal please."

CHAPTER 8

Franklin, Tennessee

Delivering the ultimate in bad news was always difficult. Mike had been called upon to perform this task numerous times during his career. The words required to communicate the dreadful news created a hurt in the victim's family that he was familiar with. He'd lost his mom, his dad and his best friend Ron Kremer. But the news that hurt him the most came nineteen years ago when he was visited by his commanding officer in Mosul, Iraq. Mike had recently returned from an investigation when he learned of his little sister Connie's brutal murder back home in Tennessee. This event changed him, his life, his future—everything.

On some days, Mike's efforts touched dozens of people, many of whom had just experienced the same devastating trauma he'd lived through himself years earlier. His was not just a job. In some cases, he was the family's only advocate for justice. He didn't want these homicide survivors forced to watch their loved one's case turn cold, like he'd watched Connie's case, due to lack of evidence, get pushed back behind more recent, more solvable murders.

Mike scrolled to the cell phone number for Reverend Cliff Charles. Cliff was one of over two dozen volunteer chaplains for the Nashville Police Department and Mike's favorite partner when it came to delivering bad news to families of homicide victims.

"Hello."

"Cliff. It's Mike Neal. Are you available?"

"At the moment, no. I'm sorry. I'm with a family at Southern Hills Hospital and I've got another visit already scheduled right behind this one."

"I'm on my way to see a young wife in Franklin to inform her of her estranged husband's murder. I need to try and move quickly on this, so I'm going to handle this one alone. If you finish early, give me a call."

"Sure."

The detectives were supposed to deliver death notifications as a team, but he needed to get on with his research while the facts were fresh. In homicide investigation, time could mean the difference between finding the truth and seeing your efforts get boxed up, labeled and placed into cold case storage. He knew it would be easier to apologize to the Lieutenant for acting alone, than to get his permission.

As he drove through the subdivision of five-acre lots and six and eight thousand square foot homes, he wondered: *What do all these people do for a living?*

He watched mailboxes and slowed to a stop in front of the residence with the matching address.

He checked to be sure his digital recorder was in his pocket in case he needed it. He grabbed his note pad. Out of habit, he looked in the rear view mirror to be sure his tie was straight and he looked professional. He was due for a haircut. His Army training taught him to keep his hair short. His vanity told him to keep the sides even shorter to conceal the increasing number of sparkling gray hairs. At forty-seven, Mike could see and feel changes taking place with his body. He wasn't ready.

He walked the long sidewalk and rang the doorbell. No answer. He rang it again. He knocked on the door. There was still no response.

He decided to take the sidewalk back to the concrete drive and check out the rear of the property.

As he rounded the back corner of the house, he saw two women working in a small garden, maybe sixty feet away. The younger of the two looked up as he approached. Soiled from her work and with her flowered dress damp from perspiration, this lady was still quite attractive.

"Can I help you?" She asked as she removed her muddy gloves and pushed her sunglasses on top of her head.

The older woman looked up from her work, but remained in the garden.

He showed his detective's shield. "I'm Sergeant Mike Neal with the Nashville Police Department. I'm looking for Allison McKinnon."

Her eyes widened as he spoke.

"Mike? Oh my goodness. Mike Neal?"

The sound of her voice completed *his* recognition.

"Allison? Wow. I didn't recognize you."

"Oh, my goodness." She looked down at her dress. "I must look like hell." She attempted to tuck her auburn hair behind her ears and in the process smeared mud across her cheek. "Please forgive my appearance."

"Don't worry. I understand." He smiled until he remembered why he was there.

"How are you?" she asked.

"I'm doing pretty good. And you?" He knew however she answered his question, it was about to change.

"I'm doing okay," she said, as she briefly looked away.

"Allison, is there somewhere," he looked around, "we can talk?"

By this time, Allison's mother had joined them.

"Mom, you remember Mike Neal don't you? We went to UT together."

She squinted. "I remember the name, but ... I'm sorry. I'm getting old and forgetful. Did you two date?"

"Mom?"

He noticed Allison checking out his left hand. "Yes, ma'am. We dated." He knew the term failed to describe their relationship.

"Oh. You're *that* Mike Neal."

A little uncomfortable, he looked at Allison, wondering what her mother meant.

"Mom, maybe you could get us some of your lemonade?"

"No, I'm fine," Mike said. "It may be best if we all sit for a minute." He gestured toward the patio chairs.

"What's the matter?" Allison's mom asked, looking at Allison for an answer. "Is it Drew?"

"I don't know, Mom."

"Drew?" he asked.

"My younger brother."

"No." He shook his head.

Both women sighed.

Once the three were seated at the patio table, he leaned forward. "I'm sorry, but I have some disturbing news. Tyler McKinnon is dead."

Allison's mother grabbed her mouth. "No."

"Wha ... What happened?" Allison asked.

Mike was about to explain what little was known about Tyler's death, when the relative quiet was broken by the roar of a car engine. A red Chevrolet Camaro sped up the inclined drive and parked at the rear of the concrete pad behind the house. A young man stepped out of the sports car and swaggered toward the patio.

"Hey, whose car is that out front?" he asked before considering the man seated with his family.

"It's Mike's."

Allison allowed her brother time to come closer.

"Drew, this is Mike Neal, a friend of mine from college."

Drew stared at Mike. "Nice to meet you."

"Same here," Mike said as he stood and took Drew's hand.

Allison waited for Drew to sit. "Drew—Mike just told us. Tyler is dead."

"What?"

"Tyler McKinnon was killed early this morning," Mike confirmed.

Drew thought for a moment as he looked from Mike to Allison. "Good riddance."

"Drew Culver," his mother shouted.

"He's an ass." Drew leaned back.

"You should be ashamed of yourself," his mother said.

"What? Are you guys serious?"

"Yes, I'm serious," Allison said.

"Damn. Sorry, Mom. What happened?"

"Mike was about to explain when you drove up."

Mike watched Drew for his reaction. "He was murdered."

Drew's face wrinkled. "What?"

"Oh, my goodness," Allison's mom said.

"Why? Where?" Allison asked.

"He was shot while driving home. In fact, he crashed his car into the oak tree in front of your home on Hillside."

"Do you have any idea who did it?" Allison asked.

"We're gathering evidence and talking to folks. That's why I'm here. We have to talk to everyone who knew him best—standard procedure."

"Hell, I don't know anybody who really *knew* Tyler," Drew said, looking at his sister. "At one time, we thought we did."

"What do you mean?" Mike asked.

"Tyler turned out to be a strange bird," Drew sat forward.

"Drew. Don't speak ill of the dead," his mother said.

"I can't help it. He treated Allison like crap. His priorities were all screwed up. He didn't deserve her." Drew turned to face Mike. "We got into it on a regular basis. The guy was a real jerk."

Mike looked at Allison for her response to Drew's statement, but saw little change.

"Tyler had problems," Allison said, sounding more forgiving than Mike expected.

"Problems?"

"Several," Allison said. "Mostly, self-image related."

"Tyler wanted to be a big shot," Drew spoke up. "He was never satisfied, always wanting more. He had a beautiful wife, plenty of money, and no idea how to be happy."

"I get the impression," Mike looked at Drew, "you and Tyler didn't get along."

Drew grunted.

"That's an understatement," Allison whispered.

"See this?" Drew pointed to a scab over his left eyebrow. "A gift from Tyler."

"Have you been fighting with him again?" Allison asked.

"Two weeks ago—outside Barney's. He took home his share of souvenirs, too. I called him a faggot. He was quicker than I remembered." Drew smirked.

Allison shook her head at Drew. "When *will* you grow up?"

"I was defending *your* honor."

"Please, spare me the pseudo chivalry. Would ya?"

Mike broke up the brother-sister squabble saying, "I'll need to speak with each of you individually a little later. For now," he turned to Allison, "I need to get your consent, as the sole home owner, to search the house, and I'll need a key."

"No problem." Allison stood. Her mother followed her into the house.

"Who do *you* think did it?" Drew asked.

" We don't know yet. That's why we're investigating all the leads we can generate. Do you have some ideas about who may have wanted Tyler dead?"

"Yeah ... anybody that knew the bastard."

Allison stepped out onto the patio. Mike stood.

"I'll keep it in mind, Mike said."

Drew went inside, leaving Mike and Allison alone.

"Here you are." Allison handed Mike the key.

"Thanks. Walk with me?" he asked. I'm sorry to have to bring you bad news like this."

Allison nodded.

"I appreciate your willingness to help us." He stopped at his car and turned back to face her.

"Do you know anything yet?"

"Not much. I'm hoping we'll find something inside the house that will help."

"He wasn't much of a housekeeper, so there's no telling what you'll find."

"No problem. I'll call you later to arrange a time for us to talk. I'm going to need as much information about Tyler and his relationships as you can recall."

"Okay."

"Is there anything I need to know about the house that you think might help me?"

"Honestly, he could have remodeled the place and I wouldn't know it. He used the back bedroom as his office when we were .... I assume he still did. You'll find a floor safe in the office closet. He wouldn't have removed it, but I have no idea if he still used it."

"Good. Any idea what the combination is?"

Allison smiled. "Tyler's memory was so bad; he couldn't remember my birthday."

"So?"

"The combination was originally *my* birthday. He had the locksmith change it to *his* birthday, November 23, 1979. So, eleven, twenty-three, seventy-nine. It's digital."

Mike wrote the numbers in his notebook.

"Frankly, I'd be surprised if it's locked. He left it unlocked most of the time. He just put the board and carpet back down and left it."

"How can I reach you?"

Allison gave him her cell number. She stepped back and crossed her arms over her chest.

Mike gave her a small wave as he pulled open the car door.

"It was good to see you, again," Allison said.
"Same here." He smiled briefly. "I'll call you later."

CHAPTER 9

Franklin, Tennessee

Mike's car disappeared around the corner and Allison turned back toward the house. As she slow-walked up the drive, memories of their first meeting at UT came back into focus; she closed her eyes for a moment and sighed as she recalled the first day of class.

She was an A student all through high school and college. Her major at UT was Landscape Design and Construction. She loved horticulture. Somehow, the doctoral scholars of the Plant Sciences Department decided her major required a course called Statistics. She knew this was not going to be a skate. She hoped to find a geek in the course that needed some cash and was willing to tutor her to at least a C average. Her plan was to sit near the back and make a list of the potential victims who could become her new Statistics coach.

She didn't know any of her classmates' names, so she made a list based upon their physical appearance and their current seating location within the class. She knew most students tend to sit in the same general area in each of their classrooms. It was habit born of comfort, and occasionally by degree of interest in the course subject matter. Distaste for the subject sent the masses to the rear of the classroom to allow for frequent nodding off. Nerdiness, on the other hand, pulled some students to the front of the room, but not nearly as many as late arrivals to class. As in church, once everything got started, that's where the empty seats could be found.

As she listened for questions from the class which might point out her prospective coach, she made notes, adding to her list of potential victims. While scribbling some less than flattering data about one of the girls in the second row, she heard the boy next to her clear his throat. She looked up to see that he was definitely not a boy. This was, without a doubt, a man.

She tried to cover the notes she'd made about her classmates, but she could tell, this guy had already seen her cryptic assessment. When the professor turned toward the blackboard he leaned toward her and whispered, "A girl as attractive as you shouldn't have to shop the class for dates."

"I, uh—I'm not..." The professor turned in their direction. She leaned forward, put her hand to her mouth and forced a cough. She was taken aback by this hunk's statement. She was wondering how she could have missed seeing those arresting eyes before now.

"I'm making notes about people and their appearance," she whispered. "I'm—a writer. I'm writing a book." *Yeah. That's it.* "I'm developing characters for a book." She nodded like a bobble-head doll, attempting to confirm her lie as fact.

"Oh, I see."

That was so dumb. She turned, closed her eyes and hoped he believed her.

"What's your genre?" He asked when the professor faced the board again.

"My what?" she whispered, squinting.

"Genre, you know. What kind of book is it? Fiction—Non-fiction, Mystery—Thriller—Romance?"

"Oh, I haven't decided."

He wrinkled his brow.

Damn. Not a good answer. "I'll tell you after class."

He nodded his head.

She turned the page in her spiral notebook to hide her notes. She tried to check him out further without turning her head. No such luck. His desk was not directly beside hers. It was back far enough she couldn't see him well without turning her head.

I hope he's at least looking at me.

She checked her watch. There were only minutes left in the class.

What can I tell him about writing a book? Oh hell, I'll just tell him the truth. What difference does it make anyway? Maybe he'll think it's funny or creative or something.

The professor doled out the reading assignment for their next session, and she wrote it down as her fellow statisticians began to exit the classroom. She stood and collected her books.

"I'm Mike."

"Allison," she said grabbing her purse and still hoping to impress him.

"So, tell me about your book," he said.

"Okay," she paused to take in her first good look at him. "I have to be honest." She took a huge breath.

"That's always best." He smiled.

Oh, my. He is beautiful. "I was scanning the room, looking for a potential tutor."

"Oh?"

"Seriously. I know nothing about this Statistics stuff."

"I understand. Heck, it is *Statistics*."

"And my major requires it for some goofy reason," she said.

"Mine, too."

"So, do you have any experience with Statistics?" she asked.

"A little," he said.

"Really?" She looked him over again. "Want to be my tutor?" *Want to be my date? Want to take me to ....*

"I don't know."

"I can pay. How much do you charge?"

"What did you write about me in your notebook?"

"Nothing," she said not wanting to be found guilty of any criticism.

"Nothing? I didn't rate *anything*? If I didn't rate at least a comment, I'm not sure—"

"I wrote about the geeky looking people," she interrupted, "thinking they were more likely to be good at this boring subject."

"I guess that's a compliment? I didn't make the geek list."

"It's certainly a compliment. You would make no one's geek list, I assure you."

"Good, I was worried about that. What class do you have now?"

"I have a break until one-fifteen."

"Want to hit the grill?"

"Sure," she said, trying not to jump up and down.

CHAPTER 10

Hillwood
West Nashville

Clayton West sat hunched over in his wheel chair, watching his beloved Golf Channel. He enjoyed the live tournaments, the recorded matches; he even enjoyed the commercials. But Clayton could no longer enjoy playing the game he'd loved for more than forty years.

He adjusted the nasal cannula again. He hated the way it irritated his nose, but he despised his damn emphysema more for the way it restricted his freedom. The disease anchored him to his home, ending his life's pleasures and reducing his human interaction to home health technicians and rare visits from friends fortunate enough to still be alive and not shackled by an attachment to a metal tank filled with life-supporting gas.

His disease had diminished his general health over the last year. It had taken him from playing three rounds of golf each week to dreaming of being able to play just one. He watched the Golf Channel daily to see other people doing what he could only remember.

Clayton was a widower. He lost his lovely wife Margaret to colon cancer in late 2008, long before his own debilitation set in.

On the rare days when there was no golf on TV that he hadn't already seen, he sat looking out the living room window at the neighborhood children playing on their lawns and in the street. He hoped they were happy children, well-balanced and cared for by their parents. God knew, in West's forty-plus years as a child psychotherapist, he'd seen hundreds that were not.

Throughout his career, his weekends with friends on the golf course and afterward in the clubhouse for drinks and cards were *his* therapy. This was necessary to help cleanse his mind from the hours he'd spent with disturbed kids who, too often, were simply a product of their parents' own mental issues or their inability as parents. He did his best to lessen the damage, but sadly when the children left him, they returned to the environment which frequently was the source, or at least the inspiration for their disorder.

As he sat staring at the kids, there was a knock at his back door.

He rolled himself through the kitchen. He could see the home health technician's uniform through the window in the back door.

"Hello, Mr. West. My name is Chad."

"Afternoon," he mumbled as he rolled his wheelchair backward from the kitchen doorway. He looked the new technician over with a suspicious scan. "What happened to Jerry?"

"Jerry?" the technician asked.

"My regular guy." He rolled himself into his den.

"Oh, that Jerry. He doesn't run this route on Monday's. I think he's on the east side today, you know Donelson, Hermitage, Mt. Juliet. Yeah, he's taking care of patients out there today. So, how have you been doing? Having any problems with your regulator or your tanks?"

"No." He watched the man work. He was still uncomfortable with someone new taking care of his lifeline.

"That's good." The technician maneuvered a large cylinder and cart to a vacant spot along the wall.

"Some guy called from the company a little while ago," West said, "telling me they were going to change my tank. What's that about?"

"That's what I brought you today. " The technician pointed to the large cylinder. "This is the new model. It has a larger capacity and doesn't have to be changed as often. You'll be able to go for maybe three weeks on this big boy."

"Why are you putting it over there? I can't reach it there."

"You won't need it until you use up your current supply. I'm sure Jerry will be by tomorrow to tell you all about it."

He was relieved Jerry would be the one helping him with it. "I'm not sure I'm comfortable going for weeks without Jerry checking my equipment."

"Oh, Jerry will still be by to check on you like always. He just won't have to change out your tank so often."

"Are you going to change my cannula today?"

"Your what?"

"The cannula." He lifted the oxygen tube coming from the flow meter to his nose.

The technician walked over to check the tube. "Oh. It looks good to me."

"Jerry changes it every week."

"It'll be fine," Chad said. "He'll probably change it his next visit."

This technician smiled a lot, but West was still uncomfortable with him.

"I have a couple of things left to do here and I'll be out of your way, sir."

The technician tightened the strap holding the larger oxygen cylinder in place and then adjusted the large regulator.

"I guess that does it, Mr. West. Have a good day." The technician waved and let himself out.

He rolled his wheelchair to the back door and secured the deadbolt.

Now in front of his large screen television, he turned the sound up in time to watch the players' introductions as they approached the first tee. He watched several players' progress through the difficult course and recalled shots of his own that resembled those facing the younger players on the PGA Tour.

He missed playing the game, and he missed his friends who used to gather at the country club three or more times each week for eighteen joy-filled holes followed by hours of poker, dinner and drinks. They spent their time together criticizing each other's golf games, laughing at their jokes and generally having a wonderful time.

Their long standing foursome was cut in half when two of the senior friends, Barrett Stone and Roy Barron passed on almost three years ago. The other player still living, was able to navigate a course, but it had to be in a cart and he was able to play only nine holes with his forty-something son.

West's memories were interrupted by the roar of voices and applause coming from his big screen TV. He looked up to see Phil Mickelson tipping the bill of his cap to the crowd. This, following his birdie on the first hole and the successful beginning to what West hoped would be another great round. Mickelson had long been his favorite.

He slowly shook his head and longed for the chance to once again experience the exhilarating feeling that came with defeating par, one more time.

Before leaving West's home, he'd adjusted the regulator and made sure the sound of the constant flow of pure oxygen coming from the new compressed gas cylinder out into the house would not be noticed by the old man.

He'd placed a small box inside the doorway to the living room and out of West's line of sight. The device was constructed using an inexpensive cell phone, some wire, a cotton ball and a single fresh drop of acetone. He'd removed the cell phone's back cover and disabled the speaker causing the device to function in silence. He soldered two small wires to the speaker's contacts and stabilized the wires so they didn't quite touch inside the expanded cotton ball.

Normally, whenever a cell phone received a call, the battery sent an electric signal to the speaker to announce the call. After his modification, the signal would now create sparks as it jumped between the wires each time the signal was sent.

When he'd tested the device, it took no more than three rings to generate enough sparks to ignite the acetone and cotton ball which were stretched apart and placed around the wires' ends. In the oxygen rich environment on the floor of West's home, he suspected the device may need only one ring. He knew from experience, pure oxygen was slightly heavier than air and would tend to settle to the lower levels of an undisturbed space.

Back at his apartment now, he changed out of the stolen technician's uniform. He pulled a beer from the refrigerator, walked outside and took a seat at his rusted patio table. He leaned back and watched a jet as it left a white contrail across the midday sky. As he took in a large mouthful of the cold beer, he wished for the day when he was on that plane traveling far, far away.

He pulled out his cell phone, checked the time and scrolled to the list of new names and numbers he'd received from Barrett Stone. At one hundred thousand dollars each, when these *accidents* were all over, he'd be a millionaire, twice over. He laughed out loud. He scrolled the list of targets and stopped at number one, 'Clayton West'. He stared at the name for a moment, tapped it to make the call and then took another large gulp of beer as he listened to the rings and envisioned the outcome.

West was focused on the incredibly difficult nine iron shot from the rough facing one of the newest young PGA professionals when he saw through the doorway something odd in the living room. He was confused, unsure of what he was seeing. He raised his glasses, rubbed his seventy-six year old eyes and squinted to see the ghostly image more clearly as it moved across the floor.

He realized what was happening not long before the smoke detector announced the threat. The flames soon reached, and began to climb, the living room drapes. The fire engulfed the upholstered sofa as if it had been soaked in an accelerant.

He fought to manipulate his wheelchair toward his fire extinguisher. As he grabbed for the extinguisher, the flames reached his feet. He pulled the extinguisher pin as the flames ignited his pajamas and burned his legs. He stomped his feet and screamed. The pain caused him to drop the heavy extinguisher.

He backed his wheelchair to the wall and slapped at the flames. Within seconds the blaze had climbed his clothing. He continued to scream as he thrashed about attempting to put out the fire. The fire burned his arms and his face. It gained momentum fueled by the oxygen being fed through the nasal cannula.

Gasping for the oxygen that was being stolen from him by the fire, his last breath took the flames down into his lungs. His unbearable pain was multiplied for an instant. Then, it ended.

The house filled with flames in less than three minutes.

CHAPTER 11

Brentwood
South Nashville

Mike was scrolling through his notes and crime scene photos when a patrol car came over the hill and rolled up behind him. He watched as the officer's dark blue uniform filled his driver side mirror. He dropped his power window and the officer laid an envelope across the window's opening.

With Allison's blessing and her house key, he didn't need the search warrant, but his concern for procedure and his years of court experience told him to submit the electronic affidavit anyway —just in case. The DA would appreciate it.

"Thanks."

"No problem," the officer said.

Mike opened the envelope and scanned the warrant.

He returned his camera and digital recorder to his pockets as he stepped from the car. He approached the officers who were huddled at the front of one of the MNPD cruisers. The criminalists were practicing their individual skills in an attempt to obtain visible and latent evidence from the Lexus while they awaited the arrival of the Medical Examiner's crew to remove the victim from the car.

Mike informed the group he wanted to make an initial walk-through before the criminalists began their search of the house.

He crossed the patio at the rear of the home and took a seat on one of the padded metal framed chairs in order to pull on his Tyvek shoe covers. After digging in his pocket for the house key, he pulled on a fresh pair of gloves as he inspected a series of pry marks on the door and door facing. The pry marks were approximately one inch wide and the scarring of the painted wood was obviously fresh.

After taking close-up photos of the pry marks with his digital camera, he inserted the key.

"Hello—Police," he shouted as he pushed on the door.

He was surprised to see the home had been ransacked. Kitchen drawers were pulled out. Some were removed and strewn across the floor with what appeared to be their former contents. Items from the cabinets were raked out onto the counters, and some onto the floor. The total amount of kitchen wares and food scattered across the floor would have filled no more than one of the twelve double cabinets. If he'd not known the homeowner's situation, he could have predicted the occupant was a single male who did not like to, or know how to, cook or clean. He took more photos.

The home looked to have been tossed by someone hurriedly in search of something, but with dirty dishes filling both sides of the sink, a stench of decaying food, a full trash bin and general disorder, it was hard to be sure what portion was Tyler's mess and what part was the result of the break-in.

What the hell did they expect to find in a single man's kitchen, anyway?

His practice of searching for what *is* at the scene that shouldn't be, and what should be there but *isn't*, was going to be made much more difficult by Tyler's own clutter.

Dodging dishes, canned goods and near empty cereal boxes, he stepped through the kitchen eating area and into the great room where he found nominal furnishings in similar disarray. The countless nail holes in the monochrome walls told him the home's artwork had not been there for Tyler's pleasure. The layer of dust on every horizontal surface proved as Allison had told him; she was the sole keeper of the house.

He moved through the home without disturbing anything. Touching only the carpet, he took the hallway off the great room which, no doubt, led to the bedrooms.

The first door to his right was a full bath which looked to be untouched by both whomever searched the home and anyone who in the past several months might have had the slightest intention of cleaning it.

He snapped photos of the next two rooms, one to his left and the other to his right. Small bedrooms—both empty. From the hallway, he could see drapery rods. The drapes were missing and the closet doors were standing open. All that remained in either room were mini-blinds and the dozen or so depressions in the carpeting, permanent signs of happier times when the home was filled with furniture and most likely some degree of emotion. Allison's departure appeared to have emptied the home of both.

As he continued down the hallway, he approached the doors to two more rooms. One room was large with clothes and personal items scattered or hanging from minimal furniture. If the room had posters of musicians taped to the walls, it would have resembled a normal teenager's bedroom. He took photographs of the room. A large mattress and box springs were poised like an anchored raft floating in a lagoon. This confirmed it was, or should be, the master bedroom.

The other room, located on the back side of the home was furnished with an inexpensive L-shaped laminate desk, a well-worn high-backed vinyl office chair and other typical furnishings, some still in their functional positions and others overturned or in pieces on the floor. Much like the kitchen, it was difficult to tell how much of the ruin in this home office was Tyler's and how much was the result of an intruder's search. Mike took more photographs.

All the drawers in the desk had been removed, emptied and thrown about the room. There were triangular gashes in the drywall which appeared to be caused by the corners of flying desk drawers, possibly propelled in anger. If the motivation for this murder was passion, it could help to shorten the suspect list.

The bottom drawer of a four drawer lateral file was open, more than likely the last one searched. Papers, legal-sized manila folders and green hanging files were strewn around the room in all directions.

He looked at the flat screen monitor, as well as a mouse and keyboard on the desk. Their cables dangled across scattered papers on the desk. There was no computer in sight.

He was headed for the room's open closet when he heard voices from the other end of the house. He retraced his steps back toward the kitchen to find Wendy on the top step outside the kitchen door.

"What a mess," Wendy said, sticking her head inside the doorway. "We're on hold out here waiting for the M.E. Are you ready for us yet?"

"Almost," he said. "The house is sparsely furnished which should speed up your search. Be thorough in the office at the far end of the hallway by the master bedroom. It looks to be the intruder's target area."

"Gotcha, Sarge. By the way, we believe your shooter was likely working alone."

"Oh? Why is that?"

"Very little visual particulate residue on the victim's face or on his white shirt collar exposed above his jacket. The gunshot must have come from at least six to eight feet away and traveled the windy distance between the two vehicles. If a front seat passenger had pulled the trigger, more than likely with his arm out the window, the shot would have come from no more than three to four feet away. There would have been considerably more particulate matter on the victim and his clothing. I'd bet residue is coating the passenger's side door upholstery in the shooter's car."

"Let's pray we get the opportunity to test the shooter's car for residue and you'll get to win that bet."

Wendy smiled.

"Did you bag the cell phone?"

"Yes. We dusted it and I turned it on. Password protected."

"Make sure it goes to Dean McMurray in the A/V lab. I'll tell him it's coming."

"You got it," Wendy said.

"I'll call you in a couple of minutes so you guys can get started. I won't be long."

"We'll be out front."

He paced the hallway thinking about Allison and Tyler and what kind of life they must have shared during their short marriage. Memories of his and Allison's college days together caused him to have trouble picturing her with someone who would live like this.

He turned on the closet light and knelt in the doorway. He pinched the fibers near the threshold and pulled up the piece of carpet, exposing an eighteen inch square section of half inch plywood which was cut to fit flush with the sub-floor. A one inch diameter hole had been drilled near the center of the square. He inserted his index finger, lifted the wood and exposed the matte black steel door to the floor safe.

He took more photographs. He called Wendy to dust the safe top for prints before he checked to see if it was locked.

He watched as Wendy pulled some smeared partial prints from the numbered buttons and a partial palm print from the chrome handle. She mounted the tape sections containing the prints on a white board and handed them to Mike for a look.

"Good luck with these. They don't look like they're going to offer us much," he said as he handed them back.

He checked to see if the safe was locked. It was. He remembered the date. Eleven, twenty-three, seventy-nine; the lock sounded a soft tone. He hoped it was confirming the proper combination. He turned the chrome handle one quarter turn and lifted the thick three-bolt steel door until it leaned over and rested on the closet floor. He pointed his flashlight inside the safe.

"Holy shit," Wendy said, as she looked over his shoulder.

The safe was filled with several bundles of cash. Lots of Benjamins and Andrews were stacked neatly in the hole. Resting on top of the cash was the most garish lady's gold jeweled brooch he'd ever seen. He took more photos.

He wasn't surprised so much by the cash, the quantity of cash, maybe. This was an item he expected to find locked in a man's safe. However, most men who lived alone didn't fill their safe with women's jewelry, particularly something as bizarre as this piece. The brooch was large, over three inches across at its widest point.

This is not jewelry a young woman would wear. He couldn't believe Allison would have any interest in such a flashy piece.

He picked up the brooch by its edges for a closer look. It appeared to contain several diamonds. The oddest thing about the piece was the center. Amidst all the gold and diamonds was the tri-star circular emblem from the middle of the Tennessee state flag. There was a diamond in the middle of each of three stars. He placed the brooch on Wendy's gloved hand so she could search for prints.

When he turned back to the safe he saw what had been lying beneath the bizarre piece of jewelry. It was a four gigabyte USB flash drive.

CHAPTER 12

Green Hills
Nashville

Somewhat back to normal following his three hour nap, Mike gripped the neck on the chilled fifth of Jack Daniel's Tennessee Honey and removed it from the refrigerator door. He transferred an ounce or so of the sweet oaky whiskey to a glass and set the bottle on the counter in front of him. As he took the first sip, his focus was drawn from the pleasant taste to the bottle's label, the Cherokee name of his home state and his college alma mater. His thoughts immediately went to Allison, his memories of their college experience and their unexpected reunion earlier today.

He walked into the den as he took another sip and scanned the wall of books above his desk. He held the whiskey in his mouth and gradually swallowed the sweet southern nectar.

His gaze stopped on his collection of college yearbooks. He tucked his index finger inside the top of the faux-leather bound 1994-95 volume and pulled *The Volunteer* senior yearbook from the shelf. He leaned back in his office chair to await his computer's boot up.

He blew the dust off the top edge of the large volume, speculated how long it had been since he looked through the college annual and then laid it across his lap. He opened it to the inside front cover and laughed as he read numerous short notes from people he hadn't thought of in two decades, some he couldn't remember at all. Inside the back cover he found what he was looking for. The sight of Allison's youthful musings from eighteen years ago produced a smile and more than a bit of emotion.

<u>Dear</u> Mike,

I can't believe the year, and our time at UT are almost over. We've had so much fun. I never thought I'd learn to love Statistics – not so much the course as the tutor.

Between skunking both Kentucky and Vanderbilt and then winning the Gator Bowl, it was truly an awesome end to our football season. Looks like this new freshman quarterback, Manning, may be exactly what UT needs.

Mike, I don't have a lot of room here to tell you all I want you to know and, for that matter, it's not the place. But, it's not like I haven't told you before. We've come a long way in the last months, and I feel it's time we thought about what's next. We'll be graduating in less than three months. I can't imagine not seeing and talking with you every day. Let's make a date and discuss our plans.

Thanks for a wonderful senior year.

Love <u>always</u>,
Allison

Rereading Allison's words reminded him of his initial thoughts when he read them nearly eighteen years ago. They scared the hell out of him. He genuinely cared for her, but she was moving way too fast. He'd had plans for his post-military life that he'd not even finished visualizing yet.

I did the right thing.

He reached for his cell phone and scrolled to the number he'd recently added.

"Hello."

"Allison, it's Mike."

"Hi."

"Listen, I have some more questions. Are you available?" He was sure Allison wished he meant this in a different way.

"I'm not too busy at the moment, if that's what you're asking."

"Yeah. We went through the house and found some items I'd like to discuss with you, if now's a good time?"

"I guess so. Are you coming over again?"

He knew it would be best if they talked in his world this time. "Actually, I'd like you to come to my office."

"Uh, okay." Allison hesitated. "Where's that?"

"My office is in the Criminal Justice Center at 200 James Robertson Parkway."

"I have a GPS. I'll find it."

"There's parking on the Third Avenue side of the building. You can ask for me at the bubble, and I'll come to the lobby."

"The what?"

"Oh, sorry. The guard's desk."

"I guess I could be there in ... maybe an hour?"

"That'll be great. Let me give you my cell in case you need it." He gave Allison his number. "I'll see you in an hour or so."

"Okay."

He closed his phone and stopped before re-shelving the yearbook. He flipped to the senior pictures.

"Hmm. No wonder I was dating her. She doesn't look all that different today. Good genes."

He pushed the book back into its reserved space and smiled at himself for being sentimental.

I did the right thing.

CHAPTER 13

Criminal Justice Center
Downtown Nashville

The Criminal Justice Center guard notified Mike that he had a guest. As he came down the stairs, he saw Allison pacing the floor near the entrance. He slowed his step. Seeing her dressed up helped him remember why he was conflicted back in 1995 when he decided it was best if they didn't rush things.

She didn't have any mud on her face. Her hair, instead of windblown, was flawless, and much like she wore it on dates back in their college days. Her makeup was perfect. When she spotted him, her expression reminded him of the way she smiled when she opened the door to her apartment in Knoxville.

This is very distracting.

"Hi." Allison unfolded her arms.

He was convinced she was preparing herself in case there was a hug coming. She used to tell him he gave the best hugs. He couldn't let himself go there.

She'd been separated from Tyler long enough that she would be missing the company of a man, and this man was the one she'd chosen first. There was no way he could allow this to move away from a professional relationship, not now. He'd considered asking one of the other detectives to take over the case, but he didn't want to offend her. She'd felt his rejection once. He couldn't do it to her again, especially after what she'd been through recently.

"Did you have any trouble finding a place to park?"

"No. I parked where you said I could."

"Good." He smiled. "Let's go this way." He gestured toward the stairs. He tried not to think about how good she looked, and how the girl he'd known intimately back in the mid-nineties had matured into such a beautiful woman.

As they passed the break room, he said, "Can I get you some coffee, a Coke or something?"

"No, I'm fine. Thanks."

"Here we are." He stopped at the door to his office. "Have a seat." He motioned to one of the sad-looking straight back chairs in front of his desk. "Pardon the furniture. Our budget doesn't allow for luxury." He turned the other chair so it faced her, removed a stack of files from his desk, and took a seat.

He opened one of the files and looked up at Allison. "How are you feeling?"

"I'm okay, I guess," she said after a somber sigh. "I met with the funeral director this afternoon and set up the arrangements once the Medical Examiner has released Tyler's body."

"They told me I should have the autopsy report in the morning," he said.

Allison nodded. "It's all so draining." She stared at him. "It brings back all the bad memories ... and a few of the good ones."

"I'm sure it does. I'm sorry you had to go through all this."

"Thanks. I'm glad at least *you're* here."

"I'll do what I can to help you." He wished there was more he could say to help with the grief, but he knew all too well there were no words equal to the task.

He shuffled the files again to create a back-to-business segue and said, "When I approached the back door of the house today, I noticed some tool marks."

"Tool marks?"

"Scars on the door facing, indicating forced entry."

"Oh?" Her brow wrinkled.

"Someone forced their way into the home and ransacked it."

"For what? I took everything of value when I moved out."

"I noticed the place was almost empty."

"It's the way Tyler wanted it. I tried to get him to keep some of the furniture and artwork so the house wouldn't look so empty, but he kept saying, 'No, take it. You picked it out. You always liked it. Take it.' So, I did. Obviously, many of the things we shared in our marriage no longer meant anything to him." Allison looked down. "I'm not so sure they *ever* did."

"As you told me, Tyler was still using the back bedroom as his office," he said attempting to redirect the focus of the discussion.

Allison nodded.

"This room was a wreck. Do you have any idea what someone could have been looking for in his office?"

"I have no idea what Tyler was into during the last months we were together, much less since that time. Drew told me he'd seen Tyler with some rough looking people."

"Did you ever know him to be involved with people who make their living from illegal enterprises?"

"Huh? He *was* a lawyer. As long as I knew him, most of the people he associated with were thugs of one type or another. The ones who weren't criminals were *lawyers*."

He smiled, knowing well what she meant.

"Sorry, I have no love for most lawyers I've known."

"What about people outside Tyler's client list?"

"I wouldn't know. I was much too far removed from any of that. I will say, Al Ricks was the best friend Tyler ever had." Allison paused. "Although, I'm not sure Tyler deserved him."

He could see Allison was reflecting and about to explain further.

"Tyler changed in the year before I left." She paused. "He began doing things that were out of character from the Tyler I knew. He was away from home a lot, and when he'd return, he never wanted to talk about where he was or what case he was working on. He became distant, a different person than the man I met and fell for." She looked down. "After several months of this kind of behavior, it was all I could handle. I was pretty sure he was into drugs. I told him I was leaving."

Mike pulled a sheet from atop a stack of files Wendy had given him. She'd made copies of several documents found scattered throughout Tyler's office. After checking the strewn files for prints, the team of criminalists did their best to organize the sheets by what appeared to be the clients' names they'd found within the files.

"This is a list of names from all the papers the crime scene team found in Tyler's office." He handed Allison the sheet of paper. "Do you recognize any of these names?"

Allison scanned the list of twenty-some names slowly, moving her finger down the page. "Some of these look familiar, his clients I think, but most of them ..." Allison shrugged. "I don't know. I'm sorry, Mike."

"That's fine." He handed her a pen. "Mark the ones you believe were his clients. It'll help us narrow down their identification. Anyone else you recognize, jot down who they are or why you feel you recognize them. Anything at all could help."

Allison began her review of the list.

"I'm going to grab some coffee while you look over the list."

"Sure."

When he returned from the break room, Allison was finished and she handed him the sheet.

"Who is this?" He pointed to a name she'd written at the bottom of the list. "Wade Powell?"

"I didn't see his name on your list. Powell's case was the one that put Tyler over the edge. He was fired after that one."

"Fired?"

"The partners at his law office said he blew it. Powell agreed. They said Tyler could have gotten Powell off with no more than involuntary manslaughter, but Tyler lost his focus and then ... the case. Powell got manslaughter and an eight year sentence. He got out of prison after about half that. I can't imagine your people not finding his files somewhere in Tyler's office."

He made a note to run Wade Powell through the National Crime Information Center (NCIC).

"Did Tyler hear from Powell after his release?"

"I have no idea." She hung her head. "That was about the time we were beginning to ... drift apart."

He looked at Allison and thought of the anxiety she must have experienced thanks to Tyler.

"Did you ever see Tyler carry a gun?"

"Not while *we* were together."

"When we searched Tyler's car today, we found a loaded .40 caliber pistol in the console of his car."

"What?"

"Can you think of anyone he might have had reason to fear?"

"I ... I don't know. He was always a little paranoid. Like I said before, Tyler associated with a questionable group, and he'd changed a lot." She looked at the floor. "I guess nothing at this point should surprise me."

"I opened the floor safe today when I made my initial walk through of the house. Do you know what Tyler kept in the safe?"

"No. I never kept anything in it myself, so I couldn't be sure. It was too much of a pain to use; that's why he frequently left it unlocked. I've always had a safe deposit box at the bank. Why he put the safe in the floor is beyond me; more paranoia, I guess. I assumed he kept some cash and maybe stock certificates or insurance policies in there, his will, deed to the house, things like that. But, I really have no idea."

"I didn't find any of those personal items, but I did find some cash."

Allison nodded.

"There was twenty-thousand dollars in the safe."

Allison's forehead wrinkled. "You're kidding?"

"No. That's not all. I also found a large lady's gold and diamond brooch." He handed Allison a photo of the brooch.

"What? What was he doing with something like that?"

"It's not yours?"

Her forehead wrinkled. "Seriously?"

Mike smiled. "It's clearly a custom piece. We're talking with jewelers trying to determine who designed it. With the center emblem from the state flag, we're fairly sure it was done locally. With any luck, the designer can tell us who it belonged to."

He'd decided not to discuss his discovery of the flash drive with anyone except Wendy until Dean McMurray in the A/V lab was able to examine it.

"The cash and jewelry are not the only items troubling us. When the criminalists finished pulling out the bundles of cash, they found a small quantity of cocaine in the bottom of the safe."

Allison put her elbow on the chair arm and held her head as she shook it. "I don't understand. I really don't." She was silent for a moment. "He wasn't like this when I met him. He was a pleasant, decent man. He had goals for his life—for us. He wanted to make partner in a law firm and eventually open his own, like my late father. He refused to let anyone help him. He wanted to make it on his own. He didn't want to be seen as having anything given to him. I can't figure out what happened."

"Do you remember when he began to change?"

" I ... I guess it was around the middle of the summer last year.

That was when he started coming home late. He seemed to have lost interest in me—in us—in anything. He didn't want to go anywhere with me. He didn't want to talk about much of anything; mostly he just made excuses for being gone." Allison hung her head. "It's all very embarrassing."

"I understand."

"He started sleeping in the guest room. He said it was because he snored and didn't want to keep me awake. Frequently, I'd get up in the morning and he'd already be gone." She held out her hands, palms up. "I don't know what happened. I just know it all came apart. I grew tired of no answers, no respect and no husband. What can I say?"

Allison was obviously still hurting from the way Tyler had treated her. Mike hated it for her. He wanted to tell her he was sorry and be the friend she needed to help her, but he knew it was best not to go there yet.

CHAPTER 14

Franklin, Tennessee

Allison had not spoken with Al Ricks since the separation. He was *Tyler's* friend. At the time of their split, she worked to distance herself from everything related to Tyler. She didn't dislike Al, but sometimes his wimpy ways got under her skin. She liked for men to act like men, strong and protective. That was one of the issues she had with Tyler in the last year. She rarely felt safe and secure with Tyler any more. He'd lost his concern for her and their life together. With Tyler gone, she could no longer comfortably maintain the detachment from her former friends. Allison liked Mary Ellen Ricks and she hated that they'd lost touch, all because of Tyler.

As she sat and made notes on who to contact, she realized there was a short list of people who knew Tyler well enough to be concerned about his death. Al Ricks was Tyler's closest friend and he deserved to hear about this from her. The phone started to ring.

"Al Ricks."

"Al—it's Allison."

"Hey, Allison. How've you been? We haven't—"

"Not so good."

"I'm sorry. What's wrong?"

"Al, I need to tell you something." She paused. "It's going to hurt."

"What do you mean?"

"Tyler is gone."

"Gone where? I've been trying to reach him all day. He's not answering his—"

"Al," she interrupted, almost shouting. "He's ... gone. Tyler's dead."

"What? No way. I was just with him yesterday afternoon and most of the night at Darcy's Bar. He was fine. He was ... Oh, my God. Did he have a wreck on the way home?"

"Not exactly."

"What are you talking about?" he shouted.

"He was killed."

"What?"

"He was shot."

"Shot? No way. Are you sure? By who?"

"I don't know. The police don't know. No one knows yet."

"Oh God, when did this happen?"

"The detective said, 'early this morning'."

"Detective?"

"Yes. They're investigating."

"Oh, Allison." He began to cry. "I knew I should have called him a cab, but no, he couldn't leave his Lexus at Darcy's. I don't—"

"Al," she interrupted his rant.

"Why? Why?"

"Listen to me, Al."

"What?"

"I told Sergeant Neal you were Tyler's best friend."

"Who?"

"The detective, I told him you were good friends with Tyler."

"Oh." He wiped his eyes.

"He's going to want to talk to you."

"Talk to me? Why?"

"You knew Tyler best."

"So?"

"If you had drinks with him last night, you may have been the last person to see him alive."

"I don't—"

"The detective said they want to talk with everyone who knew Tyler, or had been with him in the last seventy-two hours."

"He was fine when we left Darcy's," he said. "He *was* kind of high."

"Did he talk about anything that might explain why someone would want to kill him?"

"Geez, no. Not that I remember. I don't believe this."

"You need to think about it. The police are going to call you."

"Oh ... okay. I ... I don't know."

"Al, just tell them the truth so maybe they can uncover something to help them find out who killed Tyler."

"Yeah. Sure. Tell the truth. I'll tell the truth."

"Listen. I have to go. I have to call family and some other people who knew Tyler."

"Sure. Thanks. I'll uh, call you later."

"Goodbye, Al."

CHAPTER 15

Criminal Justice Center
Downtown Nashville

Detective Doug Wolfe interrupted Mike's case review with the lieutenant when he stuck his head in Burris's open door.

"Hey, Mike. Sorry Lieutenant. The guard said there's a guy out front to see you. He says you're expecting him."

"Thanks Doug." He turned back to Burris. "Drew Culver, McKinnon's brother-in-law."

"What's *his* story?"

"He showed signs of aggression toward the victim when I first spoke with him at his mother's home today. The victim's wife, Culver's sister, claims he and McKinnon have been at odds for years. I asked him to come in on the premise of helping us learn more about McKinnon's background and social contacts. I'm hoping he can offer us some helpful information to push the case in the right direction; expose *his* role in McKinnon's life or possibly his death."

"You say that like he may be a person of interest."

"Not so far. I don't have anything yet to point me there."

"Let me know how it goes." Burris checked his wall clock. "I'll talk with you tomorrow. I'm going home."

"Yes sir."

Mike met Drew in the lobby and the two of them stopped by the break room on their way to the interview room.

"Would you like some Coffee? A Coke?"

"No, I'm fine," Drew said.

"I guess I drink too much coffee," he admitted as he filled an insulated cup, "but it comes in handy when sleep is rare."

"Do you guys always work long hours?"

"More lately than normal; it runs in spurts." He stirred in his artificial cream substitute. "There's a full moon, you know."

"Really?"

He looked at Drew. "The term lunacy comes from the root word lunar, which means 'related to the moon'."

"Is that old legend true?"

"Who knows? There are studies to prove about any theory you can dream up. Let's sit in here." He motioned toward one of the small interview rooms.

"Speaking of theories, what's yours on McKinnon?"

"What do you mean?"

"Who do *you* think killed him? By the way, before we get started, I want you to be honest with me. I need to know what *you* know. Okay?"

"No problem." Drew took a seat in one of the club chairs that faced each other across a small table. He took in a large breath and released it slowly.

"I don't know who killed him, but I can assure you the odds are high whoever did it knew him. Anyone who knew Tyler could be a suspect. I used to think maybe his attitude was mostly fallout from their separation, but hell, he was that way for months before Allison left. He changed. He was simply rubbing people the wrong way."

"You don't believe your feelings toward McKinnon are the result of his behavior toward your sister?"

"I hated McKinnon. It's a fact. His mistreatment of my sister *was* one of the reasons."

"You're not concerned about how that sounds?" Mike studied his face.

Drew folded his arms across his chest. "Let me put it this way. There are dozens of people who will tell you Tyler and I didn't get along, and some on occasion have seen us come to blows. What good would it do for me to try and hide that fact?"

"None, I guess," he said. "Tell me what you know about Tyler's life as a lawyer."

"If you're referring to his work in court, he wasn't very good at it. At least, that's what Allison told me. He lost his job. Allison said his firm let him go."

"When was this?" Mike asked as if he knew nothing about it.

"I'm not sure, 2006 maybe?" Drew shifted in his chair. "Allison said the straw that broke the camel's back was the botched trial of Wade Powell. He got screwed."

There's that name again. Mike needed to locate Powell and see what this former convict could tell him about Tyler and more especially why his files were missing from Tyler's office.

"I don't know all the facts, but supposedly Tyler's coke habit had progressed to the point it was affecting his work." Drew held up his open palms. "Allison's words—not mine."

"When did he start using cocaine?"

"I don't have a clue."

"Do you know if he was still using?"

Drew shrugged. "Why would he quit? He was single, doing whatever the hell he wanted to. I'd say he was still snorting the shit, as long as he could afford it. He was a real dumb ass."

"Aren't *you* single and doing whatever you want to?"

Mike's insinuation obviously took Drew by surprise.

He stared at Mike. "Yeah, but I don't do drugs. You want me to pee in a cup?"

Mike ignored the question. "Allison tells me you ran into McKinnon on a regular basis over the last year or so. Where?"

"Different clubs here and there. I go out a lot. He did too."

"Clubs such as?"

"About a month ago I was out with a buddy of mine and we stopped in at The Home Stretch Sports Bar. They were supposed to have this great band from up north. We'd been at the bar about an hour or so, and in walks McKinnon alone. He was high."

"How do you know he was high?"

"He looked the part. He was over confident, high-energy, loud and obnoxious like normal."

"And you couldn't let it go?" he asked.

Drew leaned forward. "He walked by me, acted like he stumbled and then stomped on my toe. I shoved him. He drew back his fist. Before he could swing, I slugged him. He got up and came at me. He knocked my drink to the floor. I got pissed. I had him around the neck when the bouncer grabbed me, pried my arm loose and escorted both of us out the door. He told us not to come back. If my friend Chuck hadn't followed us out, I would have gone to jail that night. Chuck stopped me, talked me out of it. We left and went to another bar."

"This doesn't exactly paint you as an innocent party with regard to Tyler's demise."

"I know. You wanted honesty." Drew held out his hands, palms up.

"Tell me who you've seen with McKinnon."

"I don't know. Nobody in particular. Since he and Allison split, I don't believe Tyler's made a lot of friends, but each time I've seen him, he looked like he was feeling very little pain."

"What do you know about Al Ricks?"

"Allison said he was probably the only real friend Tyler had left."

"Did you ever see them together?"

"Yeah, once. I think it was at Amerigo's on West End. They were having dinner." Drew paused. "In my opinion, Tyler was simply white trash with a law degree. He was never good enough for Allison. I told her that before she married the loser and several more times while she was with him. I never figured what she saw in him."

"Did she tell you, since they split, what she saw in him?" Mike realized as soon as he asked, this question was not relative to the case. He'd asked the question out of personal interest.

"No. Once she left, she didn't want to talk about him." Drew slouched in his chair. "She never found anyone she cared about after you two left college. Until that ass hole came along and snowed her with his legalese, and his assurance of a comfortable future with his family's money."

"His family was well off?"

"His dad was in the music business, some kind of upper-level manager or something. I heard he made decent bucks."

Mike scribbled in his notepad for a couple of minutes and was about to ask Drew what he knew about the rest of Tyler's family.

"Allison said she met with you earlier."

He nodded. "Yeah, we talked."

"Allison used to talk about you a lot," Drew said, staring at Mike, "especially after she left Tyler."

He stopped writing and looked up. "Oh?"

"Yeah." Drew nodded. "I wish you guys could have hooked up before she met that asshole."

Mike knew it was best if he avoided comment. He looked back at his notes and thought about all that Allison had been through.

I still did the right thing.

CHAPTER 16

Stone Asset Management, LLC
Downtown Nashville

Shannon was re-typing Barrett's edited quarterly financial reports when her desk phone rang.

"Stone Asset Management, may I help you?"

"This is Sergeant Mike Neal with the Nashville Police Department. I'd like to speak with Mr. Al Ricks."

"Uh, yes sir. One moment." Shannon put the call on hold.

She punched in Al's extension.

"Yeah?"

"Al, there is a Sergeant Neal on line one from the police department."

"You're kidding. What does he want?"

"I don't know. He didn't say. I didn't ask."

Al hesitated. "Thanks."

Al sat with his finger positioned over the button for line one, remembering Allison's call, informing him of Tyler's death and the imminent questions from the police. He thought he'd be prepared when the call came. He wasn't.

"Al Ricks."

"Mr. Ricks, Sergeant Mike Neal from the Nashville Police

Department."

"Yes sir, what can I do for you?" Al said, breathing slowly and attempting to project calm.

"I'm investigating the death of Tyler McKinnon. Mrs. Allison McKinnon told me I should speak with you since you and Mr. McKinnon were friends for several years. Is that correct?"

"Yes. That's true. Tyler and I were friends since college."

"Good. I'd like for us to talk face to face about Mr. McKinnon. Are you available?"

"Uh, when?"

"What about now?"

Al could feel his blood pressure climb. "Well—I can be, I guess." Al's nerve meter pegged in the red as his expectations for a half dozen benign questions over the telephone dissolved.

"Good. I'm in the neighborhood. I can be there shortly."

Al's breathing accelerated and his heart raced as he looked around the office. "I, uh, yeah. Sure."

"I'll see you soon?"

"That's fine." Al heard the detective's phone go silent before he'd finished acknowledging his comment.

He gradually returned the handset to the cradle as if the detective was still on the line. Al squeezed his eye lids together and grunted. "Damn it!"

With his head in his hands he began to consider what kinds of questions the detective might ask him. He wondered what Allison may have told him.

He pushed the intercom button to call Shannon's desk.

"Yes."

"Is Barrett here?"

"No, he had a client meeting."

"Great. That's great." He slapped the handset down in the cradle and tried his best to catch himself mid-tantrum and find some composure. He held his hands out flat, palms down just above his desk pad and took a large breath. He'd never spoken to the police before in his life. Now, they were going to be asking him questions about a murder, the murder of his closest friend, and he was likely the last person to see him alive.

"Shit. This is all I need. Barrett is going to have a fit." *What if I don't say the right things? What if I look like a suspect? What if Barrett doesn't like what I tell the detective?*

"Damn it, Barrett. How come you're never here when I need you?"

Al shouted to no one.

He stood. He looked at his wristwatch. He froze behind his desk, staring into space. He thought about how to prepare for something like this. He decided he was wasting his time. Like Allison said, all he could do was tell the truth. Just tell the cop what he knew about Tyler. *Why would Tyler care? He's gone.*

"Okay," Al said to himself. *Chill out.* He tried to coach himself to self-assurance. *Just be honest. I've done nothing wrong. He can't arrest me for being Tyler's friend. What am I worried about?*

His desk phone rang, interrupting his mental preparation.

He tapped the speaker button. "Yes."

"Al, Sergeant Neal is here to see you."

"What the hell? Already? Where was he, in the freaking parking lot?"

"Uh, I'm not sure." Shannon said. She looked at the detective and smiled.

"Give me a minute. Is he upset? Does he look mean?"

"No."

"I'll be out in a minute." Al hung up the phone.

As he put on his suit jacket and examined his fear-filled reflection in the glass-covered print hanging over his credenza, he thought to himself. *How did I end up in the middle of this?*

The detective stood as Al approached with his false confidence.

"Good morning." He stuck out his hand and envisioned the detective handcuffing his wrist as he offered it. But instead, the cop shook his hand.

"Mr. Ricks. I'm Sergeant Neal." The detective offered his card.

He accepted and looked over the card. "If you'll follow me, Sergeant."

"You must have been close by," he said still looking at the detective's card, out of nervousness.

"I was in the neighborhood."

Al closed his door.

"Have a seat." He gestured toward the twin burgundy leather chairs and took his seat behind the desk. *This will keep something between us in case he gets hostile.*

"So, what did you want to know?"

Neal began with easy questions. As Al answered, he watched the detective as he scanned his office, no doubt analyzing him and his personal surroundings.

Once he realized Neal wasn't going to be quite so scary after all, he began to relax.

"I understand you and Mr. McKinnon were together Sunday evening?"

"Yes. We had dinner together and drinks afterward."

"Where did you have dinner?"

"Darcy's."

"Did you go anywhere afterward?"

"No. We were there until we left and went home."

"Tell me what you know about Mr. McKinnon's social life over the last several months. Who was he spending time with, other than you, when he wasn't working?"

"He and I saw each other maybe once each week or so. We'd have dinner and a couple of beers and share laughs about the days when we were in college. It was a method of escape for both of us. Tyler seemed to enjoy it. I did. I know he had other people he hung out with from time to time, but ... I don't know who they were."

"Do you know Wade Powell?"

"No," he answered quickly.

"I get the impression you know who he is."

"Yes." Al sighed. "He was one of Tyler's clients."

"And?"

He looked down. He could tell the detective already knew who Powell was. "He was Tyler's Waterloo. Tyler was fired after he lost Powell's case."

"Why was that?"

"That was about the time Tyler's life was hitting bottom. He was already screwing up. Losing his job drove him to make even worse choices." He paused. "He either started doing cocaine which caused his performance in court to suffer, or he became so disgruntled over his failed litigation, he turned to cocaine in order to deal with it. Honestly, I'm not sure which happened first."

"Did you share Tyler's taste for drugs?"

"No. I don't do anything like that. I like a Jack and Coke occasionally, but not drugs. I like my head to be clear when I'm working."

"Did you spend time with Tyler when he was high on drugs?"

"No. He wouldn't see me when he was high. He knew I didn't approve and I would leave. Several times I called him to get together, but he'd let the call go to voicemail and then call me back later to apologize and say he was busy." He looked down and then back at the detective. "I knew what it meant."

"Did he socialize with Mr. Stone?" Neal asked.

Al chuckled. "Mr. Stone doesn't socialize with anyone who can't improve his position in life, much less Tyler McKinnon. Barrett never cared for Tyler."

"Any idea why?"

"You'd have to know Barrett. He's different." He shook his head. "Tyler didn't measure up to Barrett's standards."

"What do you mean?"

"Barrett is headstrong. Everything has to be his way. From the day he met Tyler, Barrett treated him like shit. Pardon my language. Tyler is ... was a good guy. He had a rough life, and in the last year or so, it had gotten the best of him. I hated it for him, but ...." Al shrugged.

Neal scribbled in a note pad. "Tell me about Tyler's marriage."

"Allison was good for Tyler. I think she made him grow up a bit. They were good together for a couple of years, but Tyler screwed that up, too."

"What do you think caused that?"

"Tyler's losing streak maybe, I don't know. He never wanted to discuss his marriage."

"I understand Tyler was your attorney."

"Yes. In name anyway."

"How often did the two of you communicate with each other?"

"I'm sorry?"

"You know, on the phone or email, texting, that sort of thing."

"Oh, we shared email and talked frequently. It wasn't always about work."

"Did you and he ever share email containing attachments of some sort? Such as Word or Excel files?"

"Yes. I guess we did. Why do you ask?"

"When we obtained permission from Mrs. McKinnon to inspect Tyler's home, we found his personal computer was missing."

"That's odd."

"Do you know if Tyler used a PC or a Mac?"

"He used a PC, a laptop. It wasn't a new one."

"With it missing, one of the only ways we have to gain data about his computer is to review files we know came from his computer."

"Really?"

"Yes, and files such as email with attachments offer up some information of that type."

"Interesting."

"Mr. Ricks, I know you want us to find Tyler's killer and determine why he was killed. And I'm sure, if the roles were reversed Tyler would do all he could to help us find your killer. Wouldn't he?"

"Yes. I'm sure he would."

"Since our ability to extract data from Tyler's computer is lost, the only chance we have to gain knowledge in this area is with your help." Remarkably, his fear of this detective and his probing questions were replaced by an unexpected degree of camaraderie. He was being asked to join forces with the police to investigate Tyler's murder and play a role in bringing his killer to justice. He wasn't expecting this.

"Can we—can Tyler count on you to help us find his killer?"

"Sure. Of course."

"I need you to know, you are under no obligation to help us. You have the right to refuse to help if that's what you decide. There is no pressure."

"Oh, no. I want to help. Tell me what I can do. I know Tyler would have helped you."

"I'm sure he would have. What we need you to do is bring up your email."

He opened his email.

"Sort all your past email from Tyler for the last, let's say, six months."

He sorted his email on the sender name to put all of Tyler's email together. He sat back and put his hands in his lap.

"Is something the matter?" Neal asked.

"I was thinking. Some of these emails may contain some of my private information. I know you're the police, but there's attorney client privilege and such."

"Have there been personal topics like this which you and Tyler have discussed via email in the last six months?"

"I'm sure. But, I don't remember exactly when we discussed them?"

"If there are emails you're concerned about because they might contain private information about you or your business, take them out. I don't want you to feel you are divulging anything you shouldn't. Go ahead and take those out of the list now. It's fine. I'll wait." Neal sat back in his chair and crossed his legs.

Al couldn't come up with anything specific that fit this

description, but his gut told him he should at least look. After reviewing a few dozen of the eighty or so emails, he failed to see anything that concerned him.

"I'm ready."

"Can you print the list?"

He printed the list of email from Tyler and gave it to Neal.

"About twenty-five of these have attachments. Would you be willing to send five to ten of these to the email address there on my business card."

"No problem."

"Oh, before I forget," Neal said. "What version of Office are you using?"

"I have no idea. Let me look."

"Do the rest of the folks in the office here use this same version?"

"Yes. I'm sure they do. They were all upgraded this year. Here it is. Microsoft Office Professional 2013. Is that what you wanted?"

"Yes. In that case, would you be able to forward me also emails from the others in the office that came to you with any type of attachment so I have a comparison against Tyler's files? It could play a role in how his computer software and yours dealt with attachments. It may not be needed, but it's worth a try."

"Sure. I guess. How many do you need?"

"I don't know. Four or five from each person should be fine."

He sent the emails with attachments to the address on Neal's card. As he clicked to send the last one, he leaned back in his desk chair and said, "All done."

"Great. You've been a huge help, Al. I know Tyler would appreciate it, and I'll let Mrs. McKinnon know as well. She was right."

"Right? About what?"

"She said you had always been Tyler's best friend."

CHAPTER 17

Criminal Justice Center
Downtown Nashville

Mike stepped softly as he approached Dean McMurray from behind. The clicks of the A/V Lab manager's keystrokes were so fast they almost sounded like a buzzer.

"Does the Chief know his Audio/Visual Lab Manager spends his free time surfing the Internet for porn sites?"

Mike loved to kid around with Dean. The tech-savvy lab manager never let the consequences of his tragic accident get in the way of his work or his relationships. His devastating injury came when his police cruiser was rear-ended while he was on duty assisting an elderly motorist with her flat tire. This dedicated MNPD officer, who now spent his days supporting Nashville's detectives, was admired and well-liked by all his peers.

"I certainly hope he knows better," Dean said, without the least bit of surprise in his voice. "Does he know his best homicide investigator can't sneak up on a crippled man in a wheelchair without his squeaky shoes giving him away?"

"My shoes don't squeak," Mike said, bouncing up and down to determine who was right.

Dean pushed buttons and rotated a large volume knob.

"Here is your entrance overture from about a minute ago."

Mike didn't know if the repeating irksome sound coming from the room's large speakers was truly his shoes or some fabricated audio blurb Dean had manufactured for his embarrassment. Regardless, this geek was talented.

"How's it going, Deano?"

"If you are referring to my world in general, even from my permanently seated position, my head is above the water line, most days. However, if you are referring to the recent analyses which you have entrusted to my care, I'm sure you'll be pleased to know I have been able to determine several serviceable facts."

"Awesome. As Norm would say, 'Spill it'."

"I was able to hack the so called *smart phone*. It took me all of five minutes. I've prepared you a list of the fifteen or so names and phone numbers from the contact list."

"That's all?"

Dean shrugged and handed Mike a single sheet of paper with the list.

"I was also able to extract a list of inbound calls coming to this phone. Many of these were from numbers on the contact list. Some were not."

Dean handed him a second sheet.

"Neither list contains any calls placed prior to four and one half weeks ago," Dean said. "I assumed this was the time the phone was purchased, but I contacted the carrier to be sure. You'll be glad to hear that once again I was correct. At least *I* was glad to hear it."

"I would expect nothing less," Mike said as he began to review the lists. "What about the email?"

"The short list of electronic messages and attachments obtained from Mr. Al Ricks's inbound email, and which allegedly originated from Mr. McKinnon's PC, have several details in common. This leads me to believe they indeed originated from the same source computer. More than likely, McKinnon's PC; no surprises yet."

"Good, what else?"

"Patience, my man," Dean said without looking up at Mike.

Mike rolled his eyes, but said nothing.

"Also, the email originating from Mr. Ricks's PC, those from Ms. Richards's PC, and those from Mr. Stone's PC were all created using Microsoft Office Professional 2013."

"I told you that already."

"You told me Ricks said it. I'm confirming it to you as fact. That is significantly different. *I* do not deal in hearsay."

"Go ahead."

"The emails and attachments originating from Mr. McKinnon's PC were created using Microsoft Office version 2003. Looks like Mr. McKinnon was not tech savvy, *or* he had not kept his software up to date, *or* he didn't want to spend the extra cash for the updates, *or* maybe he liked using the older software and wasn't interested in change."

"Hmm. Interesting."

"Not so much," Dean said. "Truly, this is not the most interesting part."

"No?"

"No. The interesting part of all this is the file that was saved on the," Dean stopped, cleared his throat, and looked around the office for inquisitive ears, *"flash drive,"* he whispered, "was created in Microsoft Office Professional 2007."

"You're kidding?"

"Nope."

"Your flash drive file was created on a PC running Office 2007 software, not on Tyler McKinnon's PC with ten year old software and not on any of the PCs at Stone Asset Management, LLC."

"So, what's on the drive?"

"An Excel worksheet with three columns, forty-seven names, dollar amounts and dates."

"Hmm. Anybody we know?"

"I ran the list. They're all in our database. Local area drug arrests, all of them."

"Who are they?"

"Generally small-timers, from simple possession of marijuana or cocaine to possession with intent. A couple were arrested with some serious quantities of either marijuana or cocaine."

"Did you print me a copy?"

"Of course." Dean offered him two sheets of paper.

He scanned the names and shook his head. None of the names matched the ones found in McKinnon's files or on his phone.

"I thought it was interesting that all these arrests have taken place in the last six months. I did an Internet search on Nashville drug arrests. All these names were contained within the first twenty or so search results; most were files from local news media stories."

Mike looked at Dean for a moment.

Dean was smiling.

"Do you think someone else could have put this list together in the same way you did?"

"Could they? Yes. Did they?" Dean shook his head. "That's your area, Sergeant. I deal in facts, remember?"

"Let's get back to the software issue. What does your discovery tell us about the creation of the flash drive?"

"Not as much as you'd like it to."

"Huh?"

"As I escalated the analysis and descended into the meta data."

"The what?"

"Meta data."

"I've heard about it, but explain it anyway."

"Meta data is data about data," Dean said.

Mike squinted.

"Try to keep up, detective. Meta data is information which travels *with* data, sort of like a ... a passport. Yes, like a passport. It tells anyone who knows how to ask the questions," Dean leaned back and smiled at Mike, "who, what, when, where, and maybe even how. The *why* will be left up to the real detectives to determine."

"Boil all this down and tell me what's left."

"What we have is a flash drive with an Excel worksheet file containing data that was constructed on 04/03/13 at 19:42:10, using Excel version 2007, which if read by Tyler McKinnon's computer, would have required his PC to download an Internet file converter in order to view these files using his antiquated software."

"If this file was created less than twenty-four hours prior to his death," Mike thought out loud, "which it tells us that it was, did he ever see the file?"

"There is no data in the flash drive file meta data that says he created the file or ever viewed this worksheet using his older version of Excel."

"Are you sure?"

Dean looked around the office. "Do you see anyone else around here you'd prefer to ask about this?"

"No."

"May I continue?"

"Please."

"This doesn't mean McKinnon never saw it, only that he never saw it using his older software. None of this information is conclusive, but that does not diminish its value."

"What are the odds he would have seen it on any other PC?" Mike said in a whisper.

Dean looked around the room again. "I will assume, Sergeant, your question was rhetorical. You're the detective. You'll have to tell me."

Mike laughed and slapped Dean on the back. "Good work, buddy. Thanks."

"No problem," Dean said, with a proud smile.

"One more thing," Mike said, "I need a favor. I need you to tell me if you can find any questionable activity since 2011 by a man with the name Wade Donald Powell. According to NCIC, he was convicted here in Tennessee of voluntary manslaughter in 2006. He served almost five years at Riverbend and was released in August 2011. I need to know where he is now, where he's been and what he has been doing since his release date. He must be on his best behavior or else there'd be something in his record from his parole officer."

"You have his DOB and Social?"

He handed Dean the printout from NCIC.

"I'll work it in and call you," Dean said.

"Thanks, you're the man."

"Correct again Sergeant," Dean said.

CHAPTER 18

Stone Asset Management, LLC
Downtown Nashville

Shannon looked up to see a neatly dressed man open the door and step toward her desk. She was attracted to him—again.

"Good morning, Sergeant. How may I help you?"

"I need to speak with Mr. Barrett Stone."

"Yes, sir." She focused on the detective's left hand. This candidate's ring finger was naked, and in her active imagination, the rest of him was, too.

She rang Barrett's desk phone without taking her focus off the handsome detective.

"What?" Barrett barked at the interruption.

"There is a gentleman here to see you."

"Whoever it is, he doesn't have an appointment. Get rid of him," Barrett said.

"He's from the police department."

"What?"

"He's a detective."

"What does he want?"

"I'm not sure. You'll have to ask him."

"Fine." Barrett conceded following a lengthy exhale. "Bring him back. I'm busy."

She stood. "Sergeant, if you'll follow me please." She smiled as she took the long route around her desk in order to display her assets for the attractive cop.

She walked ahead of her visitor, doing her best to further exercise her marketing skills and give Sergeant Neal something to enjoy.

As she reached Barrett's door she turned in time to see the detective reading something on his smart phone. Disappointed by his lack of interest, she frowned, knocked on Barrett's door and opened it.

"Barrett, this is Sergeant Neal."

"Sergeant." Barrett stood but remained behind his desk. "How can I help you?"

"Mr. Stone, we're investigating the murder of Tyler McKinnon. I'm told there was a connection between Stone Asset Management and Mr. McKinnon?"

"Sergeant, the only *connection* as you put it, was between my partner Al Ricks and Tyler McKinnon. I personally had no use for the man."

"You don't sound as though you and McKinnon were close."

"Close? Not quite." He gestured toward the chairs in front of his desk.

Both men sat.

"McKinnon was my partner's friend."

"Not yours?"

"Not mine."

"Was there something about him you feel I should know?"

"For an attorney, he was a sad excuse. I'm not sure how that will help your investigation, but that was *my* experience with him. He was not an impressive thinker—more of an attorney *wannabe*. And from what I'm told, his litigation record confirmed that."

"He was a trial lawyer?"

"I was told by Al Ricks that McKinnon attempted courtroom work years ago when he was trying to find himself, but he discovered that challenge to be larger than his talents. More than *one* of his clients received an all expense paid trip to prison as the result of McKinnon's substandard representation. Truly, most of my familiarity with the man was second-hand, but as far as I'm concerned, he was a disappointment both as an attorney and as a friend to Al Ricks."

"Did Mr. Ricks think so as well?"

"Al Ricks forms his own opinions. He's—considerably easier to impress than I am."

"Do you know of anyone who might have wanted Tyler McKinnon dead?"

He shook his head as he held his hands out palm side up. "My initial response would be: anyone he may have represented, but I know you're not here for subjective critique." He leaned forward in his chair. "I didn't have enough interaction with the man to answer that question. I'm no criminal investigator, but I can't help but assume that one of his ill-represented clients might be a productive place to start."

Neal continued to make notes.

Barrett was comfortable with his ability to manipulate other people. As he watched the detective scribbling, he considered the challenge of pitching Sergeant Neal with his investment plan, but decided the level of risk could be somewhat greater than he was comfortable with. He decided against it.

When Neal looked up, Barrett glanced at his Rolex, hoping to send a message.

"Sergeant, I am quite busy." He forced a weak smile.

"I understand," Neal said. "This won't take long. Mr. Stone, can you tell me what this is?" Neal handed him a two page document.

He squinted to read the heading and recognized the contract, dated months earlier. "It appears to be a contractual agreement of some sort." He handed it back to Neal after a cursory exam.

"Correct. It's a signed agreement between Tyler McKinnon and Stone Asset Management, LLC for investment services."

He remained unruffled.

"Mr. Stone, where do you think Tyler McKinnon obtained the monies listed here on this agreement with your company?"

"How much is it?"

"Fifteen thousand dollars."

He rolled his eyes. "Sergeant, I have no way of knowing where our clients' funds originate, nor do I care."

Neal flipped backward in his note pad.

He knew what was coming.

"Mr. Stone, you stated moments ago the only connection between Tyler McKinnon and Stone Asset Management was between your partner Al Ricks and Mr. McKinnon as his attorney."

He stared at the detective, gritted his teeth and fought the urge to explode.

"Sergeant, as I told you, McKinnon was *Al's* friend. *Al* chose to employ him as his attorney, for what reason I have no idea. It was a total waste of time and money, but Al said he was trying to help out the incompetent fool. Those last words are mine, not Al's." Please tell me, what does all this have to do with me?"

"This agreement is signed by you," Neal said.

"Let me see it again," he said, buying time.

He looked over the paper. "So it is. I'd say Al must have stuck this under my nose and asked me to sign it when I was too busy to be concerned with who the investor was. It's not the first time he's done that. Frankly, I don't remember it."

He tossed the agreement toward Neal and made a display of checking his watch again. "Can we wrap this up?"

"Mr. Stone," Neal said, unaffected by his attempt at rudeness, "until we complete our investigation we're actively working to identify or eliminate all potential suspects. Our inquiries normally begin with those persons who knew or interacted with the deceased recently and who may have had some reason to do them harm."

"What is that supposed to mean?" He crossed his arms over his chest.

"It means I have questions that need to be answered so I might be better able to eliminate you as a suspect, or be better able to pin you down as a person of interest."

Barrett's eyes narrowed and his lips tightened. He couldn't believe the nerve of this cop sitting in *his* office referring to him as a *person of interest* in a homicide.

"Detective—,"

"Sergeant," Neal cut him off.

"Whatever." He stood. "I'm not going to sit here and allow you to insult me by referring to me as a suspect in a damn homicide. I am a well-respected business man in this city and I know my rights. I am *finished* speaking with you and I want you to leave. If you want to talk with me further, you can do so through my attorney, who will be contacting your superiors shortly."

Neal closed his notebook and stood.

"Mr. Stone, I understand you are a busy man. We're all busy, I'm attempting to serve the interests of the citizens of Nashville by investigating a brutal homicide. I hope your intentions are not to hinder my investigation. Attorney or no attorney, you *will* be held accountable."

Neal stepped to the door and let himself out without further comment.

Shortly afterward Al opened Barrett's door without a knock. "Well?"

"Well what?" he answered, trying to sound unconcerned.

"How did it go?"

"He asked a lot of stupid questions and I handled them masterfully. What did you expect?"

"I heard you get loud."

"*He* became offensive. I responded appropriately to his aggressive questions with fitting responses. He was in *my* world, not his. He should've shown more respect if he wanted to continue to talk with me."

"What are *you* worried about?"

Al said nothing.

"Close the door, please—as you leave."

Al pulled the door closed behind him.

CHAPTER 19

Stone Asset Management, LLC
Downtown Nashville

Barrett pulled his cell phone from his pocket and scrolled his contact list. He tapped a number with no name listed, only the number. The phone began to ring.

"Yeah?"

"It's me," he announced as he began to tap his stiletto letter opener on the desk pad.

"No shit."

If I didn't need you for the dirty work, I'd ... He rotated the stiletto into stabbing position.

"I have work for you."

"What kinda work?"

"This will be easy."

"So, you gonna tell me what it is, or is this some kinda damned riddle I gotta try and figure out?"

Barrett closed his eyes and took a deep breath before responding. He expected everyone to have regard for him and his words, but he was realizing if he was going to interact with those at the lower reaches of society, he couldn't expect their adoration or anything beyond contempt. "I need you to find out where someone lives."

"What else?"

"That's it for now."

"Seriously? I'm not your secretary, ya know."

"Just do what I ask. Will you?"

"Who is it?"

"Mike Neal."

"Who is he?"

"He's a detective with the Nashville Police Department."

"Oh, no. No."

"What? You don't want the money?"

"I don't want my *ass* back in prison. That's what I don't want."

"You can't get arrested for finding out where someone lives."

"If you have my background, you can get arrested for *nothin'* if it's what they decide to do."

"Why are you so paranoid?"

"I'm not paranoid. I'm a lot wiser than I used to be. You forget. I know how you think, and I know this ain't all you'll want from me. And, I ain't goin' back in for you or nobody else."

"Find out where he lives."

"Remember what I said."

"I'll remember," he confirmed. "You remember who's paying you."

"You ain't *got* enough money."

"Fine. Now that we've established that, can I at least expect you to honor your commitments?"

"As long as completin' your *tasks* don't sacrifice my freedom."

"I'm paying you enough to cover some significant risk," he said.

"Maybe in *your* mind. You're not the one at risk."

"Let's try and move beyond all this and focus on what I need from you. Okay?"

All he heard from the phone was a grunt.

"Wonderful. Call me when you have it. Would you?" He ended the call.

It was all Barrett could do to keep from telling this idiot to forget everything, but he knew he needed the man's morally vacant skills much more at this time than he needed the man's admiration.

The private investigator he'd hired to locate this ex-convict had earned his money. Now, if Barrett could just motivate this example of societal rubbish to do his bidding, this killer could become worth his weight in stock certificates.

CHAPTER 20

Franklin, Tennessee

Mike was accustomed to the dismal aura surrounding families recently affected by violent death. He'd learned long ago, the only way to survive the emotional distress, and preserve a level of sanity in his line of work was to maintain some isolation from the victims. He was concerned, with Allison involved in the case, this could become difficult.

He'd received a call from the Medical Examiner earlier in the afternoon. The details confirmed what he knew already and little else. Tyler Edward McKinnon was killed by a lethal gunshot wound to the left side of the head with a large caliber hollow point bullet fired from a distance of between six and twelve feet. The projectile entered the victim's head 3.6 cm forward of, and in line with, the left ear canal. Time of death is estimated at between 02:30 a.m. and 04:30 a.m. on the morning of Monday April 22, 2013.

When the M.E.'s assistant had finished giving him the basics, he asked that they email him the full report as soon as possible.

As he stepped through the rear doorway of the funeral home, Mike could smell the fragrance of fresh flowers mixed with the smell of food. Flowers were a beautiful expression of sympathy in a difficult time. In the south, food was traditionally brought to the funeral home for the family by friends of the deceased.

He looked down the long hallway to the front of the building where people were lined up waiting to sign the register, inscribing proof of their sympathy, and their presence. He nodded a reverent greeting to the funeral home's men-in-black as he walked the well-worn hall carpeting toward the front lobby.

He passed the column of serene mourners and moved into the room where the Culvers and McKinnons were greeting family and friends around the unopened, flower-topped, steel gray casket. Photos of the deceased were placed throughout the room on tables.

Mike spotted Allison. In a modest black dress with a single strand of pearls, she was the classic mourning wife and the most attractive lady in the place. He watched as she shook hands, hugged and interacted with people who were sharing their sympathy, and some, their uncomfortable questions about Tyler's death.

An elderly couple finished their chat with the widow and moved toward the coffin and the photos, Allison dabbed her nose with a tissue and glanced around the room. Her gaze locked on his and both began to walk toward each other.

He could hear her excusing herself and thanking people as she moved around them.

"Hi," she said as she raised her arms to wrap them around his chest. She closed her eyes.

He gently caressed her shoulders. He took in the fragrance of her perfume and her hair, as well as the memories and emotions that traveled with them. "How are you?"

"Much better now," she said. Allison looked up and smiled at her old lover.

"You look good," he whispered.

"Thank you. I've not heard that for a long time."

He smiled. He knew better than to comment about that. He gazed over Allison's shoulder at the multitude of visitors and family, most of whom were watching the widow and no doubt wondering who he was. Many were clustered in small groups, likely discussing Tyler McKinnon's violent demise and speculating on who was involved. One person noticeably absent from the grieving family was Drew Culver.

"Is Drew not here?"

"He's coming later," Allison mumbled. "He won't stay long, just enough to satisfy Mom."

"What was it between Tyler and Drew anyway?"

"What do you mean?"

"You know what I mean—the conflict. There had to be more than just a brother defending his sister? When Drew spoke to me about Tyler, his voice was filled with animosity. Your brother despised Tyler."

"You may have misunderstood him," Allison said.

"Oh?"

"Yes. Drew has always been protective of me, even when we were kids."

"I can understand his feelings, but when he and I were talking, his words weren't protective. At least for now, his loathing keeps him on the suspect list."

Allison inhaled and blew it out. She took his hand and said, "Let's go outside. I need to explain something."

He walked with Allison to her car. She put her hand into her pocket, pulled out tissues and her keys. She pressed the remote access and they sat in the car.

Allison turned in her seat to face him. "About a year ago, Drew proposed to his girlfriend Laura. They'd been dating for about two years and were happy together. Laura's family was not well-to-do, so Mom agreed to help with expenses. Drew asked me to lend Laura a hand in preparing the wedding. That girl didn't have a clue. I was glad to help. She spent evenings at our house talking about the wedding. Drew was working second shift at the time, so Tyler took her home each of those nights around nine o'clock."

Allison leaned back and rubbed her forehead. "I don't know when it happened or how, but Tyler developed an interest in Laura."

He was sure the look on his face convinced Allison he had already finished the story in his mind.

"Yes, they had an affair. Drew caught them together and he beat Tyler senseless."

"Did Tyler file charges?"

"I talked him out of it. I told him he deserved it, and I ought to do the same to him myself. This is when our relationship began deteriorating."

"What happened then?"

"Drew called off the wedding. He told Laura he didn't ever want to see her again. It really embarrassed Mom."

"What about Tyler?"

"He received twenty-six stitches to close up the cuts on his face. He was off work for two weeks to allow the damage to heal enough for him to convince people it was caused by a bicycle accident."

"Were there any more confrontations?"

"Oh, yes—several, but less severe. Most were shouting and shoving matches. I was able to break up some of them, but after I moved out there was no one to keep them apart. One night they got into it and Drew sent Tyler to the hospital."

"Does Drew own a pistol?"

Allison looked into his eyes. "No. And you're looking in the wrong direction. Drew didn't kill him."

He nodded, but he wasn't as confident as Allison seemed to be. "How can you be sure?"

"Mike, if Drew would have *ever* killed Tyler, it would have been the night he found out about the affair. Surely, you realize that."

"Most likely, yes. But we have to vet all potential suspects and you have to admit, unfortunately, Drew makes a pretty good one. Means, motive and opportunity; he can't be ruled out yet."

Allison looked at him, and then down at her hands.

"Speaking of suspects," he pulled a folded sheet of paper from his pocket, "do you recognize any of these names or numbers, other than your own and your mom's of course?"

She scanned the list. "I don't recognize any of the others. Who are they?"

"Names and numbers we took from Tyler's contact list in his cell phone."

"Seriously? Why would he still have my numbers in his cell?"

"My guess is, unlike you, he hadn't given up."

Allison looked at him without comment.

"His call record shows that he called your cell phone several times, but with no connection."

Allison hesitated and looked out the front window. "I made it clear to him; I was gone."

Mike shrugged. "Guys can be hard-headed like that."

"Who are the others?" Allison asked.

"The first two numbers are Al Ricks cell and home. The next four are clients. The rest are numbers for his landscaper, his Lexus dealer and two pizza delivery joints. Then there were two women who said they thought they may have met him at a club, and the last one is the number for a local escort service."

"What? An escort service?" Allison laid her head back on the head rest. "How embarrassing."

"Most of Tyler's inbound calls were from Al, but there were three from a number we've tied to a local drug dealer."

Allison shook her head.

"What about that list of clients from Tyler's files in his office?" Allison said trying to change the subject. "Have you checked them out yet? Some of those people are known criminals."

"There are about a dozen on the list we're currently investigating. Some of them were locked up when Tyler was killed."

"I guess I'd make a good suspect too, huh?" Allison stared into his eyes. "After everything he promised me and his total failure to honor his commitments?"

He looked at Allison, wondering why she'd said it. "You don't look like any of the suspects I've investigated."

"So, where does this leave us?"

"Which *us* are we talking about?" he teased. "You and Drew, or you and me?"

"Which would you rather talk about?" Allison asked, resting her elbow on the car's console as she leaned toward him and gave him a weak smile.

"We've already talked about Drew." He looked into Allison's eyes. His memories took him back to Knoxville and the early weeks of their connection when they used to park in one of the distant campus parking lots at night and talk and ....

"So tell me—where are you in life's contest of relationships and emotions."

He considered what he *should* say versus what he wanted to say. "My life is complicated by my work." He paused. "My emotions are somewhat callused on the one hand and ... raw on the other. This job makes successful relationships pretty damned difficult. Of course, I guess it depends on your definition of success."

"But, it doesn't make them impossible?"

He grunted. "No—not impossible. I know some strong folks who manage to somehow set it aside and live a separate life at home. It's tough. It has to be. You have to sort of develop a split personality, dedicating one to the work and the other to your family. You can't take the job home. That won't work. If it was easy, there wouldn't be so many failed relationships in law enforcement."

"I understand."

"Do you?" He paused. "It's difficult to do this job and do it well. It's more difficult to watch someone you care about trying to do it and maintain a sense of normality in their life."

"Does that mean you've decided to avoid taking chances at relationships outside the job?"

"It would be a safer route. But, even cops deserve a chance."

"We all deserve a chance, especially when we're coming off a monumental failure." Allison leaned toward him, put her left hand behind his neck and pulled him into her soft and engaging kiss. He didn't resist.

As their lips came apart, he looked into Allison's eyes briefly. He touched her cheek as the flash of the arriving car's headlights killed the darkness and the moment, bringing both of them back from the brief resurgence of their affection.

Allison sat back in the driver's seat and pulled down the makeup mirror. She checked her face and hair.

"I guess this isn't the place or time," he said.

Allison turned to face him. "Tell me where and when."

He laughed and looked at his watch. "You should go back and be with your family. I need to go too."

"I'm glad you came by." She reached for him.

"Me too." He squeezed her hand. "I'll call you."

CHAPTER 21

Belle Meade
Nashville

As Mike pulled forward in the long line of Mercedes, Lexus, and BMWs waiting to be valet parked at the political fundraiser, his frustration was suspended by the repetitive sound coming from his cell phone.

"Mike Neal."

"Mike, it's Dean. I ran your search on Wade Powell."

"Yeah?"

"Looks like he's behaving himself. I can find nothing of significance on him since his release other than the fact that he has a full time job as of twenty months ago and he's making all his P.O. appointments. He's living at the same apartment complex in LaVergne where he works as their maintenance man. He's remained clean, so far. What did you think I might find?"

"I don't know. If he's like so many others with his history, he may not be as clean as he looks. He may be smarter and more careful since his stay in prison. Keep an eye out and maybe run your check again in a few days. Okay?"

"Copy that. Anything else you need?"

"You can email me the name and address of the apartments where he's living in LaVergne."

"My pleasure, Sarge."

"Thanks."

Mike was finally greeted by one of the valet parkers.

"Good evening sir," the young man said, holding the door to the turd brown two-year-old slightly dented Chevy Impala sedan.

"Hello." He pulled back the right panel of his sport jacket to show the young man his shield and in doing so, his Glock was also exposed. He thought he was going to have to catch the boy to stop his stumble when he stepped back.

"Sir?"

"Nashville Police Department business, I'd like you to keep the car close. I won't be long."

"Uh, yes sir."

"And by the way, don't touch anything inside the car."

"Oh, no sir."

"If you do, I'll know."

"Yes, sir." The boy's eyes widened.

"Fingerprints, you know." Mike smiled at the boy.

"Uh, sir?"

"Yes. You can touch the steering wheel and the gear shift."

"Thank you, sir."

The young man climbed into the car and pulled his long shirt sleeves down to cover his hands before he put the car in gear and slowly pulled away.

Mike approached the multi-million dollar residence. Tonight's social event was a five thousand dollar per plate fundraiser to help relieve the campaign debt for the party's most recent failed run for the Tennessee State Congress.

His detective shield was as good as an invitation to any gathering. The large man at the front door had a coiled translucent white wire extending from the rear of his jacket's collar up to his right ear. His hands were folded across his ample gut and a serious wrinkled forehead projected his attitude. The fact Mike was underdressed for the event caused the rent-a-guard to give him a questioning look. As the large man stepped into his path, Mike again pulled back his jacket to expose his detective shield.

"On duty," he said, then waited for the man's response.

The guard stepped back and without saying a word extended his arm toward the crowd inside.

Mike nodded his thanks and stepped into the large room. He scanned the crowd from left to right and spotted Stone talking with a dapper-looking man who appeared to be in his late sixties.

As Mike came near the two men, Stone must have sensed his presence. He glanced to his right, saw Mike and then turned his back and kept talking.

Mike tactfully stood to the side and waited for a break in their conversation. He leaned toward Stone. "We need to talk."

"Pardon me? You need to contact my office during business hours for an appointment if you want to speak with me." Stone lowered his volume. "Better yet, as I told you before, contact my attorney."

"Mr. Stone—"

Stone interrupted him by once again turning his back and facing the older man, "I apologize for this man's rudeness." Stone smiled. "I'll catch up with you and we can continue our discussion."

The man nodded and assured Stone it was no problem. He turned and walked away.

"Let me make something clear," Mike said.

"Listen—"

"No, you listen." Mike raised his voice, then paused. "First of all, this *is* business hours. *My* business hours are twenty-four seven. Now, we can either step outside quietly without making a scene and have a calm discussion, or I can call in a couple of uniformed officers to join me in disrupting this pretentious event and embarrass you in front of all your friends. Then, if I don't get some answers, I can have those officers place handcuffs on your wrists, and take you through the middle of this snooty group and down to the Criminal Justice Center where we will end up doing exactly what we can more easily do outside here in about ten minutes." He gestured toward the patio doors.

Mike pulled his jacket back and put his hand in his pocket exposing his shield and his side arm to the large crowd of wealthy and influential folks. "Your call, Mr. Stone."

Stone's face reddened. He angled his head away from the crowd and scrunched his lips together. He said nothing, but turned and marched toward the French doors that led outside onto one of the patios. Mike followed him.

When Stone reached the patio, he didn't stop. He kept walking down the steps and toward one of the rear parking areas, away from earshot of his friends. Stone turned to face Mike.

"You have a lot of nerve showing up here in front of my business associates and embarrassing me."

"You didn't like the privacy of your office, so I thought you'd prefer this to being escorted out by uniformed officers. If you'd like," he pulled out his cell phone, "I can still call them."

For years he'd dealt with people who suffered from delusions of grandeur. Putting them in their place brought him considerable pleasure.

"How did you know I would be here?"

"Someone told me there would be more money represented here tonight than at the CMA Awards. So, I made the assumption. Looks like I was right."

"So, what is it that's so damned important you had to barge in here and start pushing around law abiding citizens?"

"As I attempted to explain to you when we spoke earlier today, I am conducting a homicide investigation. I am charged with the responsibility of collecting information in order to determine who was involved with the victim and what their relationship might have been."

"Fine, that's *your* problem. How does this involve me?"

"I have uncovered credible evidence that you threatened harm to Tyler McKinnon less than a week before his death."

"What? What the hell are you talking about? I've threatened Tyler McKinnon more than once. That doesn't mean I killed the dumb bastard."

"Maybe—maybe not. But this fact, along with your obstinate attitude about the seriousness of this case, and your attempt to mislead me into thinking you and McKinnon had virtually no interaction, reserves you a front row seat on our list of suspicious people."

"You've got to be kidding me."

"Mr. Stone, unless you can provide me an excellent alibi for Sunday night and early Monday morning, I'm afraid you will *remain* on our suspect list."

"I was at home in my bed by ... eleven, maybe midnight at the latest. My wife can attest to that."

"Is your wife here tonight?" He looked back toward the house.

"No. She wasn't available. She has her own set of priorities, misguided as they are."

"I see. How do I get in touch with Mrs. Stone?"

"You can do as I do. Leave her a voicemail and *wait*." Stone pulled his smart phone from his jacket pocket.

"Go," Mike said when he was ready to key in her number.

Stone gave Mike his wife's cell number and put his phone away. Standing with his arms crossed in a defiant pose and staring away from the detective, he said, "May I go back inside now?"

"Yes."

Stone took a long step back toward the home.

"Mr. Stone."

Stone stopped without turning to face him.

"Can I assume you have no plans to leave Nashville any time soon?"

Stone hesitated. "No—I do not."

"Good." He watched Stone stomp back to the illuminated mansion.

CHAPTER 22

Downtown Nashville

Mike pulled the vibrating phone from his pocket. "Mike Neal."

"Michael, what's shakin' partner?" Norm said, "I just picked up your voicemail."

Detective Norm Wallace was Mike's former partner. They'd served together in Homicide for almost three years until Norm suffered a heart attack on the job. "How long ago did you call?"

"Not long. The lieutenant tells me I might be able to warm up one of your colder homicides from a few years back."

"Just one? Hell, I have several stale ones that aren't taking me where I need to go. And at the rate I'm picking up new cases, I have less and less time to dedicate to the old ones."

"I know the feeling," Mike said.

"I got one yesterday. You have to hear this. It was a sick old man on oxygen who was burned up in a house fire. The Nashville Fire Department Arson Investigator says he believes it may have been murder. Here I've got a classic accidental death scenario with what some arson guy says is a crime scene made out of wet charcoal and I'm supposed to find evidence and a suspect?"

"We're all swamped, buddy. I know how you feel. Listen, Burris said the case I'm calling about is the late state senator's wife,

Meredith Bowles."

"Bowles. Yeah. I've been getting heat from Burris and several *political* sources for a long time now. Then I found out she was the freakin' Mayor's sister. Man, I didn't need to know that."

"It's always helpful when the pressure's jacked up by the folks in power," Mike said with a tone of sarcasm.

"A case as connected as this one will never be allowed to become a cold case. I don't have squat for meaningful evidence. The only prints, other than hers didn't show up in any AFIS search. There were tool marks on the sliding glass door and tennis shoe impressions around the patio matching half of Nashville's teenagers. I'll own this freakin' case until I retire."

"Yeah, but I can understand the mayor's perspective," he said.

"I'll bet you can buddy," Norm said, remembering the brutal murder of Mike's sister. "So, what have you got that's gonna help me clear this one?"

"I don't know if it will clear it for you, but it's got to help. I've come across a piece of jewelry Burris says may have belonged to your victim."

"Jewelry? Please tell me it's a large gaudy-ass gold brooch with three stars and diamonds in the middle of 'em."

"That's it."

"You *are* shittin' me? I've been looking in every pawn shop and second-hand jewelry store in town for that tacky-ass bling since I saw it in pictures of the Senator and Mrs. Bowles taken before his death. They said it was a gift from him and she wore it every day after he died.

"Yep. This is definitely it. There can't be two of these globs of gold."

"Where did you get it?"

"It was sitting on top of a bundle of cash inside the floor safe at my victim's home."

"What? Who's your victim?" Norm asked.

"Tyler McKinnon."

Norm thought a moment. "Doesn't ring a bell. Was he a politician?"

"No. He was a low tier lawyer who lived in the older section of Brentwood. He was shot in the head while driving home early Monday morning."

"Whoa. Do you think he could have killed Mrs. Bowles?"

"Honestly buddy, I don't know enough yet to make a call on that.

I'm thinking my victim may have received the cash, the brooch and possibly some other *gifts* as a post mortem contribution to his assets meant to fowl up my investigation."

"I thought you said it was in a safe with a bunch of money?"

"It was, but the dumb ass used his birthday as the combination on the rare occasion he decided to lock the safe."

"Brilliant. Anybody could figure out his birthday."

"So, are you thinking maybe the Bowles killer was also your victim's killer?"

"It's one scenario Burris and I are in agreement has to be considered."

"And planting the brooch was the killer's attempt at misdirection?" Norm asked.

"It's looking like it's a first rate possibility, but I can't be certain yet. There's just not enough solid evidence to support any theory. I'm hoping, between your investigation and mine; we can solve one of these murders and as a result uncover enough meaningful information to close the other one. My closure rate lately is embarrassing."

"I know the feeling. Where's the brooch now?"

"Wendy logged it in the property room. It'll be under McKinnon, Tyler."

"This is great. I could kiss you."

"Hold that thought. Better yet, why don't you kiss Cheryl when you get home and tell her it's from me. Tell her I could use some of her awesome lasagna. I'll accept it as compensation for my assistance with the Bowles case."

"It's a deal, partner. This is great news. Maybe I can get the politicos off my ass for a while."

"Don't hold your breath. This may give you the missing brooch and whatever leads it can generate, but I'm not sure Wendy was able to get any usable prints from it. I'm sure DNA results, if there are any, could be weeks away, maybe longer."

"I'll keep my fingers crossed," Norm said.

"I still need to confirm how this hunk of gold ended up in McKinnon's safe, so keep me in the loop on anything you find."

"You got it, Michael. Thanks again."

CHAPTER 23

Downtown Nashville

Before making the call to Stone's wife, Mike did as much research as time allowed. When possible, he liked to begin his interviews with questions to which he already knew the answers. This helped him discover early on whether or not people were going to be honest with him.

He was able to learn that Barrett Stone's wife of four years was the former Sarah Alexandra Ballenger, daughter of Seth and Clarene Ballenger. Mr. Ballenger is the grandson of Owen Ballenger, co-founder of Ballenger & Hart, one of the oldest law firms still operating in Nashville after almost 90 years.

Sarah was an only child, the sole heir to the law firm and her father's fortune. Seth Ballenger's assets were more than enough to attract the interest of any potential suitor, much less one who worships the dead presidents.

Sarah Stone's cell phone display read 'Nashville Police Department'. She decided to answer it. "Hello."

"Mrs. Sarah Stone?"

"Who is this?"

"Mrs. Stone, this is Sergeant Mike Neal. I'm a detective with the Nashville Police Department."

"What is this about?"

"I'm investigating the murder of Tyler McKinnon. Your husband gave me your cell number. I need to speak with you briefly."

"Why?"

"Mrs. Stone, I need to ask you some questions about your husband. I'd prefer to do this face to face if I could meet with you for a few minutes."

"What is it you need to know about my husband? I'm in the middle of something important at the moment." She took a sip of her Cabernet Sauvignon.

Sarah's fellow Bridge players looked at each other with questioning glances followed by smiles as Sarah stood and started down her hallway in search of some privacy.

"I hate to interrupt your evening, but I need to get this information. I need to verify Mr. Stone's whereabouts Sunday evening and Monday morning."

"Surely you don't suspect Barrett killed someone—do you? Sergeant, you must not know Barrett very well. He wouldn't expel sufficient energy or soil his hands enough to kill someone."

"What does that mean?"

"Barrett Stone is not the kind of man who acts as much as one who talks and tells others what to do. My husband and I are not the closest couple in town, Sergeant. You may already know that."

"I understand. What can you tell me about his whereabouts Sunday night and early Monday?"

"Let me see. Sunday, when I went to bed, Barrett was on the computer. When I got up Monday morning, he was gone as usual. He normally sleeps about five hours each night. He doesn't require as much rest as I do. Other than that, I'm not sure what I can tell you."

"So, you can confirm he was at home with you at what time?"

"Sergeant, I can confirm he was at home, but he was not *with* me. We have separate bedrooms."

"I see."

"I set the security system nightly as soon as the weather report is over. I go to bed at about ten-twenty each evening. I can't tell you when *he* went to bed or got up or left the house." She paused. "Wait a minute. Can't you request data from our security company?"

"With your permission."

"I'll call them and ask what time the alarm was turned off. That should tell you when he left, shouldn't it?"

"Within reason. Do you mind letting them know it's okay to share your access data with us? We may need to request other information."

"Such as?"

"Such as data for other days when the system was armed or disarmed. I can't think of anything else they could tell us that might be of importance."

"I'll tell them, but I'm sure they'll require me to sign some kind of release to cover their collective asses, but I'll take care of it."

"I still need to meet with you. What time tomorrow can you give me maybe an hour or so of your time?"

She hesitated. "What about one o'clock?"

"What about ten in the morning?" Mike asked.

Sarah laughed. "Can you come to my house? I don't normally get up until at least eight-thirty or nine."

"Yes. I can meet you there."

"Do you need my address?"

"No, ma'am. I know where you live."

"Oh, I'll bet you know a lot of things," Sarah said. She hung up.

This was a strong, intelligent and confident woman. Mike was not at all surprised. No other woman would stay with a man like Stone. But, why would one like *her* stay with him at all? There had to be a reason. Based upon what he knew about this affluent segment of Nashville society, in some way, it all had to involve money.

CHAPTER 24

Stone Asset Management, LLC
Downtown Nashville

"I'd hoped to go another few weeks to get our assets up over fifty million," Barrett said. "But, this infuriating detective is putting everything at risk with his relentless prying."

Al stared at Barrett, but said nothing.

"She never answers her damn cell phone when *I* call her," Barrett said as he held the cell phone to his ear. "Actually, it's for the best. I don't want to talk to her anyway."

Al wanted to tell Barrett to stop his complaining, but he found it easier to just tune him out.

"She blew her last chance to ever speak with—Hey. It's me. Al and I are going to make the conference in Atlanta after all. We're driving down tonight in order to make the early session. I'm going home now to pack."

With that brief discourse, Barrett easily ended his voice mail and his chances at Sarah Ballenger Stone's substantial inheritance. Al had watched for almost four years as their marriage dissolved into a caricature, a portrait of detachment painted by greed.

"So much for her attempt to use that sorry excuse for a prenuptial agreement her old man drew up. She's not getting a dime of my damn money. She and her father are so lame to think they could control me. I'll show you, *Daddy Ballenger*."

Al looked up as Barrett rubbed his hands together like some cartoon villain. "When are you giving your wife the news about our good fortune with the Atlanta Conference?"

"I'm going home shortly to pack," he said. "I'll tell her then."

"Face to face? Wow. That's balls, Albert."

Al shrugged his shoulders and continued to collect items from his desk that he wanted to keep. "She deserves some respect."

Barrett nodded. "More than my pain-in-the-ass wife, that's for sure. Listen, leave your PC and your cell phone on your desk."

"Why? I need them."

"I'm going to destroy the hard drive from your PC and the one from Shannon's desktop. And, I'll have you a new cell phone tonight. We'll get you a new laptop later."

"Why?" he asked again.

"I want to eliminate any potential connections. I have to destroy anything that could be used against us."

"What about *your* laptop?"

"I'll destroy it later. I have several important things I have to do first. It's going to take a while.

"I have a couple of boxes to put in the car and then I'm going to leave for a while. When I get back, I'll take care of the computers. Put anything questionable you feel needs to be destroyed in one of those boxes and I'll take care of it. Everything else in the office will be shredded or burned. I have a crew coming in later to take care of it.

"Cheer up. You're about to be born again." Barrett smiled. "Start thinking about the future, not the past. I'll call you at home in an hour and let you know what time I'll be picking you up."

"Before I forget," Al said, "I have a couple of Excel files I've updated. You're going to want these updates, so I'll send them to your email before I shut down my laptop. This way the data won't be lost."

"Good idea."

Al knew Barrett had no plans to destroy his own laptop. He just wanted to be sure he had total control over everyone else and no one could endanger him or his magnificent plan.

Al stayed busy as he watched Barrett take the last box out the door.

As soon as he was sure Barrett was gone, he pulled a thirty-two gigabyte flash drive from his pocket and plugged it into one of the USB ports on his laptop. Al pulled up the Excel files he'd talked about and attached them to his email going to Barrett.

Al had other files on his laptop he could not allow anyone to destroy.

CHAPTER 25

Oakhill
South Nashville

Barrett arrived at Al's home at half past midnight. Al was standing at the end of his driveway with his bags packed. The only help offered by Barrett was his pressing of the remote trunk release.

The BMW pulled away and Al reached back over his shoulder to grab his seatbelt. As he looked at his home for the last time, he spotted Mary Ellen's silhouette. She was standing at the dining room window in her robe, waving. Once again, he pondered his daunting decision.

"My carry-on bag in the back seat contains everything we need to support our new identities," Barrett said. "The counterfeiter in Chicago was both talented and discreet. The IDs are amazing, and he was more than affordable."

Al looked out his side window. *Of course he was affordable, now that you have much of the assets from over three dozen of your father's wealthiest friends.*

Al listened as Barrett told him in boring detail how he'd spent the day initiating the numerous steps in his scandalous plan, so that by eight o'clock tomorrow morning, when business would normally commence, Stone Asset Management, LLC, Barrett Hayden Stone III and Al Ricks would no longer exist.

As Barrett pulled onto the EuroCar dealership lot to drop off his lease car, his headlights illuminated the shining black stretched Lincoln limousine, waiting to take them on the next segment of their late night exodus from this current life.

Barrett pushed the shifter into park for the last time and triggered the trunk release for the chauffeur.

As Barrett opened his door, a gust of wind whipped through the car. Al looked at Barrett. His eyes bulged. The wind had blown Barrett's hair so that, for an instant, in the glow of the car's red dash lights Barrett's face appeared crimson red with what looked like horns projecting from the top of his head. An icy chill ran through Al's body.

"What are you looking at?" Barrett asked. The wisps of Barrett's hair fell. He shut off the car and dropped the keys into the console. "You look like you saw a ghost."

"Oh—nothing. I ... uh. I was looking at the limo."

"Let's go." Barrett said as he turned to exit the car.

Al stepped to the rear of the BMW to help with his bags. He grabbed two bags and started for the limo behind the driver. He saw Barrett approach the rear door of the limo, stand and wait for the driver. Barrett cleared his throat to clarify his proud expectation. The driver approached and opened Barrett's door. He stood back to allow his demanding customer to enter the car.

Al shook his head as he opened his own limo door.

Barrett was sitting in the car's rear seat, so Al took the long seat on the right side of the spacious black leather-lined compartment.

Barrett pushed the button to raise the solid privacy panel behind the driver's compartment. He unzipped his bag and tossed a nine by thirteen inch manila envelope onto Al's lap.

"What's this?"

"The new you."

He opened the sealed flap and dumped the contents onto his lap. "Oh."

"That should be everything you need."

He fumbled with the passport, birth certificate, Texas Driver's License, credit cards and a throw away cell phone. "T. Albert Marshall?"

"I thought it fit you. It sounds like a wealthy Texan to me." Barrett smiled. "First name is Thomas. The limit on each of the credit cards is twenty-five thousand."

Al looked up.

"If you need more, tell me."

"It should be plenty."

"My new name is Bradford S. Strong."

"Really?"

"I like it," Barrett said. "By the way, the only number programmed into your phone is my new cell number."

Al sat staring at his new plastic identity.

"What's the matter?" Barrett asked.

He hesitated, closed his eyes and shrugged. "A totally new identity; it's a big change—a lot to get used to."

"Yes, it is. It's a change you deserve. And, so do I."

He looked at Barrett and doubted if the man had ever loved his wife or anyone else in his life.

"You look like hell."

"I'm concerned about all this."

"About what? I've taken care of everything. You should be relaxed, thankful and anticipating a glorious second life. Most people never get an opportunity like this."

"There's more to it. I feel sort of ... selfish," he admitted.

"Selfish?" Barrett chuckled. "I'm feeling a lot of things right now, but selfish is not one of them."

The two men swapped stares.

"Since I was old enough to have a memory, I watched my father, and for that matter my mother, chase money with the passion they should have shown for each other. My father spent his time with his cronies and business associates while I sat home wondering why he had no time for me and guessing where he could be that was so much more important."

Al knew this memoir by heart, but he also knew better than to remind Barrett of it. As always, it was easier to let him vent. At least he wasn't yelling at *him*.

"My mother worked every day for years, seven days a week, at her real estate brokerage. For what?" Barrett paused. "She said her agents and her customers needed her. Yeah? Well—so did I." Barrett shook his head. "She knew her husband wouldn't be at home anyway. But then, *I* could have used a mother instead of a housekeeper."

"Neither one of them wanted a family. They didn't even act like they wanted each other. Hell, they must have gotten close at some point, or *I* wouldn't be here."

Barrett looked out the limo's tinted window at the city's lights racing by.

"By the time they discovered the cancer, it was too late. If my father ever loved her before, he stopped after the double mastectomy. He lost interest and she lost her mind. When he gave up on her, *she* gave up. She lost hope and let her sleeping pills heal her. That's when that damned Bowles woman tried to make her move and sink her claws into him." Barrett took an emotion-filled breath.

"These rich old fools have been doing business with me solely because they enjoyed knowing my father, and they knew young Barrett would take care of them too. I'm taking pleasure in emptying their portfolios. They *owe* me. They got my father at a time when *I* needed him, while I sat home crying and watching others my age going places and enjoying their *dads*." Barrett paused. "Selfish? I don't think so."

Barrett tossed his carry-on bag into the floor of the limo. "We have a long drive. I'm going to take a nap."

Barrett removed his jacket and hung it on the hook over the limo door. He slipped down in the soft leather seat, positioning one of the throw pillows beneath his head.

Glad Barrett had finally completed his tirade, Al pulled his soft side leather briefcase closer where he could reach the novel he'd selected yesterday as his diversion during the long trip.

He looked at Barrett. He was already snoring.

The last thing he wanted to do for the next three hours was listen to Barrett's theories on how they could have made more money than they did. He would rather listen to the man's snoring. He made himself comfortable for the long drive.

The recent dramatic changes to his settled life, and the upcoming alterations to his physical appearance in the next forty-eight hours, had Al on edge. He knew he needed to fill his mind with something besides Barrett's snoring.

He pulled the foam ear plugs from his case. He'd brought them along as his defense for wailing infants on the ten hour transatlantic flight. He pushed the ear plugs in, slipped his loafers off, and leaned back in the seat. He parked his tired feet against the seat across from him and flipped through the first half dozen pages of the hardback novel, looking to start his much needed distraction.

CHAPTER 26

Stone Asset Management, LLC
Downtown Nashville

Shannon arrived for work, expecting nothing different from any other morning, Barrett would be a jackass and Al would be suffering from the debilitating effects of a poor self image and the cumulative results of Barrett's harassment.

For the past several days, she'd been stressing over Barrett's investor quarterly reports. Barrett told her when she began she must have them completed by this morning. The clients were expected in the office throughout the afternoon, and he needed time for a final review. Her work was still unfinished when she left the office yesterday. So, she took the reports home last night and after working until well after midnight, they were completed. Barrett would have no excuse to brow beat her today, at least not about *this* project.

With the reports in their individual dark blue Stone Asset Management, LLC folders with faux gold embossing, they were ready for Barrett's examination. She entered the office building with a certain degree of confidence and with her arms full of her late night efforts. She hoped Barrett would be late today giving her time to prepare the conference room for his clients. Barrett always wanted his clients to be more than impressed with his financial expertise. A professional presentation was the proper first step. She knew he wanted them charmed from the start.

She set the box of reports next to the office door and fished in her purse for her key. Once she had the door unlocked and propped open with her foot, she placed her purse on top of the box, picked it all up and pushed the door open with her butt.

When she turned from the door to approach her desk and park the heavy box, the sight before her interrupted her plan. Her head swiveled back and forth. She was looking for her desk, her credenza or anything on which to set the box.

Feeling as if she was in a sudden stupor, she set the box and her purse on the floor in front of her and then stood hoping that when she looked again everything would be as she left it last evening. It was not. The office was empty—totally empty. Nothing she was accustomed to seeing on her morning arrival was anywhere in sight, except carpeting and drywall.

"This makes no sense."

Searching for a logical explanation, she went back to the door, opened it and turned to look at the two-toned brown plaque with Stone Asset Management, LLC. The plaque was gone. In its place were four small holes in the drywall to the right of the office door. She hadn't noticed the plaque was missing when she arrived. She scanned the hallway in both directions hoping somehow she was in the wrong office or maybe on the wrong floor.

While she ran a list of potential explanations through her mind, she pulled her cell phone from her purse and dialed Al's number. After three rings she was informed the number she was calling had been disconnected or was no longer in service.

Convinced she had somehow called the wrong number, she tried again. She received the same recording. This was too much of a coincidence. She knew her next option was something she never did. She called Barrett's cell phone.

When she heard the same recorded message as the one for Al's number, she backed to the edge of the room and leaned against the wall to keep from falling. She was running out of possibilities. Her gaze darted back and forth, searching the vacant space around her for anything that might suggest an answer. She allowed her back to slide down the wall until she was sitting on the floor in a less than ladylike position.

She closed her eyes and willed the morning to go away. It didn't.

This was the most surreal feeling she had ever encountered. She needed something to make sense soon, to explain what, and most of all, why.

She asked herself, *Did Barrett fail to pay the rent and we were evicted? Al would have called me. We were robbed? They wouldn't have taken furniture. Barrett decided to move the office and couldn't bring himself to fire me?*

"Hell, that jerk would relish firing me," She said to no one and stared at her phone. "There has to be someone I can call." She scrolled her contact list. "I'll call Sarah."

After three rings, Sarah's voicemail message began and she decided to leave her a message.

"Sarah, it's Shannon Richards at Barrett's office," she said masking her nerves with a pleasant tone. "I was wondering if you could give me a call. I sort of have an issue here at the office and at the moment I can't reach Barrett or Al. Can you call me back, please? I really need to speak with you soon. I appreciate it. I hope you're doing well. Thanks."

She ended the call and expelled a huge breath, wondering if Sarah would be concerned enough about her vague dilemma to return her call. They hardly knew each other.

She thought about calling Mary Ellen Ricks, but as she scrolled the contact list on her phone she realized she didn't have Al's home number. He'd told her to always call his cell.

She bowed her head and for the first time in a long time confessed to God she didn't know what to do, and she asked Him for help. She began to cry. The more she cried the more hopeless she felt and the more bewildered she became.

The click of the office door startled her. She grabbed her mouth to help silence her sobs and watched the answer to her prayer walk in.

"Hello?"

Shannon climbed to her feet and acknowledged Sergeant Neal.

"Hi," Shannon said, dabbing the corners of her eyes with the back of her hand.

He looked around. "What happened?"

"I wish I knew." Shannon straightened her dress.

"What do you mean? Where are Stone and Ricks?"

"I don't know," Shannon said. "I arrived about twenty minutes ago and found it like this."

"You didn't have any warning something was about to happen?"

"Nothing."

"Can I assume you've called those two?"

"Yes. I called both of them. Their cell phones are disconnected."

He nodded, thinking his investigation into Tyler McKinnon's murder may have helped to inspire Stone's departure. He stood looking around the vacant office, and then back at Shannon. He was confident he knew what had happened.

"Was there anything Stone was involved in lately that could have resulted in this? Any sign of nervousness or anxiety that might have caused him to want to run?"

"I ... I don't know of anything. He had me prepare all these investor reports that *had* to be completed by today. He was supposed to meet with several clients this afternoon."

He listened as he pulled his note pad from his pocket.

"Barrett's always been private with regard to his business. His office door was closed most of the time." Shannon crossed her arms over her chest and looked at the floor. "I've never felt a part of the team here. More like a spectator. He never allowed me to help with his company records."

"Why not?"

"I'm not sure." She looked up at him and shrugged. "Where I used to work, I did everything. I knew what was going on with every client. Here, I answer the phone and prepare whatever paperwork Barrett asked me to put together. I learned quickly not to ask questions. I do what I'm told, and I usually don't get yelled at so much any more. Hell, I don't do fifty percent of what I know how to do, and I make the same salary as where I used to work, plus a small bonus, thanks to Al. It works, I guess. Or—it did."

"What about bookkeeping?"

"He never wanted me to help with anything involving *his* books. He didn't care about me working on his clients' financials, but he wouldn't allow anyone, not even Al, to be involved with the company's accounting."

Mike looked at his watch and decided he needed to call Sarah Stone to ask for a later meeting, maybe this afternoon. It looked like this was going to add significantly to the questions he'd planned for her.

"I need to make a couple of calls."

"Sure," Shannon said.

He turned, pulled his phone from his pocket and crossed to the other side of the empty office space.

After leaving Sarah Stone a message requesting a meeting later in the day, he called Sergeant Brent Spangler from the Nashville Police Department's Fraud Unit and explained the situation. He and Brent had both worked patrol out of the South Precinct in their early days with the MNPD.

"I can't be sure yet. I don't have all the facts," he told Spangler, "but based on a couple of brief interviews with Stone and the feedback I've received from his associates, it appears he may have absconded with more than *his* assets."

"I can be there in less than an hour," Brent said. "Will you still be there?"

"I'll need to leave as soon as you get here. I have an interview with Stone's wife."

"His wife?"

"Yes, I'm still looking at him for the murder of a man who was an associate of Stone's partner as well as an investor with Stone Asset Management."

"Sounds like this guy's been busy."

"He's an odd bird, a real peculiar type. You'll realize that for yourself when you begin *your* investigation."

"I'll see you shortly," Brent said.

Mike walked back to Shannon. "Tell me what you can about the people who did business with Stone."

"I met some of them as they'd come in to meet with him, and I've talked with some on the phone, but I didn't *know* any of them. Most of them were middle aged or older, married or widowed. Many of them, based on what Al told me, were actually friends of Barrett's father."

"His father?"

"Yes. Al told me Barrett's father was a financial guy too. He was also a venture capitalist in addition to being a financial advisor. He did a lot of investing with individuals and groups. He invested in companies by himself too, according to Al anyway."

"I see. Where can I find Stone's father?"

"Mt. Olivet Cemetery. He passed some years back. Barrett's mother is gone too."

"I see. Do you have access to any data on Barrett's clients?"

"Everything is gone." As Shannon held out her hand to indicate the absence of all information, she saw the box on the floor with the quarterly reports. "Wait a minute."

Shannon walked over to the box and pulled out one of the blue folders.

"These reports represent some of Barrett's clients. These are the clients he was supposed to meet with today. I would think there could be information in here that would be helpful to you." She handed one of the folders to him.

As he flipped through the folder, he could see addresses and phone numbers. These reports were exactly what Brent Spangler needed to initiate his fraud investigation.

CHAPTER 27

Hartsfield-Jackson Airport
Atlanta, Georgia

Al watched Barrett approach the long line of people waiting to remove their shoes and have their carry-on luggage x-rayed. He turned back to Al.

"With all our technology, you'd think they could find a way to do this faster."

Al looked ahead at the lines and tried not to focus on Barrett's whining. He was on maximum alert as he approached the first TSA agent. Breathing deeply and slowly, he was trying not to look anxious. He handed his ID and boarding pass to the male agent seated on a stool at the podium.

"Morning," the agent said.

"Morning," Al mirrored the man's brief greeting so as not to allow his nerves to produce an attention-getting response. The man looked back and forth at the photo ID and at him three times. His nerves shifted into overdrive. He watched the agent, absorbed in his examination of the bogus ID. Al ran through all the personal information on T. Albert Marshall that Barrett had given him to memorize.

"Thank you, Mr. Marshall." The agent handed back his boarding pass and ID, looked at the woman behind him and indicated for her to step forward.

He breathed a quiet sigh and marched forward to the line of people who were emptying their possessions into what looked like old restaurant bus pans and placing them onto the rollers feeding the X-ray machine.

As the line of travelers was absorbed through the scanners, he stepped forward. He placed his bag into one of the plastic pans, his shoes, belt and the contents of his pockets into another pan and shoved both onto the rollers.

He was third in line behind the man currently inside the full-body scanner. He watched as his belongings were pulled into the x-ray tunnel. He stared at the tunnel and wondered if anyone ever had their belongings stolen while they were waiting to have their private parts inspected.

The agent standing on the far side of the scanner yelled, "Next." He motioned for Al to walk inside the large frame and place his feet on top of the yellow images painted on the floor. He walked into the scanner slowly, put his feet in position and held up his arms as if someone had pointed a gun at him. He stood still. The machine rotated and the agent said, "Step out please." He smiled at the agent, hoping he had something to smile about.

More relaxed now, he approached the output side of the scanner to retrieve his belongings from the grey pans. He dropped his loafers to the floor and slipped them on as he refilled his pockets. He collected his things and was about to walk toward the concourse when he spotted Barrett. His face held a confused stare.

"Sir."

Al felt something tug at his elbow. As a reflex, he jerked it away and spun his head to see a man's broad chest, white shirt and shining TSA badge opposite his name tag: Rodney Jackson. Al tilted his head back until he was able to see the man's face looking down at him. The man was so big, so tall, and so black; he looked like he could have been a lineman in the NFL.

"Come with me sir," The giant said in a deep baritone voice. Al's eyes widened as the man removed the bag from his grasp.

"What's the matter?"

"Come with me. We need to check your bag."

He looked back for Barrett, but he couldn't find him this time. As he followed the man, he knew whatever this was about; it would likely not turn out well.

They entered a high-walled private cubicle where another stone-faced TSA agent was waiting. Al grew more nervous with each step. His bladder weakened. His mouth was desert dry. He looked down, trying hard not to let his face communicate his anxiety.

The big agent set the bag atop a long table and indicated for Al to stand on the opposite side of the table. The big man stood behind the new agent who was obviously of a higher rank.

Al tried to think of what in his bag could be concerning them. He didn't have a weapon.

"Step back," the second agent said.

Al complied.

"Did you pack your own bags today?"

"Yes sir."

"Have your bags been under your control since you packed them?"

He thought a moment. "Yes."

The man unzipped the bag and without comment removed the neatly packed clothes and toiletries Al always carried with him in case his luggage was ever lost or late. He piled them on the table next to the bag.

Al was still unsure what they were looking for. He knew what was inside the bag. There was nothing that should have garnered any attention.

He watched as the agent unzipped the side compartments. When his gloved hand removed the small Gerber multi-tool from the side pouch, he forgot himself and said aloud, "Oh, shit."

The agent held up the tool and said with a theatrical tone, "This is prohibited. It is contraband."

"I am so sorry." He shook his head. "I forgot it was in there. I used it when I was packing up some boxes the last time I traveled. I was driving then not flying—like now—driving my car. I ... I wasn't thinking. I'm sorry."

The agent handed the tool to the big man, checked the rest of the compartments and randomly stuffed Al's things back inside the bag. As he zipped close the bag, he said, "Stay aware of what's going into your luggage."

"Yes, sir. I'm sorry." He hung his head. "It won't happen again."

The agent pushed the bag toward him and extended his arm toward the concourse granting permission for his departure.

He grabbed the bag and hurried from the cubicle. He walked

toward the concourse and spotted Barrett who was already approaching him. He knew he was about to hear a lengthy diatribe on why we can't afford to draw attention to ourselves at this stage of the plan.

"What the hell was that about?" Barrett asked.

He rolled his eyes. "I'll tell you later. Let's go."

As they entered the Delta Airlines Sky Club, he followed Barrett like an obedient pup. It was the way Barrett wanted it. If Al had entered the room ahead of Barrett and selected their seats, Barrett would have walked away and sat elsewhere.

They dropped their carry-on bags and sat across a small table from each other.

"So tell me," Barrett demanded with a look of disgust.

"I accidently left a small multi-tool in my carry-on bag. It was no big deal."

"What an idiot."

"I forgot about it," he said, attempting to defend himself. He wanted to tell Barrett what he could do to himself, but could not yet satisfy that urge.

"You forgot?" Barrett stared at him. "That could have blown every—."

"It didn't," Al interrupted in a terse tone that surprised Barrett.

"Fortunately." Barrett snatched the newspaper from the table between them. He held up the paper in front of him and began to read.

Al's nerves were still shaken, but his disdain for Barrett's manner was dominating his current focus.

From behind the newspaper Barrett began to laugh.

Al scanned the area around them, embarrassed. "What's so funny?"

"There's an article here on incompetence in the workplace and it reminded me of Shannon. I was imagining how she must have felt this morning when she unlocked the door to the office and saw nothing but bare walls inside." He chuckled out loud again. "She's going to think she's dreaming, and then she'll be mad as hell."

"She did a good job for us." He looked at Barrett with disgust. "Sometimes ... you amaze me."

He lowered the newspaper. "What the hell is that supposed to mean?" Barrett said, mounting his defense.

"It means that, too often, I wonder whether or not you respect or fear *anything*. I'm not sure it's healthy."

Barrett folded up the paper, leaned back in his club chair and started laughing again. "Not healthy?"

Al looked around the room at the half-dozen people staring at the two of them.

When Barrett stopped laughing, he looked Al directly in the eyes. "No," Barrett said at a more tactful volume. "I don't fear anything, except losing—losing at anything. It's not an option for me and it shouldn't be for you either. Sooner or later, you're going to get tired of other people taking advantage of you. I did. What you see," Barrett tapped his chest several times, "is the product of that."

Barrett stood, straightened his clothes, and walked away without another word.

He strolled the noisy concourse in search of a place to make a private phone call. He realized there were no quiet places in an airport as busy as this one. The concourse itself could be his best option in order to not be overheard. Half the people here were on their cell phones and the other half were listening to various flavors of audio on an assortment of electronic devices. His clandestine conversation would be masked by the low-pitched roar from the crowd of travelers navigating the terminal and scrambling for positions at their gates.

He walked until he found a vacant gate with several empty seats. He pushed a speed dial number he had entered yesterday and approached the huge windows overlooking the tarmac. The phone rang until he thought it would go to voice mail.

"Yeah?"

"Does it always take you this long to answer your phone?"

"Only when I think it's *you* callin'."

"Funny."

"*I* thought so."

"I wanted to touch base with you since I'll be unavailable for the next ten to twelve hours."

"What are you gonna be doin', countin' your money?"

"Your wit escapes me."

"I've found humor is good for the soul."

"You have one?" Barrett asked.

"Now, who's the funny man?"

"Listen. I have another job for you."

"What now? More addresses to look up for your Christmas card list?"

Barrett paused before answering. "You know, the last time I checked, I was paying you quite well for everything you do."

"You said that before." He paused. "What do you want—sir?"

Barrett didn't want to get into an argument at this point, so he took a moment to calm himself. "Remember the address I had you locate?"

"The cop?"

"Yes, the detective."

"I knew it. You *are* crazy."

Barrett held his temper to keep from creating another rift.

"I ain't killin' no damn cop. I got you what you wanted. I took his picture off the Internet, followed him home and got you his address, just like you asked. I'm done."

"The address was for you, so *you'd* know where he lived. This way you can catch him away from his cop friends and take care of him."

"You say that like he's just another dumb ass thug on the street. Killin' these old farts for you is one thing. Hell, they're almost dead anyway. Not a cop. Not me. Forget it."

"These pricks locked you up for doing less than half the crimes others did who are out walking the street on probation. Isn't it time for your retribution?"

"My what?"

"Payback," Barrett barked into the phone.

"The payback I was due was from McKinnon for bein' a world-class shitty lawyer, allowin' me to get screwed by the system, and costin' me damn near five years of my life."

"Yeah, well. You don't have to worry about him anymore, now do you?"

"Gee, thanks."

"You don't sound pleased."

"Nobody gives a damn when a lawyer gets his just reward. I know several guys who would throw a party if their lawyer bit the dust. Do you know what cops do when one of theirs gets it? Nobody gets away with that shit—*nobody*. They'll drop everything to catch a cop-killer. So, forget it."

"We discussed this. You're not killing anyone. You are merely setting the stage for them to have an unfortunate mishap which cannot be traced back to you, or me." Barrett did his best to sell the accident setup as if it was legal. "They're doing the deed themselves."

"Right. You can sugarcoat this all you want. I've stared down the uniformed hacks and their metal batons. I've seen the pitted concrete and rustin' steel bars from the *inside*. I ain't goin' back. You want him dead? *You* kill him."

"Listen, this has to be done or we're both going to be looking through those bars. I'm not going to be there to do the job. You have to. Besides, when this cop goes away, the risk for both of us goes with him."

"That's easy to say. You're not the one doin' the deed. Besides, nobody in their right mind would take on this kinda risk at these prices."

"I realize that. That's why I'm doubling it for this one."

"Right. Try again."

"He's a man; he's no wiser than you."

"Flattery don't fit in my wallet."

Barrett hated for anyone to get the better of him. It wasn't the money. He didn't give a damn about the money. It was unacceptable to lose any negotiation when you had his intelligence and his resources. At this point, his options were few and dwindling. Time was short before this cop ruined everything. "I'll *quadruple* it under one condition."

"Say that again."

"I will pay you four times the agreed upon per person amount if you complete this task—under one condition."

"Which is?"

Barrett explained the lucrative stipulation and told him he had to go. They'd announced his flight was boarding.

"You *have* lost it, dude."

"And you'll be rich ... *dude*," Barrett reminded him.

The phone was quiet on both ends.

Barrett looked at his watch. "Move Neal up the list. I have to go."

"I ain't promisin' nothin'," he said with a tone that whispered his interest.

Barrett disconnected the call. He'd learned enough about Wade Powell to know his love of money and his failure to say 'No' gave him the answer he needed.

He smiled as he walked back to the Sky Club.

He'll do it. And I won't even be suspected. With the pre-nup bitch gone too, that'll be one less parasite trying to find me and take my money.

"They called Flight #114," Al said as he stood.

"I heard them." Barrett pulled the strap of his carry-on bag onto his shoulder, raised his arm and said, "*Arrivederci*, America."

CHAPTER 28

Downtown Nashville

"You had to have known something was up, didn't you?" Detective Spangler asked. "You were right here in the middle of it all every day."

"You don't know Barrett Stone," Shannon said. "He's a control freak. He doesn't want anyone to know his business. He keeps all his own financials, and anything else of importance, to himself. But that kind of explains all this now, doesn't it?"

"What work *did* he give you to do?"

"Like I explained to Sergeant Neal, all I was allowed to do was basic receptionist and secretarial chores. I ran errands. I made coffee. I had no access to any of his personal information, client data only. I did what he asked and tried to keep him from chewing on my ass, which he did too often already. He paid me. That was it."

She didn't mind repeating to Sergeant Spangler what she'd told Mike, but she was beginning to lose her poise. She was defending herself, and she hadn't done anything except her job. Barrett was the one they needed to be interrogating. Spangler pulled one of the reports from the box. "Sergeant Neal told me this box of reports represents several of the firm's clients."

"Yes."

"Do you believe it may have been a diversion, meant to keep you busy while he was planning all this?"

"If it was supposed to keep me busy, he succeeded. I was up until after midnight last night finishing them in order to keep him happy and off my ass. A lot of good it did, huh?" She folded her arms across her chest. "Bastard," she said, just above a whisper.

"Are there any clients represented here who you would recommend I speak with first; some who may know more than others about what he's done or where he may have gone?"

"I didn't know any of these folks personally. They came in occasionally, but when they did, they were here to see Barrett. I escorted them to his office and served coffee. As you'll see when you read their information, most of them are older, in their sixties and seventies. Some are retired. Those are the ones I have to wonder about. How much of their life's savings did they hand over to him? How badly will they suffer from his greed?"

"You've worked for Stone how long?"

"Too damned long. I started here a little over two years ago."

"So, what's *your* take on all this? What do you think these two did other than disappear with a bundle of money and abandon everything and everyone?"

"First of all, Al was a follower. Like me, he simply found himself doing Barrett's will in order to avoid his wrath. However, I'd put *nothing* past Barrett Stone." She paused. "The one thing about Barrett I saw daily was his total lack of concern for anyone other than himself. Oh, when he was on the phone or face to face with a client, you'd think he was a saint with only their best financial interest at heart. But, he talked another game when there was no one around. I've never known anyone else like him and I hope I never do."

"Did he ever get violent?"

"I remember once not long after I started here. I hadn't seen his bizarre behavior yet. He and I had a confrontation over his expectations. Al and I had a discussion after Barrett left that day. He stopped me from quitting. He said he'd talked with Barrett after a similar episode with the girl I replaced. She'd had all of Barrett she could handle and one day she walked out. Al said he asked Barrett, 'How can you so easily treat people like shit?' I'll never forget what Al said was Barrett's self-righteous response. He said Barrett told him, 'It's basic Darwinian theory—survival of the fittest. You have to make the decision. Are you going to be one of the survivors or you are going to become food for the survivors? You need to make that decision soon, before you find yourself being digested by someone who's already made the decision.'" She stared at the detective. "Can you believe that?"

"Did either of them explain what happens when *everyone* practices that demented philosophy?"

She shook her head.

"It's called anarchy." Spangler paused. "When society's conventions become unimportant to some, the police step in. We take those violators out of the picture, and reestablish order. If *everyone* decides to abandon the rules and pursue self-interest, we all move backward fast ... into chaos."

She nodded her head. "Makes sense."

"This Stone character sounds like a real piece of work," Spangler said. "Fortunately, his type for the most part seems to be rare."

"Let's hope."

"Can you give me your cell number?" He gave her his card and wrote her cell number in his notes.

Spangler picked up the box of quarterly reports and looked at Shannon, "I'm going to speak with each of these folks and I'll call you if I have questions. I appreciate your help."

"You're welcome. I hate that I've been a part of all this."

"This fiasco was not your responsibility."

"No, but it doesn't stop me from considering maybe I should have seen it happening. Maybe I should have been suspicious."

"Don't beat yourself up over this. You're the only one here helping us unravel the crime and hopefully finding justice for these old folks."

"Do me a favor?"

"Sure."

"Tell them I'm sorry."

Spangler nodded. "Done."

CHAPTER 29

Hartsfield-Jackson Airport
Atlanta, Georgia

The moment Barrett crossed the metallic threshold of the mammoth Boeing 777-200, and before any one of the attendants could form the words 'Welcome aboard', he began dispensing assignments. His desires were paramount in *his* mind and he was determined to place them at the top of the flight attendants' morning agenda.

"I need a Stoli martini with two olives and I need to see the menu and wine list as soon as possible. The name is Strong. I'm in Business Elite."

Barrett didn't pause for a response or wait to gain any form of acknowledgement. With his plan currently moving along without issue, Barrett's ego was in overdrive.

As Barrett turned away, Al looked at the attractive flight attendant Barrett had targeted and who was now checking her watch, no doubt thinking ten-thirty was a bit early for a martini. He shook his head and mouthed the word "Sorry." She smiled. He knew, in her profession, she had no doubt encountered plenty of jackasses.

As they arrived at their assigned seats, Barrett set his carry-on bag on the floor. He inspected the space with a wrinkled look of disgust on his face.

"Where am I supposed to hang my coat?" Barrett said as he removed his suit jacket. He hooked his finger under the corner of the recessed monitor for the entertainment center and pulled it out. He removed his handkerchief, dusted the monitor as if it was filthy, covered it with the handkerchief and hung his jacket over it like it was meant for that purpose. "Finally, a good use for a television."

Al watched as Barrett sat back in the leather seat, wiggled his ass to evaluate the seat and examined the rows of electronic controls to his left. He looked at his Rolex, no doubt tracking how long it was going to take for his cabin service. He glanced to his right and looked at Al.

"I can't believe they expect us to be comfortable in these cubby holes they're calling luxurious. That is such a sham." Barrett shrugged his shoulders acting as if he was confined. "I feel like a sardine trapped in a can."

Sham? Interesting comment considering the source. "I was just thinking how nice it was to be flying first class with all these amenities." He knew he was regrettably trapped in the seat next to Barrett for eleven hours. His best effort to deal with it would have to involve ear plugs.

"It's all about your standards. I expect better service, and because I do, I get it. You need to learn this philosophy. With the changes coming to you in this new life, you should demand superior service. It's what these people are here for. They're here to serve *us*."

He forced himself to ignore Barrett's comment. *If your philosophy involves being an ass like you, I'll pass. It's not in my nature.*

His thoughts moved to his iPod. He knew this device would block out Barrett's supremacy rhetoric and give him an excuse to ignore the criticism.

A flight attendant walked down the aisle and approached Barrett with his martini and a big smile. "Here you are, sir. It was prepared as you ordered. Can I hang up your jacket for you?"

"Yes."

"Is there anything else I can get for you?"

"What about the menu and the wine list, as I requested earlier?"

"I'll be glad to get those for you." She turned to Al in time to see him slowly shake his head. "Anything for you, sir?" She smiled again.

"What about a Coke whenever you get time. No rush."

"I'll take care of it. Anything else?"

"No. I'm fine. Thank you." He returned her pleasant smile.

"That's not it," Barrett said as the attendant walked toward the rear of the airplane.

"What are you talking about?"

"That is not how you communicate with people who are in place to serve you. They expect to be told what to do. You should accommodate them by telling them what you want and when you expect it. It's why they're paid."

"I understand. That's what I did. But, doing so doesn't mean I have to treat them as if they were indentured servants."

Barrett leaned toward him. "They will respect you if your manner says you insist on it."

"I'm not so sure about that one." He pushed the ear buds back into his ears and began to rotate the iPod's selector to one of his favorite smooth jazz albums. He leaned back against the head rest, closed his eyes and turned up the volume. He could still hear Barrett talking, but he refused to acknowledge him. He increased the volume again.

He knew he was a stronger person than Barrett realized. Anyone who could tolerate Barrett's demanding personality and his incessant criticism had to have a sturdy inner make up. He learned, over their frustrating years together, to ignore as much as possible and to choose his battles. Most weren't winnable anyway.

He was in another world enjoying Paul Taylor's saxophone when he heard some loud talking over the jazz. He turned, pulled out one of the ear buds and raised his seat back.

"I wasn't rude," Barrett insisted with an adamant volume. "*She* was rude. I simply asked for Cristal. She said you didn't offer Cristal. I told her you people should upgrade your offerings and while you were at it, hire better looking flight attendants with more deferential attitudes."

"What did she say?" asked the senior flight attendant.

"She didn't say anything. She pushed her glasses up on her nose with her middle finger, turned and walked away. That's when I insisted the other attendant contact you."

Al turned his head away and grabbed his mouth to stifle his

laughter.

Way to go, girl.

"Mr. Strong, I agree her response was inappropriate. I will speak to her immediately. Please let me know if you need anything else during your flight. I will take care of it personally." The senior attendant handed Barrett his card.

"Thank you," Barrett said. "I will."

Al looked at Barrett, trying not to allow his disgust to show. He knew this acquiescence on the part of the supervisor would only fuel Barrett's demanding fire. This was one of the reasons why Barrett was so spoiled. He'd found that most people would give in to his belligerence in order to shut him up.

"What happened?" he asked Barrett.

"Just another hypersensitive woman," Barrett said. "What can I say?"

Al sat back in his seat, replaced his ear bud and glanced at the curtain separating the seating areas in time to see the senior attendant pass through it. Before the curtain closed behind him, Al got a glimpse of the man giving the flight attendant a high five.

CHAPTER 30

Belle Meade
Nashville

"Good afternoon," Sarah said, as she stepped back to allow Mike to enter the huge marble foyer.

"Thank you. You have a beautiful home, Mrs. Stone."

"Please, call me Sarah. Let's sit in here."

Mike followed her into a sitting room off the foyer, and waited for her to take her seat. Sarah was an attractive lady. Her appearance and her actions made it clear; she not only had money, but also class. He couldn't imagine what she saw in Barrett Stone.

"Please." Sarah gestured toward the chair across the coffee table from her. "Can I get you some tea or coffee?"

"No, thank you. And thanks for allowing me to reschedule our meeting."

"Fortunately," Sarah took a sip of her green tea. "I had the time available."

"I need to explain something," Mike said.

"Oh?"

"I just came from Stone Asset Management. Shannon Richards is there and she's upset."

"I received her voicemail earlier," Sarah said, "but I don't get involved in Barrett's business. I'm sorry if she expected me to respond."

"I understand. But, you may feel differently when you hear what's happened."

"What's that?" Sarah asked.

"When I dropped by your husband's office not long after Shannon arrived, I discovered like she did, the office was completely empty."

"Empty? I don't understand."

"There was nothing left in the entire office."

"Nothing? What happened?"

"We don't know yet, but it looks as though Barrett and Al Ricks have disappeared."

Sarah closed her eyes for a moment and took in a calming breath. "Barrett left me a voicemail last evening saying he and Al were leaving for some financial conference. I don't know anything about it, and I don't know what it has to do with all this."

"You say they went to a conference? Where was it?"

"He said Atlanta in his voicemail. I would be glad to play it for you, but I delete his messages soon after I hear them."

Mike made a note about the Atlanta conference. "Do you know the conference venue or the name?"

"He didn't say where it was being held or what it was called. He knows I don't care about those things."

"I'll have someone check it out. By the way, I do need to tell you I was able to reach the central station manager at your security company. He told me that on Sunday night and Monday morning your system was never armed."

"Excuse me? I always ..." She squinted her eyes as she relived the evening. "I came home around nine because that was the night Sheila Thomas and I went to dinner at Tayst. I changed into my loungewear, poured myself a glass of Pinot Grigio and watched the news. I went to the kitchen to rinse my glass. I saw Barrett on the computer. Oh, wow." She looked at Mike. "He said he had to get some things from his car, and for me to not set the alarm. He said he would set it when he was through." She looked up at Mike. "I'm sorry I didn't remember this earlier."

"This kills his alibi and elevates him back up the list of suspects." Mike made some notes. "Tell me about you and Barrett."

She sighed. "Where should I begin?"

"How did you come to know him?"

Sarah sat back and crossed her arms across her lap. "I obtained my law degree. My father insisted on it. However, I didn't follow him to Vanderbilt. I graduated, like my beloved mother, from the University of Kentucky and the law school in Lexington. Much to my daddy's disdain, I sought a path after college that did not involve the practice of law.

I took after my mother in many ways. She is a social being, more of a political type than my father. Until recently, I'd not established a clear-cut objective with my life, but many of my friends expected me to test the waters of local government. I've not made a final decision, but I am leaning in that direction."

He made notes as Sarah sipped her tea.

"In 2008, I met Barrett Stone at a function near my parents' home in Belle Meade, where I grew up. It was a fund raising effort to get some young stud's nest egg started so he could pursue his political aspirations in Tennessee state government."

"How'd he do?"

"His first inept effort tripped up his larger plan and he fell on his face."

"Oh?"

"His baseless confidence and his inability to garner public support helped convince me it was possible for me to make a positive impact in government. But, that's not my point. That night I met Barrett. Back then he wasn't so much of an ass as he was just a bit cocky. I've always been partial to a man with a little extra self-confidence. You seem to be a confident man yourself Sergeant." She smiled.

"Yes ma'am. Back to Barrett."

"After that night, he called me and we started seeing each other. We dated for several months. One thing became another. We fit together, at least back then. So, we set a date."

"This was what, 2009?" Mike asked.

"April, 2009. It was about six or seven weeks before the wedding when Barrett and I came back to my house following a dinner party. I drove his car back since we were both somewhat inebriated, him much more than me, by my plan. As soon as we came in, I prepared him another cocktail and me a Jack and Coke, without the Jack. We made ourselves comfortable on the sofa in front of the fireplace."

Mike wanted to stop her and ask her to leave out the intimate details he was sure were coming next, but he was afraid doing so might cost him some useful information so he sat and waited.

"I knew Barrett. He always started getting frisky about this time. I was ready and played along in order to fuel his fire. Then, I stopped and told him I needed him to look at something. He was confused at first by my request, but he began to flip through the pages I'd handed him."

"A pre-nup?" Mike asked.

"You *are* the detective."

"What did he say?"

"At first, as I expected, he was put off by it. But, the timing was on my side. At that point in the evening, his libido, fueled somewhat by the booze and my manual stimulation had grown stronger than his greed. I told him he had to sign it before I would —well, before he could ... he had to sign it first. My pre-nup did to Barrett Hayden Stone III what he tries to do to everyone else."

Mike wasn't sure what to say.

"I guess I did a pretty good job of persuading him." She looked at Mike and gave him a smirk. "He signed it."

"I'm not sure you'll get the agreement to hold up in court since he was drunk."

"Drunk? He wasn't drunk. He was able to ... perform. It'll be my word against his. If it ever comes down to it, I'm prepared to settle for less than we agreed to, but he doesn't know that."

"Why are you telling *me* this?"

"I thought it was still against the law to lie to the police?"

"Go on," Mike said.

Sarah poured herself more tea.

"Sergeant, Barrett Stone is a predator. As he's bragged to me on several occasions, he works his diversion to better position himself for the strike. He strives to be accepted socially for one reason only: to get close to his prey. He says, 'Reducing the striking distance, quickens the blow. It decreases the victim's awareness and ability to respond, exposing them and putting them on the defensive'."

Mike shook his head. "He has a perverted perspective on his fellow man."

"Yes, he does. As my daddy says, Barrett Stone is a man with malleable morals."

Sarah sat for a moment, and then continued. "Barrett has become a lot of ugly things, but he's an intelligent man. He knows my father's law firm has been in business for a long time and he also knows I'm my father's sole heir. He knew this when we met. I'm not so delusional that I believe love was Barrett's sole inspiration. I believe greed and lust occupied position one and two with love coming in a sad third. Today, the only changes to this win, place and show ranking would be to scratch love from the race entirely.

"When we married, my wonderful daddy had cancer. Barrett knew that. He'd known it for a while. It's not something you can hide from your fiancé. I can't help but think this fact could have been his stimulus to so easily agree to sign the pre-nuptial agreement that night.

"Since that time, the magic of today's medical treatments has afforded my daddy remission, where he remains today. I thank God for that glorious blessing. I'm confident this good news is playing a role in Barrett's current behavior. I feel he's lost interest in me and lost hope of getting his greedy hands on my daddy's millions."

"So, if you don't mind me asking, with virtually no hope of gaining access to your father's fortune, and since the two of you aren't sharing a bed, what's keeping him at home?"

"My daddy's skills as an attorney."

"Excuse me?"

Sarah smiled. "This is where the fine print of the pre-nup, which Barrett failed to read until recently, comes into play. Daddy put a limiting clause in the agreement. If Barrett leaves me, moves out, is caught cheating, or in any other way violates his marital vows, the agreed upon pre-nuptial settlement amount automatically doubles."

"Do you mind me asking?"

She smiled again. "Fifteen million—would become thirty."

Mike nodded. "That *is* motivating."

"Isn't it?" Sarah reached for her tea.

"Your relationship has turned into a financial stalemate."

"You could say that. I'm not about to give up my share of compensation for living with a maniacal millionaire. Barrett has no plans to share what he feels is his, and he has no trouble biding his time down the hall in one of the guest rooms."

"Can I assume you realize with Barrett gone, and until he's found, your pre-nuptial agreement is, for the most part, paper?"

Sarah laughed. "Yes, I know. But, I plan to give you something that should help you to spoil his escape."

"What's that?"

"Come with me." Sarah stood and walked toward the rear of the mansion.

"Before I forget," Mike said, "I need to borrow a recent photograph of your husband before I leave."

Sarah stopped. "I'll have to think about that. I don't recall any taken recently. Is it okay if there are other people in the photo?"

"Sure," Mike said. "We can copy it and remove the others from the shot."

"I may have something for you, assuming I can find it."

She stopped in what appeared to be the breakfast room off the kitchen where there were several sheets of printed paper on the table. The papers appeared to contain lists of some sort.

"A little over a year ago, I began to see Barrett staying up late at night, using the computer. I didn't think much of it until one day during a bridge game, one of my friends Tracey Grimes told us about her sister. She had asked Tracey how to check on her teenage son who she suspected was porn-surfing at night. Tracey was an IT technician before she got smart and married the IT Director at their company. Anyway, Tracey loaded this special software on her nephew's computer and it started collecting information about where he was going on the Internet and what he was looking at. She said it was amazing and disturbing."

"Software like that has been available for a while," Mike said.

"I had no idea. I'm not as computer savvy as most folks. I use it to do my banking and some email with family who I don't get to see often. Other than that, I have to turn to Tracey."

"What happened next?"

"I asked Tracey if she could do the same with this computer so I could see what Barrett was up to. I didn't suspect him surfing porn sites as much as meeting up with another woman. I thought I might catch him violating the pre-nup. The thought of catching him and doubling the settlement was, as you can imagine, exciting."

"I'm sure."

"Tracey said she could help. So, one day while he was at work, she came over and loaded the software. I waited a week, so I could be sure he had been on the computer, and I asked Tracey to come back. The software had collected some rather bizarre information."

"Such as?"

"These lists here are the websites Tracey said Barrett was looking at. The websites I highlighted here in yellow are doctors; all plastic surgeons."

Mike scanned the printouts.

"The sites in orange are hospitals in and around the Lazio region of Italy. The websites highlighted in blue are hotels in the general vicinity of the hospitals. Lazio, by the way, is the region where Rome is located."

Mike knew he had to be careful with his next question, but he needed to probe for as much information as she could provide him. "Had either of you discussed any kind of plastic surgery?"

"Sergeant," Sarah said, looking as if she was offended, "do you feel I look like I need work?"

"No ma'am. Absolutely not."

"When Tracey first gave me this data I was livid. Of all the nerve, for that inconsiderate son of a bitch to be assuming he could schedule me a facelift or liposuction or whatever else he had in mind, and then sell the idea to me under the cover of an Italian vacation. I couldn't believe even *he* could do that. But, as time went on, he never spoke of it; never hinted about it. I assumed maybe he realized it was a bad idea."

"What about a relative of Barrett's? Could he be looking to pay for the surgery on behalf of a family member?"

"Since Barrett's father passed, he has no family other than Al."

"Al?"

"Al Ricks. Didn't you meet Al?"

"Yes, Barrett told me Al was his partner."

"His partner, and his step brother."

"Really?"

"A couple of years after Barrett's mother killed herself, Barrett's father met Al's mom; they were neighbors at the time. One day when Barrett and Al were playing in the Stone's backyard she came looking for Al and ran into Barrett's father. They began seeing each other, and widow married widower less than a year later."

"How long did that last?"

"Not long. Al told me when Barrett was twelve and he was almost ten, Al's mom contracted some kind of respiratory illness and she died at home in her bed."

"How sad."

"After she became so ill, Barrett's father couldn't care for her or the boys properly and still run his business, so he hired a governess to watch over them. Al said the governess was a young woman in her early twenties, the daughter of an Italian couple who'd moved here when she was a young girl. She was educated here in America. Her father was a journeyman tile mason and had to move around the country wherever the work took him. The girl's mother had no choice but to go with him. Now that the girl had a home and a good job, she could make it on her own. Al said Barrett really cared about her."

"So, Al is not just his partner, he's family."

"And Barrett treats him like his servant," Sarah said.

"Why?" Mike asked. "Because he can, and he knows Al will take it?"

"Al is a nice guy, too nice. I asked him once why he put up with Barrett. He didn't have an answer. He did tell me the only person he'd ever seen Barrett show any true respect, other than his father, was the young governess."

Mike grunted his bewilderment, shook his head and scratched more notes on his pad.

"What about Al's wife?"

"Mary Ellen? She's sort of reserved and quiet like Al. They've been married a little longer than us. I don't socialize with her. I've only met her twice, so I can't tell you much. She was nice."

"I guess you wouldn't have her number?"

"Sorry."

"Are these lists for me?"

"Yes. I can get Tracey to print out others if you need them."

"Is there anything else you can tell me about Barrett that might help me find him?"

"Give me a minute while I look for that photograph."

Mike scanned the reports during the few minutes it took Sarah to locate the photo.

She handed Mike the photo. It was one from their wedding. "He hasn't changed much—physically."

"Are you sure you want me to have this?"

"Yes, and for all I care, you can keep it," she said with a somber expression on her face.

Mike nodded.

"If you're interested, I do have an opinion on where he may be."

"Absolutely."

"My intuition and these lists tell me Barrett and Al went to Italy. Barrett and I spent our honeymoon in Rome four years ago. While we were there, he left the hotel on his own several times. He told me I should go shopping. He didn't like shopping. Each time he returned I asked where he'd gone. He always said he was exploring the picturesque countryside.

"I had no idea what he'd been up to until one day a year or so ago when Al and I were talking, he told me more about the governess. Barrett had still never mentioned the girl to me. It turns out, the small town her family came from was less than six miles from Rome."

CHAPTER 31

Ashcroft Apartments
LaVergne, Tennessee

Powell was back from the plumbing supply company with a half-dozen Fluidmaster kits and some PVC drain fittings. He'd repaired the two leaking toilet tanks that were reported to maintenance and stocked the rest of the repair kits in his maintenance shop at the rear of the complex. He was ready to stop by his apartment and grab some lunch before tackling the damaged kitchen P-trap in Unit B-9.

As he pushed his key into the deadbolt on his front door, he spotted a business card that was pushed between the door and the trim next to the doorknob.

"Damned pest control freaks." He pulled out the card and was wadding it up when he noticed something different about it. He flattened out the card and saw the round seal of the Metropolitan Nashville Police Department. He read the name, "Sergeant Mike Neal, Homicide Unit."

He stared at the card. "Now, what the hell does he want?" He whispered to himself as he unlocked his door.

He walked by the end table next to his sofa, dropped the detective's card and pushed the flashing red button on the answering machine his employer had installed. Knowing his apartment manager, he'd have another list of emergency repairs to deal with before the end of the day.

The machine beeped and the first message began, "This is Sergeant Mike Neal from the Nashville Police Department. I came by your apartment this morning and left a card in your door. I'd like to speak with you if you could give me a call at the number on the card."

It had been over two years since he'd encountered law enforcement in any way. He'd met all his appointments with his parole officer, and he'd made a point to not exceed the speed limit; not by much anyway.

Since his release, he'd lived within society's expectations. He had not come across anything that tempted him to endanger his reclaimed freedom ... until he was contacted and propositioned by Barrett Stone.

He sat at the kitchen table eating his lunch and considering his options. He couldn't afford to have a bunch of cops come to the apartment complex and take him away for one of their group discussions. The apartment manager was willing to give him a chance, a job and a roof over his head as long as he stayed clean. He didn't want to spoil his current situation by losing his manager's confidence. This apartment gig was a good thing.

He knew the police were highly trained to manipulate people and conversations to their advantage. They prided themselves in their legal right to lie to people in order to elicit the information they needed, even to the point of coercing a confession. He'd been in one of their 'little rooms for big problems' more than once.

He decided to call Sergeant Neal and arrange a meeting. Powell knew it was risky. But, he'd never met a cop that was smarter than him.

CHAPTER 32

Criminal Justice Center
Downtown Nashville

Mike and Detective Spangler agreed to meet for coffee and bring each other up to speed on both the Tyler McKinnon murder and the Stone Asset Management fraud investigation.

"Did you get to talk with the investors?" Mike asked as he parked his coffee on the table between them.

"Yes, nine of the ones who had appointments with Stone today. A few failed to answer. I left voicemail. I hope they call back. The responses of the ones I was able to meet with covered the range of emotions. Some were angry as hell; one old guy yelled at me like the whole situation was my fault. I understood his perspective. He said he wanted Stone arrested for grand theft. Afterward he started crying. It was sad.

"Some others were more embarrassed than anything. This is a typical response after affinity fraud. I've seen it before. They don't want their friends and family to know they were gullible enough to be taken like this by someone they knew and trusted, and especially for so much money."

"That's understandable."

"One elderly couple said they were devastated not only from the loss of income, but from having trusted Stone based upon their long relationship with his father. Seems the husband was a golfing buddy of the senior Stone.

"I wasn't ready for the next one. I met with two other golfers who knew Stone's father. They invested a couple of hundred thousand each with Stone. They asked me to restrict discussion of the issue with them only. Not their wives. It appears they promised their wives they wouldn't invest with him, and then changed their minds. They said they couldn't stand the thought of having to face their wives, admit they lied and then have to eat crow because they lost their investment. I agreed to their request.

"Oh, I forgot. One old guy begged me to keep the whole thing quiet. He said he was a CPA prior to retirement and if this ever got out, his friends at the club would never let it die.

"These folks are all in the autumn of life and they shouldn't have to worry about this kind of intrusion. The more of them I met with, the madder *I* got at Stone. I want to strangle him myself. Most of these folks are now forced to prepare for a significant reduction in their lifestyle during retirement.

"All totaled, this small group I interviewed invested over 8.7 million dollars with Stone, and lost it all."

"I hate it for them," Mike said. "I hope we can get it back."

"We have to find him first. What about you? Have you uncovered anything new on Stone or Ricks?"

"I met with Sarah Stone today. She was able to add considerable data to our profile of Stone. This guy has led a bizarre life. I'm not sure his disappearing act was all that much of a surprise to her. She's nobody's fool. She comes from a family of lawyers."

"Can I assume their relationship was equally strange?"

"You can. These people amaze me with their lifestyle. It appears the marriage, from day one, has been a contest to see who can outlast the other and take the most money from the relationship *when*, not *if*, it dissolves. There has been no resemblance to what you and I would call a marriage. He was after her father's fortune made from his second generation law practice. She's been after his father's investment wealth. It's like a damned soap opera on cable TV, only worse."

CHAPTER 33

Downtown Nashville

Mike's cell phone vibrated in his pocket.

"Mike Neal."

"Sergeant, did you get me what I need?"

"Hey, Deano. What are you referring to?"

"If I'm going to be able to tell you who, or at least which computer, created this flash drive, you have to find out which version of Microsoft Office each of the potential perpetrator machines are using. So, what version is Sarah Stone's home computer running? You did visit her, didn't you?"

"I did."

"And?"

"And, I forgot to get that for you."

"It's not for me Sergeant. It's for you."

"Gotcha. Call you back." He ended the call and without delay dialed Sarah Stone.

"Hello."

"Sarah—Mike Neal."

"Hello, Sergeant."

"I meant to ask you when I was there what version of Microsoft Office do you have on the desktop PC there in your kitchen."

"I have no idea. How am I supposed to tell?"

"Do you have it running now?"

"Yes. Actually, I was in the middle of an email to my cousin when you called."

"Sorry for the interruption. This won't take but a second, and it won't have any affect on your email."

"Okay."

"What software do you use for your email?"

"I don't know."

"What does it say on the top line of the screen on the far left?"

"Inbox – Microsoft Outlook. Is that what you're talking about?"

"Yes. On the row of words below that, it says: 'File, Edit, View', etc. Do you see the line of words?"

"Yes."

"On the far right end of the line it should say 'Help'."

"Yes, I use it often when I'm on the computer and then I call Tracey."

"I want you to left click once on Help. It will open a drop down list of options."

"It did."

"What is the last option on the list?"

"About Microsoft Office Outlook."

"Good. Left click it once and read me what it says at the top of the new window."

"It says, Microsoft Office Outlook 2007, Part of Microsoft—."

"That's it," Mike interrupted. "That's all I needed. You've been a big help."

"I didn't do anything."

"You did plenty. Thanks. I have to run."

"Sure. Goodbye."

He called Dean to share the new information.

"A/V Lab, McMurray."

"Deano."

"Yes?"

"You were right."

"Hang on. Your signal broke up. Say again."

"You were right." Mike heard his voice echo, and he knew the reason.

"Sergeant, who is it you are saying was right?"

"You were, Dean. Take me off the PA system."

"You're off. Thanks. There are folks here who needed to hear that."

"Listen. I just got off the phone with Sarah Stone. Her home PC is running Office 2007. It looks like Barrett Stone could have loaded the flash drive using their desktop at home."

"That's good news. Now, in order to to prove for the District Attorney it was *that* PC and not some other one also using 2007. Can you ask her to send you a few example emails?"

"Sure. Be watching for them."

"10-4."

CHAPTER 34

Hilton Hotel
Rome, Italy

In an attempt to recover from jet lag, fifty-two year old Beverly Hills plastic surgeon Dr. Mitchell Groom planned a much needed nap as his first Italian adventure. He and his thirty year-old nurse Lee Ann were scheduled to be in Italy for three days.

"Come on," Lee Ann said as the elevator doors opened on their floor. "You can nap by the pool while you work on your tan. A *little* sun is good for your complexion," Lee Ann laughed, "like you don't know that. Put on your swimsuit and let's go. I have the sun block. I'll meet you outside the elevator here in fifteen minutes."

"Whatever." He just wanted to sleep.

Dr. Groom had been asleep for a half-hour on one of the pool's chaise lounges he'd pulled into the shade when Lee Ann fell onto the chair next to him and splattered him with water from the pool. He gasped and sat up.

"What the ...?"

"Can you believe this sunshine and temperature? I'm *not* missing Southern California at all."

He fell back onto the reclining chair. "What I can't believe is that I allowed you to talk me out of sleeping in a bed." He rubbed his lower back. "This chair is as hard as a rock."

"Oh, Mitchell. Don't be so persnickety. How often do you get to see beauty like this?" She spread her arms wide and scanned the expansive view and striking architecture surrounding their hotel.

"You're right. I should be glad we don't have to work until tomorrow."

"Exactly. Here, rub some of this sun-block on my back. My first dose has to be gone by now. I'll rub some on you when you're done."

He looked at Lee Ann as she rolled onto her stomach and untied her bikini top. He thought about his wife back in California.

Delta flight number #114 completed its transatlantic crossing without incident and pulled into the gate eighteen minutes earlier than scheduled. Barrett and Al walked the jet way with more than two hundred others and arrived in Rome as Bradford S. Strong and T. Albert Marshall.

So far, Barrett's plan was working. But, they still needed to get past the agents in Passport Control and Customs.

"Remember." He turned to Al. "Marshall—T. Albert Marshall."

"I know," Al said, "from Texas—Dallas born and raised," Al said with a heavy southern drawl.

"Don't overplay it," he said, "and call me Bradford."

As the escalator descended to baggage claim, they spotted uniformed Polizia in every direction, several were carrying assault rifles. Barrett could tell Al's senses were on high alert at the sight of these officers and their weapons.

"What's the matter?" he asked when he heard Al's wheezing.

"Police. They're everywhere. Why are they carrying assault weapons?"

"Well Dorothy," he said, leaning toward Al. "You're not in Kansas anymore. You're in the real world where bad people aren't as hesitant to impose their will on others."

"What's different about that?" Al asked.

"Relax. They're not here looking for T. Albert Marshall. Let's take our time, work our way through the lines at Passport Control and collect our bags from the carousel. Customs should be a breeze. They don't worry so much about Americans here."

"Okay."

"We just don't need to do anything that draws attention."

By the time they reached the Passport Control booths, Al had a smile on his face and appeared calm. Barrett went first and then watched as Al pushed his passport through the opening at the bottom of the glass.

"Mr. Marshall," the agent said as he read from the photo page and then looked up at Al, "are you here on business or pleasure?"

"Vacation," Al said, as he'd been coached, "My first time here." Al gave the man a big smile.

The agent said, "Enjoy Italy sir," as he pushed Al's passport back to him.

"Oh, I will. Thank you."

Al stepped away from the booth, smiling.

With no concern shown for their baggage by Customs officials, the two men took their belongings and exited the terminal at Ground Transportation. They spotted a limo driver with a sign that read: *Strong*.

"I'm Bradford Strong," he said to the driver, as he dropped his bags at the man's feet and climbed through the open door into the car.

Al parked his luggage along side Barrett's and thanked the young man for his efforts.

Barrett was punching the buttons on his satellite phone when Al climbed inside the limo.

"Hello,"

"Doctor Groom, this is Bradford Strong."

"Hello, Mr. Strong. Have you arrived in Rome yet?"

"Yes, we are just now leaving the airport. Where are *you*?"

"We are at the Hilton. How was your flight?"

"Long," Barrett said, "Do we need to meet for any reason today or just plan to see you in the morning at the hospital?"

"Tomorrow morning is fine. I have already spoken with the San Mateo staff and will meet with the Chief of Surgery later this afternoon. Their staff is skilled at this procedure. They're prepared for us tomorrow."

"Good."

"Everything is on schedule. We have the operating room booked from eight o'clock until we are finished. Be sure you and Mr. Marshall are at the hospital admitting office no later than six o'clock for preparation. Surgery should take no more than four hours for each of you. Your time in recovery could vary, but should be one to two hours. At that time you will be moved to your private rooms.

"It sounds like you have everything under control."

"As I told you when the two of you came to Beverly Hills, I've been doing surgery like this for twenty-five years. Faces haven't changed much over the years."

"We'll try to relax."

"Good, and by dinner time tomorrow evening, you and Mr. Marshall will have your new looks. You will be in bandages for several days, but your alterations will be as you requested. Enjoy your first evening in Rome, but be sure to get a good night's sleep. It's best for the healing process."

"I'll see you in the morning." Barrett ended the call.

CHAPTER 35

Criminal Justice Center
Downtown Nashville

As he descended the stairs to the first floor lobby of the Criminal Justice Center, Mike could see Wade Powell sitting on one of the polished wooden slat benches. Dressed in jeans, a plaid shirt and a jeans jacket, he looked a little older and healthier than in the photograph attached to his record in the NCIC database.

He knew a man's bouncing leg was normally a product of nerves, but Powell's pleasant tone and temperament during their phone conversation earlier in the day caused him to think Powell was comfortable talking with the police. He would soon know for sure.

When Mike came around the corner and approached him, Powell stood and offered his hand.

"Wade Powell, Sergeant."

"Mike Neal." He took Powell's hand. "Thanks for coming down."

"No problem."

He noticed Powell was making good eye contact, smiling and showing no outward discomfort with his surroundings.

"Come with me. We'll talk back here. Can I get you a Coke or some coffee?"

"Coffee, if you have it."

"I'm sure we have some, but the question will be how fresh it is," he said, working on his attempt to relate to his interviewee.

"I'm used to drinkin' it however I find it," Powell said. "I learned that in the Army."

"When were you in?" Mike asked.

"Ninety-seven to ninety-nine."

"What was your assignment?" Mike poured them both some dark coffee in Styrofoam cups.

"I was an E-4, Logistics. I was in Bosnia, then Iraq and back to Bosnia before I got my DD 214."

"I was stationed in Iraq in the early nineties myself," Mike said.

"Desert Storm?"

"Yes, and afterward. Eight years in all. Six with CID. I was a W-3."

"Impressive." Powell nodded.

Mike gestured. "Let's sit in here."

Powell pulled out one of the club chairs and sat across the table from Mike.

"The reason I asked you to come down and talk with me concerns the recent death of Tyler McKinnon."

"I sorta figured that was it when I got your phone message. I saw the story on the news Monday night."

"How long since you've had any type of contact with Mr. McKinnon?"

"The day I was sentenced to eight years in prison, they cuffed me and escorted me out. I looked back in the courtroom as I left. I saw my mama and my aunt crying. I saw McKinnon looking at the floor." Powell paused. "That's the last time I saw him."

"You've not heard from him since?"

"No, sir." Powell said as he looked directly at Mike.

"Where were you Sunday night and early Monday morning?"

"Well, Sunday night I was at The BlueBird Café for Writers Night with my girlfriend Jamie until they closed about ... eleven or eleven-thirty. There's no cover on Writer's Night and sometimes you can hear some pretty good music. We go there a lot." Powell shifted in his seat and leaned forward toward Mike. "We left there and went downtown. We hit Legends Corner ... oh, and The Stage. They closed The Stage about three o'clock and we went back to my apartment. Not the first time we've done that." Powell smiled. "By the way, Monday is my day off, so Jamie and I like to party late."

"What's Jamie's last name?"

"Bell."

"I'll need to speak with her also."

"No problem. I can give you her cell."

"I'll need her address as well."

"I can write it down for you."

He slid a piece of paper to Powell and watched him scribble his girlfriend's data. "How long have you known Jamie?"

"We've been friends for several years, but we just started datin' earlier this year. She was datin' a friend of mine a while back. They broke up. You know how it goes."

"While you were out Sunday night, did you pay for anything with a credit card?"

Powell chuckled. "You know, since I got out, no one's been all that interested in offerin' me credit."

"What about a parking receipt?"

Powell shrugged. "I would have tossed it."

He nodded. "Do you know of anyone, other than Jamie who can confirm your whereabouts early Monday morning?"

"I'm sure The Blue Bird has video cams and I'm pretty sure The Stage does too. Would that work?"

"If you're in their video during the times you stated, yes."

"I know—our waitress. Jamie talked with our waitress at The Stage off and on the whole time we were there. You know how women are. She'll remember us."

"What was her name?"

"I have no idea. Jamie should remember. I'll ask her, or you can ask her if you'd like."

"I'll talk with her about it."

"Sergeant, can I say somethin'?"

"Sure."

"I can understand why you'd think I might be involved in this. Hell, Tyler McKinnon cost me a good chunk of my life—but I didn't kill him." Powell hesitated. "I wasn't as level-headed back when I was locked up as I am nowadays. Life for me is different now. I paid my debt to society, as they say. I've done some serious growin' up since then. I've got a good job and a roof over my head. I'm thinkin' about askin' Jamie to marry me. I ain't gonna mess that up."

He looked at Powell, who was looking straight into Mike's eyes. That was normally a good sign he was telling the truth, but Mike had interviewed several liars who could easily do the same.

"When we searched McKinnon's home office we found files on his clients going all the way back to when he began his practice as an attorney." Mike watched for a telling response. "Do you have any idea why we weren't able to find any files or anything else related to *your* case?"

Powell's brow wrinkled. "Nothin'?"

"Nothing."

Hmm. Powell grunted. "I don't know unless ... maybe he destroyed my files."

"Why would he do that?" Mike was confident Tyler McKinnon was aware that he was bound by law not to destroy those files. He made himself a note to call the law firm who employed Tyler at the time of his termination.

"I got a feelin' that case may have done about as much to damage him as it did me." Powell hesitated. "I'm just sayin'."

"What makes you think that?"

"McKinnon's life was headed down the shitter the last weeks of the trial. It was kinda obvious."

"Really?"

"His attitude sucked. He was distracted. He was defeated even before he started presentin' my side of the case. Based on my limited experience, I thought he was usin' drugs. I still think he was."

"Did you confront him about this?"

"Did I? Hell, we almost came to blows over it. I even asked for a new lawyer, but the damn judge said it wasn't gonna happen." Powell sat back in his chair. "I was screwed."

Mike made notes. "Do you know Al Ricks or Barrett Stone?"

Powell was quiet for a moment. "No sir. Should I?"

"Not necessarily."

"Do you own a hand gun?"

Powell laughed. "Sergeant, I know you're aware, that would be a felony and a first class ticket back to prison. No, I do not own a hand gun or a long gun of any kind. I used to love to hunt, but I love my freedom a helluva lot more."

Mike looked at Powell and wondered how much of the man's story he should believe. His years of experience as an investigator were not populated with large numbers of honest ex-cons. He knew he would have to validate or discredit each of Powell's assertions, but he was going to start by contacting Tyler McKinnon's former law firm to see what they knew about Powell's files and McKinnon's demeanor during the last days of Powell's trial.

He scribbled at the bottom of his note pad.
Means – likely
Motive – definitely
Opportunity – to be determined.

CHAPTER 36

Oakhill
South Nashville

The phone rang again. Mary Ellen stood over the desk phone looking down at the Caller ID display. It read 'Unknown'. She never answered calls from numbers she didn't recognize or that didn't display the caller's name. Al programmed the answering machine's Caller ID to include all her family from the upper Mid-West. When they called she could decide which of her aunts or cousins she wanted to talk to.

Since Al left, the phone had rung more frequently, but the display didn't always identify the caller. She knew there was a good chance several of these calls were from the police. They'd left three messages already stating they would like to talk with her about Al's disappearance.

After Al and Barrett's sudden departure, she knew it was inevitable she would have to talk with the police about what she knew, and didn't know. But, she didn't want to talk with anyone, not about Al's work or Barrett Stone or even about Al. She wanted to be left alone. She was worried she might say something she shouldn't.

She was on her way to the kitchen when the doorbell jolted her from her thoughts. She tiptoed into the hallway where she could see the driveway through the gaps in the living room mini-blinds. The car was brown, an ugly brown. She stepped into the living room enough to see the light bar along the top of the dash; the police.

Her heart rate was climbing and her blood pressure too. She clamped her hands tight together. She whispered to herself, "Please leave."

There was a loud knock.

"Oh!" she said out loud, unable to control her nerves.

"Mrs. Ricks?"

He knows I'm here. She pulled three tissues from the box on the foyer table.

"Mrs. Ricks, my name is Sergeant Mike Neal. I'm with the Nashville Police Department. I'd like to speak with you briefly. I won't take much of your time. Can you open the door please, so we can talk?"

What choice do I have?

She walked to the door, sighed and unlocked both dead bolts. The door hadn't been opened in weeks. She pulled hard and it released.

"Hello, Mrs. Ricks."

She squinted in response to the bright sunshine behind him. She shaded her eyes with her hand. He was holding up his badge and identification against the storm door for her to see.

She unlocked the storm door and pushed it open. The detective took the handle. She stepped back to allow him to enter.

"Mrs. Ricks, thank you for allowing me to speak with you."

"Come in." She dabbed her eyes. "You can sit there if you like." She gestured toward the sofa. She took the box of tissues from the table and brought them with her to her chair and sat across the coffee table from the detective.

"Mrs. Ricks, can I assume you are aware of your husband's disappearance?

She covered her mouth with the tissues and, after a moment, nodded.

"I'm sorry to have to bother you with questions right now. I'm sure this is a trying time, but we need to know if there is anything you can tell us that might help explain what's happened regarding Stone Asset Management and the disappearance of your husband and Barrett Stone."

"I don't know anything. Al didn't discuss his work with me." She sighed. "He kept all that to himself, or else he left it at work. When he was home, he read books, he watched sports and we watched movies. Occasionally, we just sat and talked. I have no idea what's happened," she began to cry, "other than my life has been destroyed."

"What did you and your husband talk about?"

She grabbed more tissues and hid her face.

The detective waited for her to collect her composure.

"I work part time at a daycare center and sometimes we talked about the kids I worked with. We talked about the future. We talked about places we wanted to visit and the things we planned to do in our later years together, when we retired." She hung her head and wiped more tears. "I'm sorry. This has simply devastated me. I don't know what I'm going to do."

"Was your husband different lately? Was he upset? Did he talk about anything new or did his attitude seem unusual in any way?"

"Not that I noticed. He didn't like to talk about his work."

"Did he seem troubled about anything?"

"No. He was normal." She shrugged.

"Do you and Mr. Ricks have children?"

"We weren't able to have children." She avoided eye contact with the detective.

"Do you have other family here to help you?"

"No. My family lives in Michigan and Wisconsin. I have some friends here, mostly ladies I work with, but I may have to sell and move back up north. I don't know yet. I don't want to do the wrong thing." She wiped her eyes.

"I understand. Can you tell me what you know about Barrett Stone?"

Slowly, her expression changed. She took her time and then looked up at Mike. "I know he's an ass. I know he's treated Al like a slave for most of his life. And I know he can't be trusted in any way by anyone." Her anger and contempt for Stone replaced her grief. "He is the most callous, insensitive and egotistical man I've ever known. I hate him for what he's done to Al, and now what he did to me." She began to cry again. "I cannot believe Al left with him. This is all his doing."

The detective waited. "Have you heard from your husband since he left?"

"No."

"Do you expect him to contact you?"

"I ... I don't know. I don't know what to expect from anyone anymore. I feel lost. How am I supposed to feel, Sergeant?" She made direct eye contact with the detective.

"I'm not sure. I'd say your feelings are pretty normal, considering the situation." He paused. "If you do hear from your husband, I need you to contact me. Can I get you to do that?"

She nodded. "I guess so."

The detective stood and offered her his card.

She stood, glad the questions were over and anxious for him to leave.

"I have one more request. I need a recent photograph of your husband. I'll give it back, but I need it to make copies."

She thought for a moment and then turned toward the mantle above the fireplace. She pulled down a five by seven inch frame and removed a photo of the two of them. "This is the most recent one I have."

"I'll be sure to get it back to you. Thank you for speaking with me and if you think of anything else you feel I should know, please contact me anytime. Okay?"

She nodded. "Okay."

She followed the detective to the door.

"Thanks again," he said as he stepped across the threshold.

She waited for a moment, and then shut and latched the door. She leaned against the door, put her head in her hand and took several large breaths to ease the built-up stress.

CHAPTER 37

St. Regis Hotel
Rome, Italy

"When will you begin the search?"

"I cannot leave Munich until tomorrow."

"What's the problem?" Barrett asked. "I am paying you quite well for your services. I expect a sense of urgency."

"Yes. But, you cannot pay me enough to miss my daughter's violin recital this evening."

"Seriously?"

"You do not have children?"

"No, thank goodness."

"It is best."

"Whatever. I will expect you to be working by late morning."

"Herr Strong, Rome is over nine hundred kilometers from here."

"You should leave early—on a fast plane. And don't forget the accessories I asked you about."

"I will have to take care of that after I arrive in Italy. The airlines frown upon such, you know. I will call you and we can get to work on finding your friend. *Auf Wiedersehen, herr Strong.*"

He couldn't believe there were so many people who were inadequately motivated by money. This private investigator came highly recommended by Barrett II's attorney friend, Leo Brunn in Vienna, but in Barrett's opinion, this man had priority issues.

He dialed the number for Al's room.

"Yes."

"Are you ready for dinner?"

"Sure. I just called your room to ask you the same question."

"Oh?"

"The line was busy."

"I ... called the front desk for better pillows. These pillows are too damned soft."

"I'll meet you in the restaurant."

Barrett hung up the phone. He walked to the tall dressing mirror and straightened his clothes. He thought about how much he'd changed since his late teens when Elena left him. He contemplated what he might say to her, assuming this mediocre private investigator was able to locate her. Like him, she was seventeen years older now. But, he knew she would still be beautiful.

Barrett was already seated and examining the menu when Al approached the maître d' podium. He indicated his intention to be seated with Barrett.

Once seated, he requested a Jack Daniel's and Coke from the maître d'.

"So, what looks good?" he asked, attempting to initiate some benign conversation.

"I just started looking at the menu. The waiter told me about today's fresh catch and the specials. If you were on time you could have heard for yourself."

He has to be an ass. Al wanted to know about the specials, but he decided he would be damned if he was going to ask Barrett about them. He continued to peruse the menu as though Barrett had said nothing.

After a moment, the waiter returned. "Good evening."

The waiter repeated the specials for Al. He took their orders and left his guests to enjoy their drinks.

"Are you prepared for tomorrow?" Barrett asked.

Al looked at Barrett and said, "As prepared as I can be."

"You don't seem excited about it, but like you've said, it's a drastic step and few have ever taken it." Barrett opened the wine list.

"Even though Groom showed us the computer version of what we're supposed to look like when he's finished—I still have to wonder."

"Wonder?"

"What if? What if he can't do what he said he'd do? What if he drops a scalpel? What if he pokes me in the eye or cuts your nose off?"

Barrett laughed. "He's surely better at it than that. I would guess if he's prone to accidents, he'd have sheared off a Hollywood starlet's nipple by now."

"It's possible." Al wasn't laughing. "It's enough to be concerned about."

"You be concerned for me, too. I'm going to relax and look forward to being a rich, unknown and strong Bradford Strong." Barrett waved down the sommelier. "Bring us a bottle of Perrier-Jouet."

"Isn't that expensive?"

"Does it really matter any more? It's one of the best French champagnes ever bottled, and I've never had any. So, we're having some tonight to celebrate Mr. T. Albert Marshall and Mr. Bradford S. Strong. Now, doesn't that sound like an excellent reason to toast the best champagne in the world?"

"I guess so."

Once the wine steward had finished preparing and pouring the sparkling extravagance, he left their table. Barrett lifted his flute of champagne. Al followed suit.

"To our wealth, our new lives and tomorrow's new faces." Barrett touched his glass to Al's, and both sipped the French champagne.

Al acted as though he was analyzing the sparkling wine. He wasn't sure how to respond, so he said, "It's very good."

"It better be." Barrett grunted.

When dinner was finished, the two men left the restaurant. Al was impressed with the quality of the food and the exceptional service. As usual, Barrett had no compliments to offer.

As the brass and velvet lined elevator made its slow climb to their top floor rooms, Barrett looked at him and said, "Mr. Marshall, this is the way you'll be able to live the rest of your life."

"So far," Al said, "it feels like I'm living a dream."

As they reached their rooms, Barrett said, "The limo will be here to pick us up at 5:30am."

"I'll be ready."

CHAPTER 38

Offices of Metropolitan Government
Downtown Nashville

"Hi," Mike said as he approached the receptionist's desk.

"Hello. How can I help you?"

"Sergeant Neal to see Mayor Rowe." He offered his card. "He's expecting me."

"Just a moment."

He turned from the receptionist's desk, but before he could reach the sitting area, she hung up her phone, stood and announced, "He'll see you now."

"Thanks."

She led the way to a red oak door with a brass plaque that read 'Mayor Harrison Rowe'. After two quick knocks, she opened the door and stepped back to allow him to enter.

"Sergeant. Come in, come in." The six foot four inch Mayor stood and stepped around his desk.

"Mayor."

"How's the battle?" Rowe offered his sizable hand.

Mike was asked this same question by the mayor both times he'd seen him in the last three years. He knew it was coming.

"The criminals are convinced they're smarter than we are, sir. It's what makes *them* vulnerable and *us* advantaged."

"Good news. Have a seat, Mike." Rowe motioned toward the matching wingback leather chairs as he rounded his desk.

"I know you're as busy as I am, so I'll get to the point." Rowe sat and rolled his chair forward. "Recently, you were assigned the homicide of Tyler McKinnon. Is that right?"

Mike nodded.

"What is the status of your investigation?"

Even with the Mayor, he was hesitant to open up completely about any active homicide. "We have some potentially solid leads, but as yet we're still interviewing and collecting evidence. Why do you ask, sir?"

"I have reason to believe McKinnon's murder may be connected to another crime."

"Would that be your sister's murder?"

"Yes. What do you know about Meredith's case?"

"The detective investigating her murder is my former partner, Norm Wallace. He and I have discussed the case. I called him when Lieutenant Burris told me about her brooch."

"I understand you found the brooch in McKinnon's floor safe?"

"Yes sir. But, that's still not public knowledge."

"I understand. How do you think it got in his safe?"

"I can't be sure, but based upon the aggregate evidence we have so far; I'd say it's likely it was planted there in an attempt to frame McKinnon."

Rowe sat looking at him as if he was still waiting for him to answer. "You may be right. At first, I believed McKinnon was our man. Lieutenant Burris told me, even with the brooch, you and Detective Wallace found no viable connection between McKinnon and Meredith."

"No sir."

"However, there is a significant connection between Meredith and Barrett Stone. He was against his father's plans to marry Meredith. It wasn't a secret. I'd hoped Detective Wallace could make that connection by now and put Stone's ass in jail."

"He's still trying to do that, sir. But, as I'm sure you already know, there isn't sufficient physical evidence to give the DA the case he needs to indict, much less convict. No witnesses, no prints on the two brass casings found at the scene and no impressions other than those made by a pair of old Nike tennis shoes which are much like those owned by several thousand Nashville teenagers. Similar shoe impressions were also taken from the scenes of the other Belle Meade burglaries. None of the neighbors that were interviewed saw or heard anything. There's not much that points to anything other than a burglary leading to a robbery and subsequent murder."

"But that's not what happened," Rowe barked. "I'm certain of it."

Mike waited to respond. "I understand, sir. Stone is intelligent. He's smart enough to properly stage a crime to hide his involvement. We just haven't found the piece of evidence he failed to cover. Norm is good. I believe he'll find it. I'll help him in any way I can."

"Thank you. We may not be making the progress we want at the moment, but we're not going to let this one get labeled a cold case, Sergeant."

"No sir."

"Mike, I doubt you're aware of this, but the day before Stone's disappearance he attended a political fund raiser at the home of Hugh Blanchard in Belle Meade. Hugh and his wife have been friends of ours for years. I'm not sure Stone planned this, but once again he found a way to get to my family.

"I was unable to attend the function due to a scheduling conflict, so I asked my daughter, Samantha to represent me and the Mayor's office. She graciously accepted and offered our family's donation for Josh Foreman's campaign.

"While at the event, Samantha was approached by this animal, Stone. She didn't have a clue who he was or that she needed to be on the defensive. She's an attractive young woman, a recent college graduate, and she has no trouble making friends. Sometimes in today's society, this can be a liability."

"I understand."

"It seems Stone spotted my Samantha and decided he would seize the opportunity to approach a beautiful woman and take advantage of her."

"Did he make unwanted advances?"

"Not exactly, thank God. He just stole her money."

"Sir?"

Rowe nodded. "About four months ago, my mother suffered a heart attack and passed on."

"I'm sorry, sir."

Rowe nodded. "She was eighty-nine. She lived a good life." Rowe paused. "When mother passed, she left a nice inheritance to her only granddaughter. She wanted Samantha to be able to start her life with nice things that she didn't have back in the forties when she was starting out. It was a sizable legacy for a young woman in her twenties."

He listened to the mayor's emotional explanation.

"Stone told Samantha all about his company and how he was on the cutting edge of a huge opportunity for investors to make significant returns. He told her he was in the process of signing up Hugh Blanchard himself. She verified this fact with Hugh before she agreed to get involved. Hugh gave Stone five hundred thousand."

Mike grunted. "How much did your daughter give him?"

"All of her inheritance. One hundred and thirty thousand dollars."

"Oh, you're kidding?"

"Mike, she's twenty-five. Her degree is in Fine Arts, not finance. All she had on her mind at the time was impressing her daddy and showing him she knew how to make money too. She's devastated. She cried all day when she heard Stone disappeared. She said she knows her Gramma would be disappointed in her."

"It's not her fault. She was scammed."

"Exactly what I told her."

"I'm convinced with Stone's apparent flight from the country he's not only guilty of multiple flavors of fraud and outright theft, but he is unquestionably guilty of Meredith's murder and possibly others whose cases remain unsolved."

"So, you know about our suspicions of his flight to Italy?"

"I'm kept up to speed daily by Captain Moretti."

"Yes sir."

"This is why I've asked you here today, Mike."

He nodded, not sure what else to say or do.

"Sergeant, I want you to find Stone."

"Sir?"

"I want you to go to Italy and find this murdering bastard, and I want you to bring him back to Nashville. I want you to bring him back in shackles so he can answer for his crimes. He has to face the music."

"Sir, can we do that?"

The mayor leaned forward over his desk pad, his hands clasped before him like a judge about to issue a ruling.

"Mike, I know about your sister's murder. Connie, right?"

"Yes sir."

"Burris told me. I know what it meant to you to finally discover the man who killed her. I want this thieving bastard who killed Meredith caught and in prison," Rowe said. "I want *you* to be the one who locks his smug ass up. I don't give a damn what it costs, where you have to go, or how long it takes. I want it done. I want him suffering for his crimes. Am I clear on this, Sergeant?"

"Yes sir." Mike was hesitant to offer up anything more that could be construed as opposing the mayor's request, but he knew this investigation would tread well beyond his or the mayor's jurisdiction. Not sure what else to do, he continued to nod his head slowly, hoping some gem of wisdom might present itself and make all this go away.

"Sir, if I might offer up a couple of minor concerns?"

Rowe exhaled. "Go ahead."

"We are currently maxed out on man-power. The recent detective retirements have increased the caseload and we're approaching vacation season. I don't see—"

"Good idea, Sergeant," Rowe interrupted.

"Sir?"

"That's an excellent idea. I'll submit to Captain Moretti today the official mayoral request for your *extended* paid vacation."

Mike was losing ground.

Rowe stood, walked slowly as he contemplated, and sat on the corner of his huge desk facing Mike at close range.

"I know several good and decent folks who know this son-of-a-bitch and have invested with him. He's out for number one, and everyone else *be damned*. He has no plans to stop. He'll continue to be a moving target until someone stops him. That someone needs to be you."

Mike focused on the mayor's eyes and knew he was dead serious.

"I'm convinced, once you boys get his ass back here to Nashville, you'll be able to hold him with the fraud charges and position him for the murder charge. Hell, with your interrogation skills, you may even get a confession."

Mike was trying to think of any other information he could bring up that might impact the mayor's approach. "Sir, I don't speak Italian. That could be a problem with communication over there."

"Most people in Europe, especially governmental officials, have made the effort to learn English, but that won't be a problem anyway. You'll have a translator."

"A translator?"

"You're not going to Italy alone."

"Pardon me?"

"Detective Vega is going with you."

"Cris?"

"Yes."

"Cris speaks Spanish sir, not Italian."

"She speaks Italian too."

"If you don't mind me asking sir, how do you know this?"

"Her uncle told me."

"Uncle?"

"Yes, her Uncle Alberto."

Mike had heard that name used referencing only one person.

"Yes," the mayor said. "Captain Alberto Moretti is her uncle."

"Seriously?"

"Cris's mom is the Captain's sister."

He stared at the mayor in disbelief. He realized his mouth was standing open and he closed it.

"If she'd stayed in Houston, she would have been her daddy's little girl the rest of her career. That's why she came to Nashville, so she could make her own way—be what she could be on her own, not because of her Houston Police Sergeant father. We welcomed her."

"I didn't know."

"I'm sure she would appreciate your discretion in the matter."

"No problem." Mike continued to listen.

"Lieutenant Burris has agreed to the two of you making the trip. You will need to let Cris know after you leave here, so she can prepare. If she's like my wife Marie, it'll take her hours to decide what to pack." Rowe smiled. "Tell her she should not dress like a tourist. Both of you should try to fit in with the locals. No white tennis shoes."

"Yes sir. What about expenses and connections with the Italian Police?"

Rowe pulled open his desk drawer and removed a credit card.

"This card is registered in your name. It has a twenty-five thousand dollar limit."

Mike's eyes communicated his anxiety.

"Don't worry. If you need more, you'll have it."

"That wasn't what I was thinking, sir."

"I won't ask you to act like paupers while you're there, Mike. I don't want you concerned about anything except locating Stone and Ricks and bringing them back."

He stared at the card in the mayor's hand and tried to imagine what the next days were going to be like.

"Three years ago, Marie and I went to a mayor's conference in Atlanta. The conference was an international event attended by several mayoral dignitaries from around the world. At our dinner table the first evening we enjoyed the company of three other mayors and their wives. Seated next to Marie and I were Agostino Vitali, the Mayor of Rome and his lovely wife, Oriana. We enjoyed each other's company so much I invited them to visit us here in Nashville. We were pleased to welcome them last year when they vacationed in the United States."

Rowe looked at Mike's intent stare. "I'm sure you're ahead of me, Sergeant. Yes, Agostino has arranged complete cooperation by the Polizia di Stato and access to one of his best Lieutenants."

"Without assistance we would be severely handicapped," Mike said. "Trying to find our way through an unfamiliar city, asking questions with no authority; it would be hopeless."

"Mike, you're one of the best investigators Nashville has. I don't know Agostino's detectives and I can't trust them to be committed to this case. But, I trust you to do what you do best. Find the bastard who killed my sister."

The mayor stood, offered Mike the credit card with his left hand and his appreciation with his right. "Good luck."

"Thank you, sir. I hope we won't need it."

"Lieutenant Burris will have your airline tickets and a satellite telephone for you. I need you to stay in touch and keep me informed."

"Yes, sir."

Mike turned and walked from the mayor's office. He was focused on what the mayor had said, 'Find the bastard who killed my sister.'

Mike hadn't found the bastard that killed *his* sister until after the man was already dead. His interest in helping the mayor was building, as he thought about the chance to help him see *his* sister's killer imprisoned for the rest of his life.

He wasn't sure what he would face in Italy, but he knew with certainty it was not going to be a vacation.

CHAPTER 39

Starbucks
Downtown Nashville

"So, what on earth possessed you to invite me for coffee?" Detective Cris Vega asked.

"I invited everyone else I know, and they all turned me down so you were the only one left?"

"Very funny."

"I ... just thought," Mike said, "it's been a while since we've shared war stories and we needed to talk."

"Why do I have trouble believing that was your sole intent?"

"You're a tough audience, Vega."

"I do better with the truth." She grinned.

Mike nodded. "Is your passport current?"

She turned her head and scrunched her brow. "Why would you ask a question like that?"

"Just curious." Mike leaned back and folded his arms across his chest. "I haven't been out of the country in a while myself."

"I took a cruise to Nassau a couple of years ago. I don't believe it's expired."

"You may want to check, to be sure."

"Mike. Why are we discussing this?"

"The mayor has a task he wants me to take care of for him. He thinks I don't have all the skills required and I need to have someone along to assist with communication."

"Oh? Since when do you have trouble talking."

"Since I don't speak Italian. He says I need a translator." Mike stared into Cris's eyes.

"Italian?" The word clearly doubled her curiosity. Why would you need someone to speak Italian?"

"Exactly, and why would he think *you* know how to speak Italian?" Mike raised his eyebrows.

"Hmmm, I don't know," she looked down.

"Bullshit." Mike stared at Cris. "Why didn't you tell me?"

"Tell you what?" She sipped her coffee.

"You know what I'm talking about. Did you think it would make a difference with *me*?"

She inhaled and looked out the restaurant window for a few moments. "It would make a helluva difference with a lot of people and the smaller number who know, the better."

"Cris, I can understand your feelings. I don't care. You know me. It makes no difference."

She tucked a strand of her thick black hair behind her ear, interlaced her fingers and rested her hands on the table. "Okay." She looked at Mike with an expression that let him know she was about to open up. "When I was in Houston, starting out at the academy and then later as a rookie, it was the favorite topic of discussion. "That's *Vega's* little girl. Don't mess with her. The *Sarge* will kick your ass. Better not let Sergeant Vega's baby girl get hurt." She paused. "It got old … real old."

"I'm sure it did. Were there many other women on the force?"

"No, and that made it worse. I was not only picked on for being my dad's kid, but also along with the other ladies for being a woman in a macho world. There were about fifteen females in the entire department. We caught hell daily from the men. None of them wanted us in the car with them. They were afraid we wouldn't be able to back them up when things got thick. Or, they were afraid we would become just another distraction on the street. It was much harder back then. It made for a hostile work environment. That's the main reason I came here. There were several more ladies on the force here, some even in leadership positions."

"I guess with the name difference it wasn't so hard to keep it quiet."

"No, it helped. Captain Moretti—Uncle Al has always kept it to himself, except for the mayor, the chief and the lieutenant. He had to tell the chief up front, and he believed the Lieutenant deserved to know. But, that's it. Now *you* know."

"You're safe with me, kiddo. Like I said, it makes no difference. It's not about who you know. It's about what *you* do as a detective. And you do good work. I've seen it, many times."

"Thanks, Mike. So, tell me about the mayor's idea." She relaxed a bit after having shared her secret.

"You and I are going to Rome."

"Don't kid around. I've always wanted to go to Rome."

"I'm not kidding, but this will not be a sight-seeing visit."

"But we're really going to Italy?"

"Yep."

"Wow. Why?"

"To locate and bring back an alleged murderer, possible multi. He is also about to be charged with securities, investment, wire and mail fraud."

"The fraud is sort of out of our area isn't it?"

"The mayor considers it to be that much more reason for us to bring him back."

"Who is this altar boy?"

"His name is Barrett Hayden Stone III. We're also looking for his partner, Al Ricks, but Ricks is not the brains of the team. According to my investigation so far, he is more the sidekick-follower type."

"With a name like that, it sounds like Stone comes from old money."

"He comes from old and substantial money." He has a dysfunctional past as well as an equally sociopathic present."

"Who did he kill?"

"This is all still alleged, but the mayor is convinced Stone killed his sister Meredith."

"Really?"

"It's one of Norm's older cases. After Stone's flight from Nashville, he's also at the top of the suspect list on one of *my* homicides from earlier this week. I'm working with Brent Spangler on the fraud charges. And now, you're in."

"Sounds good. What are we supposed to do with our active cases while we're chasing this monster?"

"That's why we're meeting with the Lieutenant." Mike checked his wristwatch. "Finish your cookie and we'll go see Burris."

"I'm too excited to eat. Let's go now."

Cris Vega was small in stature compared to the men in the department, but even at five-foot five, her ability as a detective established a sizable competence that gained her respect throughout the MNPD.

Her confidence was fortified by her years as a Mexican-American growing up on the streets of Houston, Texas, where even the boys respected her rather than risk having to admit they lost a fight to a girl. She was tough, straight by the book and no bullshit.

Her success as an investigator and her dedication to her work helped make her one of Mike's favorite people.

"Are you available?" Mike asked as he stuck his head inside Lieutenant D.W. Burris's office.

"Yes. Come on in. Shut the door. Hi, Cris."

"Hey, Lieutenant."

Mike and Cris took their seats in front of Burris's desk.

"Lieutenant, before we get started I want to update you on my discussions at Drummond and Whyte, Tyler McKinnon's former employer."

"Go ahead."

"They told me when I went by their office this morning, that about two weeks after McKinnon was terminated, they received a large box via UPS containing all of his personal files related to Wade Powell's manslaughter case. They said there was a short note included which explained McKinnon's motive to get everything having to do with the tainted case out of his possession and out of his life."

"Based upon his quality of life after his debacle," Burris said, "purging himself of this case doesn't appear to have accomplished much for him."

"No sir, but at least it answers questions for us on why we found nothing related to Powell's case in McKinnon's office. By the way, I interviewed Powell's girlfriend, Jamie Bell and the waitress at The Stage. So far, it appears Powell's alibi holds up for his whereabouts Sunday night and early Monday, but I haven't been able to view any of the club's video yet to confirm it."

"What about the names that were collected from the other files in McKinnon's office?"

"Other than the five who remained incarcerated at the time of McKinnon's death, there are seven who may still be in the Middle Tennessee area. I was able to locate three, none of which have offered up anything helpful so far. I have the TBI and the respective county sheriffs helping to locate the ones outside Davidson County. The sheriffs know the information I'm looking for, in case I'm not available when they locate the rest of the men. They know to contact you."

"Good. How much have you told Detective Vega about the plan?"

He looked at Cris. "Everything, I think."

"You good with this?"

"Yes sir." She nodded. "*Very* good."

"How's your Italian?"

Cris smiled. *"Il mio Italiano e buono e non vedo l'ora di andare a Roma."*

"I don't have a clue what you said, but it sounded like Italian to me."

Cris looked at Mike and both smiled.

"Here is the satellite phone the mayor wants on your person at all times. His number, my number and the captain's are programmed in. I assume he gave you the credit card?"

"Yes sir." Mike took the phone.

"He wants a check-in no less than once each day."

"Gotcha."

"These are your e-tickets. Your flight to Atlanta leaves Nashville in the morning at 11:45 and you'll arrive in Rome the next morning. As you probably know, there is a seven hour time difference. I recommend you get some sleep both tonight and on the flight. This is your confirmation for the hotel." Burris handed Mike the papers. "It's only blocks from the police station."

"Your contact with the, correct me if I'm wrong Cris, Polizia di Stato, who will meet you when you arrive at Fiumicino Airport is Lieutenant Giancarlo Petrelli."

"Excellent, Lieutenant. You pronounced all the vowels."

"Burris tried not to smile, but failed."

"He's been briefed by the Chief of Police and the Mayor of Rome who was briefed by Mayor Rowe. They were sent a copy of Stone's package including the photographs of him and Ricks. According to Mayor Rowe, they have already begun searching for both men. With four million residents in Metropolitan Rome spanning well over five hundred square miles, it's best if they get started right away."

"Lieutenant, the data I received from Stone's wife leads me to believe he and Ricks are planning to have facial reconstruction. If they do, our photographs won't help."

"Until we know for sure, this is all we have to go on. Do you have any information on the doctor or the hospital?"

"No sir, not yet."

"I'd say that's a priority. This Lieutenant Petrelli should be able to help with this. If they do have surgery, they'll have to remain in the hospital for recovery. That could buy us some time. Do either of you have any questions?"

Mike and Cris looked at each other. Both looked back at Burris.

"I guess not," he said.

"Before you leave the CJC, I want your active cases with current status on my desk. If the other detectives have any questions, they'll be calling you on the satellite phone. And, don't forget the check-ins. I don't need Mayor Rowe up my wazoo because you aren't keeping us in the loop.

"Oh, I almost forgot. I received a call this morning from Burton Jarvis, Special Agent in Charge at the FBI's Nashville office. You may remember him."

"Definitely," Mike said.

Cris nodded.

"He called to tell me there was an explosion at an apartment building on Staten Island in New York. At first they thought it was another meth lab, but when the criminalists got in there they discovered it was an improvised explosive device—a suicide vest. They decided something must have gone wrong. Three bodies were discovered in the remains. Long story short; two of them appeared to be young Middle Eastern men, but the other one was the Syrian terrorist Abdul Malik Kadir who tried to kill the folks at the Kurdish-American Conference here back in 2003."

"Karma." Cris smiled.

Mike nodded. "Delayed justice."

"It is, isn't it? Sometimes it takes a while. Now get out of here and get packed. Good luck."

"Thanks."

"See ya, Lieutenant." Cris said. "And thanks."

"Get your books to the lieutenant and I'll meet you downstairs in the break room," Mike said. "We can leave your car here. I'll give you a ride home and pick you up tomorrow."

"Okay, see you in five." Cris checked her wristwatch. "By the way."

"Yeah?"

"Thanks for the opportunity."

"It's Rome, but you still have to work." He pointed at Cris and smiled. He knew, with Cris's work ethic, no one ever had to tell her to work.

"Lavorare a Roma?"

He laughed. Judging from her inflection, he was pretty sure he knew what she'd said. "Yes, even in Rome."

As he pulled his car out of the parking space and headed toward I-65, Cris's excitement and the abundance of her enthusiasm about the trip were occupying his attention. Mike didn't see the car following him.

CHAPTER 40

San Mateo Hospital
Rome, Italy

Barrett marched to the desk and announced, "We're here to check in for surgery. Is Dr. Groom here?"

"Mi scusi?"

"Don't you speak English? You've got to be kidding me." He looked around at Al.

"Non parlano inglese. Un minuto per favore."

The young lady left her seat, holding up her index finger as she stepped away from the desk."

"Where did she go?" Al asked.

"I hope she went to find somebody who can speak English."

Another young woman approached the desk.

"May I help you gentlemen this morning?"

"Finally. Yes. Dr. Groom from America told us to be here by six o'clock to be admitted for surgery."

"Both of you?"

"Yes, both of us." Barrett's tone confirmed his frustration.

"Your names please?"

"Bradford Strong and Albert Marshall."

She fingered a file and said, "I have your papers here. May I see your passports, please?"

Both men offered their passports.

"Thank you. If you would please sign these releases allowing Dr. Groom and our team to complete your surgery." She pushed the papers forward.

He pushed a copy to Al, raised his eyebrows and said, "Mr. Marshall."

"Dr. Groom has noted here the charges have been prepaid?"

"That's correct." He pushed both the signed pages back to her.

The clerk attached hospital identification bracelets to both men's wrists. "I'll contact patient transportation so we can get you started. You can have a seat over there while you wait." She gestured toward a group of chairs.

They took seats across from each other. Barrett picked up an Italian magazine from a table and began looking at the photographs.

He could tell from Al's body language he was still nervous about the surgery. Barrett wasn't about to let it show, but he also had concerns.

There were voices. Barrett heard voices, women's voices. They were talking fast and laughing, but the voices were muffled and he couldn't understand what they were saying. Their words echoed as if they were in a tunnel. He wished they would stop mumbling so he could understand what they were saying.

His eye lids opened enough to see he was in a place he did not remember. At first he thought he must be hung over from a significant bout of drinking. His eyes wouldn't stay open. He couldn't focus. After forcing his eyes open long enough to scan the room, it came to him. This looked like a hospital. He lost consciousness and fell back to sleep.

When he woke the next time he was still groggy and disoriented, but he remembered where he was supposed to be and he could see other people in beds around him. He was not in a private room. He'd insisted on a private room and as soon as he could get his parched mouth to form words and his lungs to push them out, he was going to find out why he'd not received what he'd demanded and paid for up front.

In speech much softer in volume than he normally used, he was at last able to say, "Nurse."

At first the nurse continued her data entry without acknowledging him.

"Nurse," he said with a stronger exhale.

Still, no response.

He cleared his throat hoping the sound would get her attention. She turned and offered him a glance.

"Where is ..." He coughed. "Where is Dr. Groom?"

"The doctor had to leave unexpectedly sir," she said with a heavy Italian intonation, and then turned back to her work.

He tried to clear the fog from his head. This made no sense. "He what?"

"Dr. Groom was called away." She didn't turn around this time.

"Get his ass back in here. I ordered a private room."

The nurse put down her chart and walked to his bedside.

"Dr. Groom asked me to extend his apologies. He said he would be in touch with you as soon as his wife was out of danger."

"Out of danger? What the hell does that mean? What are you talking about?" He struggled to keep his eyes open.

"Dr. Groom received an emergency call after you were given anesthesia this morning. His wife, back in America, suffered a stroke."

"What?" He put his hand to his face and felt no bandages, nothing. "What's going on here? I'm supposed to have reconstructive surgery today. Where the hell is Groom?"

"I'd say he's in the air about now, on his way back home to be with his wife."

"What? That son of a bitch," he yelled. "When I get through with him, *he'll* be the one in danger. Get me out of here." He attempted to get up, but he fell back in the bed, too dazed by the drugs to sit up. "Damn it!"

CHAPTER 41

East of Rome, Italy

Before leaving Nashville, Barrett used the Internet to rent cars and a villa outside the city for their extended recovery and stay while in Rome. The house was isolated near the rear of a ten hectare, or twenty-four acre plot of land surrounded by mature olive groves. The two thousand square foot villa offered adequate room for Barrett and Al, but more than anything, it offered a concealed location away from the rest of the world—a place for them to heal and their new identities to be born.

With the failed surgeries, the secluded house provided a place for the two men to hide out, while Barrett attempted to reconstruct his fragmented plans.

The cab driver unloaded their luggage and placed it outside the aged home's entrance. He turned to Al with a look that asked for the fare.

Al glanced toward Barrett who had already entered the house. Al pulled cash from his pants pocket and enunciated, "How much?"

The driver looked at the American dollars and said in accented English, "Thirty dollars American will cover it."

Al handed him two twenties.

"*Grazie.*" The man said, nodding. He reentered the cab and started back down the long gravel road to the highway.

Al grabbed his bags and made his way into the house. As he entered the front room, he could tell the home was easily a hundred years old. Fortunately, the furnishings were not. Through a doorway he saw Barrett with his back to him in the kitchen.

"I'm making a drink," Barrett shouted. "You want one?"

"Sure," Al said with no thought other than to appease Barrett.

Al piled his bags on top of each other and walked toward the kitchen as he inspected the home.

"I had the real estate agent install a new refrigerator and stock the bar for us," Barrett said. "She also filled the fridge and pantry with her ideas on what two transplanted American males might like to eat. Hopefully she got some things right."

Off the kitchen and outside a pair of French doors, Al could see a patio of sorts covered by a vine-thick pergola. The patio was made of individual odd-shaped flat stones that were placed side by side forming a large rectangle. The gaps between the stones were filled with earth, sand and moss.

Barrett turned from the counter and handed Al his Jack and Coke. "So—not bad, huh?"

"Not bad," Al agreed, looking around at the villa. He knew Barrett didn't care what he thought about the house, but he found it interesting that he was making an effort to obtain his approval. *Must be the vodka.*

Barrett pulled open the French doors. The cool breeze was inviting. Al stepped out onto the patio. He and Barrett took seats opposite each other at a wrought iron table and looked out over the groves that covered the rolling hills behind the house.

"What a view," Al said.

Barrett was quiet, nursing his drink. Al liked it when he was quiet. It helped him imagine what it would be like if Barrett wasn't there.

Barrett emptied his glass and sucked on the ice. He stood and returned to the kitchen. He poured himself another drink, and this time, decided to bring the bottle of Stolichnaya back to the patio with him.

"I was thinking on the way here from the hospital."

Here we go.

"You remember Elena."

"Of course, I remember Elena."

"When I made the decision to pull the plug and move us here, it wasn't without motivation. I've always loved Italy. I know that when Elena left, she not only left Nashville, she left the U.S. and moved back here—back to Italy, and to *Frascati* where her mother's family lives."

Barrett's objective was becoming clear.

"I want to see her again. It may be for the best that the facial reconstruction didn't happen before I have a chance to see her."

Al had never seen Barrett act sentimental. It was out of character and so sickening.

"You do know she's not going to look the same," Al said. "She's almost twenty years older now; both of you are.

"I know that," Barrett barked. "But, I don't care. I want to see her."

"How do you plan to find her?"

"I've tried already, but I can't communicate in Italian in order to make myself clear. I've hired an investigator to find her. He speaks Italian. I'm hoping he'll be able to locate her."

"What if she's married and taken her husband's name? That'll make it difficult to find her won't it?"

"I know all this, Al." Barrett shouted. He stood and turned his back to Al. "You're not being any help, talking about how difficult it's going to be."

"Sorry." Al could tell that Barrett's cycle from jackass to sentimental was phasing back to ass, so he went mute and listened rather than fueling Barrett's fire with more reality.

"I'm trying to focus on something productive here, something other than choking the living shit out of Dr. Groom for abandoning us after I'd already paid the son of a bitch in order to get him over here for the surgery.

"That reminds me," Barrett said. "I need to call the head of surgery or the hospital administrator and let them know I was ripped off." Barrett stood and stumbled toward the kitchen. "Where's the damned phone?"

Al followed him. "Barrett, listen. You don't need to call them right now."

"Why the hell not?"

"Think. If you call now and start slurring your words, letting them know you've been drinking, they will give you no credibility and write your complaint off to the vodka. Either wait until tomorrow when you're sober, or let me make the call."

"You can't make the call. Hell, you're no negotiator. I'm the one who knows how to get his way without giving everything away."

"Barrett, you know I'm right. Wait until tomorrow and increase the odds of getting things done and having the hospital see your point. Your negotiating skills are best when you haven't been drinking. Afterward, you can call Dr. Groom in California and see about getting him back over here. It'll be for the best."

Al could tell Barrett wasn't happy with his suggestion, but his look confirmed he must have realized Al was right.

"Alright, damn it. I'll wait until tomorrow. But, only because I don't feel like sobering up today."

Barrett turned and headed toward the back of the house with his glass in one hand and the bottle of Stoli in the other.

CHAPTER 42

Green Hills
Nashville

"Think about somewhere we haven't been to eat in a while, and when I get back I'll treat you to dinner and a movie."

"By the time you get back, there will be only one treat I'll want, and we can make our own movie."

Mike laughed. "Whoa—it's a date."

"Maybe," Carol said. "You just keep your eyes off those hot-blooded women with their raven hair and sultry lips."

"Do you realize you just described a beautiful police department photographer I know? I don't have to look over there. I have a hot one to look at right here in Nashville."

"That's right mister, and don't you forget it."

"Yes ma'am." He laughed. "Although, that's more than likely a promise I'll have trouble keeping. Besides, looking should not be considered a crime."

"For you men, looking is the misdemeanor that's too often the precursor to the felony."

"What felony would that be, your honor?"

"Murder," she said, "if you don't stop looking."

He laughed. "I'm glad you won't have access to any convicting evidence."

"At least you can't speak Italian," Carol said. "That should slow you down a little."

"Cris speaks Italian."

"Who?"

"Uh—Cris Vega is going too," he winced. "Did I forget to tell you?"

"Uh—yes, conveniently."

"She's going so there'll be a translator."

"Cris? She's Latina, not Italian. Now what's your story, detective?"

"Yeah, well. She also speaks Italian, according to Mayor Rowe. It was his idea."

"The mayor's idea?"

"There's no need to be jealous."

"Jealous? Me? Of Cris?

"We've already had this discussion," he reminded her.

"Yeah. I know. But, when we had it, you weren't taking her to Italy for who knows how long and leaving me here taking pictures of dead people while you're touring Europe. When you go to Italy, it should be *me* you're taking with you."

"I'm not *taking* her to Italy and we're not *touring* Europe. The mayor is sending her to Rome, just like he's sending me. Both of us are on duty, working to find a fugitive and bring him back to face justice."

"You're going to Italy together. Right?"

Mike clamped his lips together to prevent himself from saying something that would only get him into trouble. "Okay, listen. Can you translate Italian? I'll call the mayor back."

"Very funny. I suggest you conduct yourself over there with some self-control or you may find yourself *treat-less* when you return. *Capese?*"

"Oooh. Maybe you *can* speak Italian."

"Mike—be safe." Carol's tone changed.

"I will. I'll call you when I get back. I'm gonna miss you."

"*Arrivederce, mi amore,*" Carol said, and then she made a kissing sound.

"*Cara mia,*" Mike moaned into the phone. "If I didn't have to pack right now I'd ...." He smiled when he heard Carol's laughter as she disconnected the call.

Over a period of ten years, their relationship had matured, evolved, come close to matrimony, and come equally close to being dissolved. Currently they were close, but discreet enough so no one could convict them of breaking Captain Moretti's Law banning fraternization within the unit. As far as Mike knew, only Cris and Norm were privy to their infrequent liaisons.

He was debating with himself on which slacks to pack when his cell phone rang.

"Mike Neal."

"Hello, Sergeant."

"Hi, Sarah. What can I do for you?"

"I've been thinking. I realized I didn't tell you about Barrett's issues during his childhood. Over the last few years, Al has told me quite a bit about Barrett's younger years. Some of it could be helpful for you."

"Okay. If you don't mind, I'm going to put you on speaker so I can continue packing while we talk. I'm a little tight on time."

"That's fine."

"Go ahead." He turned up the volume and placed the phone on the bed near his suitcase.

"When Barrett's mother was diagnosed with stage three breast cancer, he was seven years old. Her ability to care for him and care *about* him was negatively affected. Her illness progressed rather quickly and when Barrett was eight she overdosed—intentionally."

"Was no one looking out for her to prevent that sort of thing?"

"Barrett's father was driven by his business success. He wasn't so big on family relations and such. He paid a nurse housekeeper to be there. When she went to the grocery that day, Pamela Stone ate all her pills. Barrett was distraught. I'm not so sure he didn't get some of *his* psychiatric issues from his mother and the way she decided to resolve *hers*."

"Al told me about a day when they were young kids playing in the woods behind Barrett's house. He said they had about a hundred little plastic army soldiers between them along with little green tanks and trucks. He said they would position their men as if they were in a war against each other, and then yell and make explosion sounds.

"One day, he and Barrett were setting up their men. Al went to gather some sticks. Barrett pulled a can of lighter fluid from his jacket and sprayed all of Al's soldiers. He asked Barrett what he was doing and Barrett struck a match, tossed it and yelled *napalm*.

All of Al's soldiers and tanks were melted."

"Hmm."

"Al said Barrett laughed about it for days."

"That's sad. Did Al attempt to retaliate?"

"He said he knew better. It wasn't worth the risk. Al's taken this approach to most of Barrett's affronts over the years.

"He told me when Barrett found out his father was going to marry his mom, he pitched a tantrum. He ran to his room, slammed the door in Al's face and tore his room apart. The next day, Al's cat disappeared. Al said they never saw it again."

"Did he suspect Barrett did something to it?"

"He said he was sure of it, but he was afraid to confront him, for fear of what else he might do. It appears Barrett and Al got along only because Barrett needed someone to dominate and little Al needed a friend at any cost. So, he was willing to put up with Barrett's domination and let him have his way if he would play with him."

"Did Barrett not get any professional help as a child?"

"Al said his mom talked Barrett's father into getting him into psychotherapy. Barrett saw a child psychologist his father knew twice each week for several months. Al said at first it seemed like it was helping and then one day he heard Barrett talking to himself in his room and laughing about how stupid everyone was if they thought this freak doctor was going to change him. Before long, the child psychologist asked Barrett's father to seek a psychiatrist. He said Barrett's deep-rooted personality issues were far beyond his expertise."

"He had some serious problems."

"Yes. And unfortunately, I didn't find out about them until after we were married."

"That reminds me," he said. "What, if anything, do you know about Meredith Bowles?"

"Meredith Bowles." Sarah thought for a minute. "I remember my dad told me Meredith Bowles and Barrett's father were a couple back when Barrett was in college. He said when Meredith's home was broken into and she was killed, they were about to announce their engagement. I've never heard Barrett speak of her. All I know is what Daddy told me. Why do you ask?"

"I was talking with the detective on her case yesterday. She also lived in Belle Meade and I wondered if you knew her."

"No, sorry," Sarah said. "By the way, my friend Tracey still has some data to pull from that software of hers. You didn't get the searches from the week before Barrett left. Also, I was looking through some of Barrett's business documents I found here at the house. I can send those to you if you'd like. Obviously, it's in my interest to help you find him, any way I can."

"Can you fax them?"

"There's too much for that. I'll Fed-Ex them to you. I don't mind. What's the address of your hotel?"

Mike read her the hotel's address from his itinerary.

"Sergeant, be careful. Barrett will stop at nothing to get whatever he wants. I wish you luck."

"Thanks."

He ended the call and noticed the digital time registered on his phone. He hadn't spoken with Allison since yesterday. She deserved an update before he left for Rome. He scrolled to her number and made the call.

His thoughts of Allison and their reconnection in the funeral home parking lot caused him to smile before she answered.

"Allison? It's Mike."

"Hi."

"I wanted to touch base with you before I leave."

"Leave?"

He updated Allison on the basics of what he could tell her about his recent mayoral assignment.

"This doesn't sound like Al. Are you sure he's involved in this?"

"I'm afraid the evidence points that way. He's missing too."

"Stone has done more damage to him than I thought."

"I'll call you when I get back. If you need anything before then, contact Lieutenant D.W. Burris. He can help you or he can get in touch with me."

"Do you think Stone killed Tyler?"

"I can't be sure yet," he said, not wanting to offer an opinion at this point.

"I hope you can find him."

"We'll do our best."

"Mike."

"Yeah?"

"Have a safe trip."

CHAPTER 43

Hartsfield-Jackson Airport
Atlanta, Georgia

Mike realized there would be insufficient time on the Nashville to Atlanta leg of their trip for meaningful discussion of the Stone case. So, he spent the one hour flight from Nashville catching a nap while Cris escaped into her romantic suspense novel by Nancy Naigle.

Their flight from Atlanta to Rome was scheduled to board in International Concourse E. Their arrival gate from Nashville was near the end of Concourse B. They had some time before their flight, but walking from their arrival gate to the underground train, riding the distance between concourses and then hiking from the train out to their departure gate could almost qualify as a cardio workout.

"What luck." Mike said as they reached their international gate and discovered the flight was boarding. "They waited on us."

The attendant laughed and accepted their boarding passes.

"Where are our seats?" Cris asked as they navigated the right side aisle of coach on the broad-bodied Boeing 777-200.

"They're in this aisle." He scanned the numbers beneath the overhead compartments. "26 A and B. I'm in the aisle seat."

"Why the *aisle* seat?"

"On a flight this long, if anything weakens my digestive constitution, I'll be able to run to the bathroom without climbing over you."

"You're pretty funny."

"I do what I can," Mike said. "Here we are."

Mike stood next to his seat as Cris side-stepped from the aisle to her seat. After pulling a spiral notebook from her carry-on, she tucked the bag beneath the seat in front of her with her feet.

Mike's carry-on bag was considerably larger than hers and he knew it wouldn't fit under the seat. He removed the murder book on the McKinnon case, all his notes on the related parties and what he'd received from Brent Spangler on the fraud charges. In between fellow passengers making their way down the aisle, he stood to cram the bag into the overhead above his seat before someone else claimed the valuable space.

"So," Cris said as she looked up at him, "you said you spoke with Norm recently. How is he?"

Mike dropped into his seat. "Like you and me, he's been covered up."

"Our absence won't help them any," Cris said.

"I know, but the mayor runs the show."

"Thank goodness."

"You've been partnered with Ramon Cordero lately haven't you?"

"Yeah." Cris looked out the window at the workers pitching the checked bags onto the conveyor. "It's good that we're apart for a while."

"That sounds like a statement with a truckload of implicit information behind it. You want to explain?"

"What?"

"You know what. If you didn't want to tell me you wouldn't have said it that way. So, spill it."

"I don't know," Cris whined. "We needed a break."

"Why?"

"He ... lately ... he's been making comments."

"What kind of comments?"

"You know."

"No, I don't know. Why don't we stop this verbal salsa dance and you tell me what he's saying to you?"

"It sounds like he's flirting."

"*Sounds* like flirting?"

"Cris, you're sneaking up on forty years of age and you can't determine for certain if a man's flirting with you?"

Cris took a deep breath. "All right. He's flirting."

"Is he married?"

"Of course. They're separated."

"Tell him to back off. You don't need that crap," he insisted, sounding like her big brother. "If you don't tell him, I will."

"I'm not sure I want him to."

"Hello. Earth to Cris. Earth to Cris. Do you copy? Have you forgotten Moretti's Law?"

Cris stared at Mike. "What is this? Do as I say, not as I do, Sergeant Hypocrite? What about you and Carol?" Cris's volume rose with her defense.

"Shhhhh. Careful."

"What? Are you pulling rank? Are you gonna tell me *your* game is somehow different?"

"I *was*. But—"

"But what?"

"Just be careful." He hesitated. "Carol and I aren't partners. Neither one of us is married. We sometimes go a couple of weeks we don't even see each other at work. Riding with someone like that every day ... ." He shook his head. "That kinda crap can ruin both your careers, fast. *You've* worked too hard to get where you are. You don't need some horny husband skirt-chaser ruining everything you've worked for."

Cris looked out the window. "He is sort of young. He's thirty-two, a freakin' baby."

"I remember when somebody else was thirty-two."

"I was much farther along than he is. He's still wet behind the ears."

He laughed out loud. "But you were an old hand, right?"

Cris shook her head without an answer and changed the subject. "So, how are you and Carol?"

He nodded and pursed his lips. "We're good."

"That's great. How long now?"

"A long time. Enough social inquiry. Okay? Let's talk. I need to update you on the McKinnon case, Barrett Stone and all the additional players that have surfaced since McKinnon's murder."

Mike and Cris had discussed the facts of the McKinnon murder since lift-off and they were now two hours closer to Italy.

"I have to get up now. My butt's numb. I can't sit here any longer without a break." Cris stood at her seat and waited for Mike to collect his paperwork and get up.

He stepped out into the aisle and Cris headed for the facilities at the rear of the plane. While he was up, Mike stood a while and then stretched before returning to his seat.

He reread a few of his notes and then checked his watch. It had been at least ten minutes since Cris's trip to the facilities. He turned in his seat to look down the aisle toward the rear of the plane and started laughing. Cris was doing pushups in the aisle in front of the toilet. A flight attendant smiled at him. She was standing guard near Cris's head to keep other folks from tripping over her as she did her reps.

Cris was an athlete. She was small in height, but that was all. Her physical ability was proven to all the officers during Police Officers Physical Agility Tests (POPAT) each September. She frequently posted the best scores of all the female officers throughout the department, and topped nearly half the men.

Her hand-to-hand combat skills were exceptional. Only a small group of officers had ever accepted her challenge on the mats. She was instructor caliber at judo. More than a few guys had been embarrassed facing her. She regularly heard responses like 'Give me a rain check. I'm getting over a muscle strain.'

Cris appeared next to Mike's seat.

"Are you good, now," he asked as he stood.

"I'm good for another two thousand miles."

"Where were we?" Cris dropped into her seat.

"We were about to look at Spangler's data on Stone's fraud."

He pulled some files from the pouch in front of him and lowered his tray. He took Cris through Brent Spangler's data, his own interviews with Stone and Ricks and a few facts on the disappearance of the two men shortly afterward. He shared the information he'd obtained from Sarah Stone and Shannon Richards and his brief and emotional time with Mary Ellen Ricks. He also gave Cris photographs of Stone and Ricks.

"This Stone character is a real piece of work. Has he been diagnosed by a professional? He sounds like he could be sociopathic."

"That's what I was about to tell you. Last night Sarah Stone called me to add one more piece to the puzzle. She knew we were leaving today and wanted to share this before I left. She hadn't discussed with me any details on Barrett's childhood problems following his mother's suicide. She learned most of this from Al Ricks since Barrett would never discuss it.

Stone began to have issues at his private school; fighting and name calling, lashing out toward teachers, principals and the first governess his father hired to care for him. His father was asked to remove him from the private school."

"Wow."

"Due to the reputation the boy garnered for himself, all the private schools in Nashville were made aware of his antics and refused his enrollment, regardless of the additional donation his father dangled in their faces. Sarah said that the senior Stone was forced to bring in a private tutor to teach Barrett in their home."

"A real handful, huh?"

"Yes, until the first governess threatened to leave. This forced his father to search for a new governess. The new one, twelve-year-old Barrett liked. He was a little older now. She was only ten years his senior and young enough to relate to him.

"Seems she'd been raised in a happy but strict Italian home and she handled young Stone with the authority and concern no one else had used. Sarah said it took a while, but with a combination of positive feedback and corrective reinforcement, she began to have an impact on him. According to Ricks, the governess taught him self-discipline and his behavior, as well as his studies, began to improve."

"This governess may have become a turning point in his life," Cris said.

"Maybe, but there may have been more there than she was able to change with five years of tough love."

"And, it may have come too late in his life for a permanent transformation."

"Sarah is still working on collecting some usable data on his last week's surfing on the PC. She is going to send them to us at the hotel."

"Why is she working so hard on this?"

"It's in her best interest for us to locate Stone. His departure from Nashville represents a violation of their pre-nup and the doubling of her settlement amount."

"That would explain it." Cris nodded. "Nice."

CHAPTER 44

East of Rome, Italy

"That son of a bitch is not the only damn investigator in Europe. He'd better call soon or I'm going to make him wish he'd never heard of me."

"When was he supposed to call?"

"He said he would call when he arrived in Rome. He should have been here and working yesterday like I'd asked him to be, but he had a recital to go to last night. What is it? Am I asking too much for someone to earn their money? I don't—"

The sound of Barrett's phone interrupted his rant.

"Yes?"

"Herr Strong."

"It's about time," he said.

"I've been working for you since this morning."

"Oh?"

"Yes. I have been arranging for the ... accessory you asked me to acquire for you. It is not that easy."

"Did you get it?"

"I did. Are you available now?"

"I've *been* available." He paused, but heard no response from the German. "Are you familiar with the Villa Borghese Gardens?"

"Of course."

"Meet me in the Piazza del Popolo in an hour. I will be near the Egyptian Obelisk on the west side."

"I will see you there."

"Don't forget the accessory. Have it in a retail bag so it will not look suspicious."

"Herr Strong, Piazza del Popolo is a public place. The Carabinieri, they are everywhere."

"Yes. I know." Barrett disconnected the call.

Barrett arrived early at the piazza and stayed back near the perimeter waiting to observe his investigator as he arrived.

The elaborate Baroque architecture was breathtaking even for someone with no appreciation for it. The area was a popular tourist attraction. People strolled about the piazza in all directions during most hours of the day.

The German was right. The Carabinieri in their Valentino designed uniforms with white leather duty belts and holsters were patrolling in pairs everywhere he looked.

It was time for their meeting and he hadn't seen anyone he imagined could be his investigator. He ambled toward the west side of the piazza's centerpiece, and as he slowed he heard a German accent behind him, "You are looking for someone?"

The German caught him by surprise, but he would never admit it.

"Let's go. Follow me."

He walked quickly at first, but only to get away from the throng of people near the Obelisk. He slowed as they reached the outer area of the piazza where no one was standing. He allowed the German to catch up to him.

"The woman I need you to locate is named Elena Triano. She'll soon be forty-four years old. Her family is from the area east of Frascati and I believe she will be found somewhere near there."

"Do you have a photograph?"

"No."

"How will I know how she looks?"

"She looks like a forty-four year old Italian woman," he said with sarcasm. "If I have to tell you how to do your job, why am I paying you?"

The two men walked a while without talking.

"I have not seen her in more than fifteen years." He looked into the distance. "I do not know how much she has changed during that time, but I know that she was quite beautiful back then."

"This girl, was she your lover?"

"Who she was," his eyes widened, "is none of your concern. You should be focused only on locating her and telling me where she is. Then, and only then, will you collect the generous balance of your fee. Understood?"

"Yes."

"Is that mine?"

He handed the bag to Barrett.

"I'll expect to hear from you soon and regularly." He turned and walked away, leaving the German staring at his back.

CHAPTER 45

Woodmont
South Nashville

Powell had followed the detective from his home in Green Hills back to the Latin woman's house and then to the Nashville airport's Satellite Parking.

Neal and the woman exited the airport shuttle at the Delta gate. Powell knew that Delta flew international destinations out of several U.S. cities, but not Nashville. However, there were always connecting flights through other hub cities.

There was no way for him to confirm their destination, but the circumstantial evidence coupled with recent news reports on Stone's exploits convinced Powell; Neal and the woman were on the hunt for Barrett Stone.

Circumstantial evidence was enough to send me away for almost five years. It should be enough to prove Neal's intentions.

As Powell left the airport, he'd wondered who the Latin woman was. Since she was with Neal at the Justice Center downtown yesterday, she had to be either his girlfriend or another cop; either way, the taller blonde who came out of the Latin woman's house to hug her and wave goodbye, ought to know where the two of them were going, even if *she* was the Latin woman's lover.

If the two of them were indeed looking for Stone, he should be willing to pay for that information.

It was now after nine o'clock. The neighborhood was dark. The street lights were on. The overgrown tree canopies prevented much of the light from reaching the street. Powell left his truck two blocks away and began his stroll, checking the area for activity as he went. Neighborhood dogs barked their concern as he walked the street. Dressed in dark clothes and a baseball cap, he was difficult to see.

The homes on the cul de sac where the two women lived were at least fifty years old. The lawns were full of large trees, shrubs and great places to conceal his approach.

Lights inside the Latin woman's home were off. The carport was empty; no sign of anyone. Powell worked his way to the rear of the house and found what he expected. The door with a nine pane window was made of wood with an aluminum storm door on the outside, locked. He saw no sign of a security system, so he pulled the small pry bar from his pants and easily moved the storm door away from the frame enough to disengage the latch and open it.

He wrapped a heavy cloth around the bent end of the pry bar and punched the small window nearest the door knob. It cracked. He struck it again and the glass separated enough for him to get hold of the large pieces. He worked them free from the glazing putty and tossed them out into the soft grass. They made no sound.

Powell reached his gloved hand through the jagged hole, unlocked the deadbolt and the doorknob lock. He readied himself in case he was wrong about the security system. He pushed the door open and listened. Nothing happened. He wasted no time checking. He knew a security control panel would be near one of the home's entrances. He found nothing.

He'd brought with him all the tools he needed to convince the roommate to talk, giving up her roommate's destination. He had a full roll of duct tape, a gag, and most importantly, a pair of needle nosed pliers. It shouldn't take her losing more than one or maybe two fingernails before the information began to flow.

Powell decided to search the refrigerator for a beer while he waited for the roommate to return. He shined his penlight on the white refrigerator covered with magnets and trinkets. It was a woman's refrigerator, for sure. He started laughing.

On the front of the refrigerator near the handle was a sheet of stationary held in place by two magnets. At the top of the paper was the embossed name 'Detective Cris Vega'. Below the name was scribbled a note. My hotel in Rome – Hotel Sonya, Via del Viminale, 58, 00184.

"So she's a cop too." He jerked the note from beneath the magnets. He read the note again, folded and shoved it into his pocket.

He opened the refrigerator door, scanned the shelves and found a six pack of beer. He broke two of the cans loose from the plastic six-pack holder and put them in his jacket pockets. Still laughing, he walked out the back door and pulled it closed behind him.

CHAPTER 46

Fiumicino Airport
Rome, Italy

As he and Cris cleared the jet way behind the horde of unhurried passengers, Mike spotted a well-dressed man he was certain must be the lieutenant. The light gray suit, his longish black hair and dark complexion made him resemble a television detective. He was waiting at the edge of the concourse to welcome his arriving guests.

As soon as Cris stepped out from behind Mike and got a look at him, her inner thoughts escaped.

"Oh ... my—"

"What?" Mike interrupted with a tone of disgust.

"Oh, nothing."

"Nothing?"

"He's hot," she whispered.

"Ah, hell."

"Gimme a break. I'm not married."

"No, but I'm pretty sure he is."

"Hey, no double standards. You guys get to window shop. So can I."

Mike chuckled to himself.

The smiling lieutenant moved toward the pair as they reached the concourse.

I guess we must look as much like cops as he does.

"Welcome to Rome," he said in English with the expected heavy accent. "I'm Lieutenant Giancarlo Petrelli. You may call me Carlo."

"Mike Neal." Mike shook the detective's hand. "Lieutenant, this is Detective Cris Vega."

"Detective, welcome."

"Thanks." She offered her hand, not wanting to miss out on any physical contact with *Signore* Beefcake.

"Your flight was acceptable?" The lieutenant looked from Mike to Cris.

"Not bad," Mike said. "I tried to sleep through as much of it as possible."

"His snoring drowned out *most* of the engine noise," Cris joked.

The lieutenant laughed. "Baggage Claim is this way."

At the police station, Lieutenant Petrelli brought them up to date on the current status of his department's search for Stone and Ricks.

Petrelli introduced the detectives to Sergeant Nico Barone who was to serve as Departmental Liaison whenever the Lieutenant was unavailable.

Mike had never seen Cris smile so much as she did when either of the two Italian detectives was in the room. Barone was not helping with his six foot two inch Clive Owen high-testosterone look and his bare naked ring finger. It was all Mike could do to keep from playfully harassing Cris about it in front of the two detectives.

"Here are your cell phones. All the local numbers you might need are programmed, including each of yours as well as mine and Sergeant Barone's."

A uniformed officer entered the room and handed Petrelli two holstered semi-automatic pistols and four loaded twenty-round nine millimeter magazines, two of which were in black leather magazine holders.

"Here are your sidearms and carry permits while you are our guests. I'll need you to sign for these." Petrelli pushed the forms toward the two detectives.

"92FS," Cris said as she signed her name. "Nice weapon."

"You didn't expect a Glock, did you?" Petrelli said with a solemn expression followed by a smile.

"No way" Cris said. "Not here at the home of Beretta. Even the U.S. military carries these bad boys."

"Smart soldiers." Petrelli smiled.

"I like my Glock," Mike whispered to Cris.

She shook her head and smiled.

Both detectives stood to slide the black leather holsters and magazine holders onto their belts.

"Try to always keep your weapons concealed and your permits available. Some of our officers will not be familiar with you and it could prevent a great deal of misunderstanding. We received special permission for you to be armed. Someone in Nashville knows someone here."

"No problem," Mike said. "We will be discreet." He chose not to respond to the Nashville comment.

"I have notified the Carabinieri of your visit and our search," Petrelli said. "They have assured us of their support and I have forwarded to their investigators throughout Lazio the photos of Signore Stone and Ricks."

"Excellent. I have some facts we've uncovered in the last few days that I'd like to share with you gentlemen," Mike said. "When we're finished, you may want to issue an update to the Carabinieri."

"Of course," Petrelli said.

He opened his case folder and brought Petrelli and Barone up to speed on the latest information from Sarah Stone on where she thought her estranged husband might be headed.

"Also, since the initial information was sent to you a couple of days ago on the list of fraud, grand theft and misrepresentation charges, we have since obtained enough evidence to issue a murder warrant for Stone."

"That changes things," Petrelli said.

"And," Mike said, "there could be a second murder warrant issued soon."

"I see." Petrelli turned to speak to Barone, who nodded. "I recommend that we contact INTERPOL and issue a Red Notice for Barrett Stone's arrest in case he decides to leave the area."

"Red Notice." Cris said. "I've heard of those."

"Yes. The notice calling for his arrest will go out to all one hundred and ninety INTERPOL members. And, in addition to the widespread police cooperation, there are diplomatic advantages to the issuance. Some countries have Red Notices built into their extradition treaties. Having issued the notice can accelerate extradition of wanted persons once they are captured."

Cris nodded and shared a smile with Barone.

Cris leaned over and mumbled something to Barone in Italian. He laughed. It made Mike uncomfortable since his Italian language skills were near non-existent.

He gave her a questioning look.

"I told him I hoped we caught Stone soon so we could have some time to see Rome before we have to leave."

Mike rolled his eyes.

CHAPTER 47

Lavergne, Tennessee

As much as Powell hated to talk with Barrett and listen to his haughty attitude, he knew if he was going to receive all the money Barrett agreed to pay him and solicit the additional money in exchange for the hotel where Neal was staying, he had no choice. He dialed Barrett's number and listened to several rings.

"Yes?"

"Hey, I thought you might want to know, I called the Criminal Justice Center to speak with your Detective Neal."

"Why the hell did you do that?"

Powell hesitated. "If you could possibly contain your criticism for a few minutes and let me finish, you might hear the answers you're lookin' for." He paused for some sign of Barrett's willingness.

"Hurry up."

"Thank you." He paused again for the hell of it. "I called Neal's office to confirm what I'd been told by another source. I informed the guy who answered in the Homicide Unit that I was an informant from Shelbyville, and I had information for Sergeant Neal. He said Neal wasn't there. I assured him the sergeant was waitin' for this information in order to close one of his active homicides and lock up the killer. They offered to put me into his voicemail, or give me the detective who was workin' the case I was callin' about, since Neal was unavailable. I told them I could not do that because 'me and the sergeant have a special relationship'. I got sort of shitty with the guy and told him I needed to see Neal face to face *today* to give him this information he'd been waitin' for or he was gonna lose this guy. I told him there was no other way. He said it was impossible. I insisted. He said to forget it 'cause Neal was out of the country. I said son of a bitch like I was real mad and I hung up." Powell laughed.

"So, what does this flurry of fascinating conversation prove?"

"What it proves is the Justice Center guard, who told me earlier that Neal was out of the country, was tellin' the truth. I'll let you figure out what country he's gone to, since you're the brain trust of the group."

"Why would he think I was in Italy? He has no jurisdiction here anyway," Barrett said. "What are the odds he could find me?"

"I don't know about all that, but I would expect the Italian police would be anxious to assist American cops in the location of a criminal who was fleein' our country to avoid prosecution. If American cops ask for cooperation from the Italian police to locate a man who entered their country illegally, with a fake passport, stolen funds, and a murder warrant against him, I'd say they would likely be pretty damned helpful."

I should have gone to Dubai. "Where did you hear all this anyway?"

"Hey, you're famous back here. The news report last night said you stole more than forty million from local elderly residents, and that the Nashville Police Department had, in addition to numerous warrants for theft, fraud and flight to avoid prosecution, a murder warrant for you and they were investigatin' the possibility of a second one."

"They're crazy. They're trying to pin all their unsolved cases on somebody that's gone and they'll never catch."

"That could be true, I guess." Powell hesitated. "You know, I was thinkin'. If you knew where Neal was gonna be stayin' in Rome, that could help you avoid whatever effort he might muster to locate you."

"And how in the hell am I supposed to find that out?"

"There are people," Powell said, "who are more resourceful than other folks believe, and these people know how to uncover valuable information. This valuable information can be priceless to people who are at increased risk without the information. Do you feel like you're beginnin' to relate to this *fascinatin' conversation*, as you put it?"

"Tell me where he is."

"I'd love to."

Barrett waited. "Well?"

"I'd love to, as soon as you transfer into my numbered account an extra half million dollars over and above the funds I have already earned, or agreed to earn, by settin' up creative situations for your elderly friends back here in Music City. Remember, this information could save your prosperous ass. And, we both know you can easily afford it."

"You're insane."

"Whatever. Did I tell you I followed your friend Neal from his office to the home of a female detective and then on to *his* home. Then, I followed him as he picked her up and the two of them parked at the airport in Satellite Parkin'. You know, Satellite Parkin' is where you park when you're goin' on a long trip. I watched through my binoculars as they unloaded their luggage. He must have asked her if she had her passport, cause I could see her pull it out and wave it at him and laugh. The shuttle dropped the two of them at Delta's outdoor counter. They must have boarded a Delta flight out of Nashville, no doubt to a Delta hub for their connection to Rome. If I were a bettin' man, I'd say you need to keep your eyes open. And unless *you* are a bettin' man, I'd say you need to know where they're stayin'."

"Maybe."

"You may also want to know, not only do I know where he lives so that I can stage *his* surprise, but after visitin' her home, I have the note the female detective left for her roommate givin' her the name, address and phone number of their hotel in Rome where she could be reached if necessary.

"Now, back to your decision on whether or not you want to know where to find Sergeant Neal in Rome."

"You're being unreasonable."

"I guess we'll talk later then. See ya."

"Wait a minute."

"I thought you said I was unreasonable?"

"You are," Barrett said.

"So?"

"So, tell me where he is, and I'll send the money."

"You sorta have things out of order here. Try transferrin' the money and I'll verify the transfer. *Then* I'll email you the hotel info. Now, that sounds more like a plan, doesn't it?"

"Fine. I'll transfer the money."

"Today?" Powell asked.

"Today."

"I'll watch for it. You'll know I've got it when you get the hotel address."

Barrett disconnected the call.

Powell laughed.

CHAPTER 48

Hillwood
West Nashville

Norm inherited a couple of Mike's newest cases. His visit today with Bobby Gaston's neighbors at the apartment complex took longer than he'd planned. He was thirty minutes late for his meeting with the Nashville Fire Department Fire Inspector, Kerry Hawke. Fortunately, when the two men first spoke they'd exchanged cell phone numbers and Norm had been able to call to let the inspector know about his delay.

"Mr. Hawke?" Norm asked as he marched his wide body onto the front lawn of the burned home.

"Yes."

"Detective Norm Wallace." Norm offered his hand. "I'm sorry to keep you cooling your heels waiting on me. I had a meeting with some folks and it took longer than I'd planned."

Norm fished his digital camera from his pocket as he looked over the blackened remains from the fire. Norm had learned from his years partnered with Mike Neal, it was best to take some of your own crime scene photos. The crime scene photographers were experts, no doubt. But, more chances at more evidence could not be a bad thing.

"The time was not wasted Detective. I reexamined my findings while I was waiting. Let me show you what I feel happened here."

Norm trailed the young man to the place where the home's back door used to be.

"This is likely the entrance where any home delivery people would have accessed the home. If you'll follow me; here is where the victim Mr. West was discovered." Hawke pointed. "His body collapsed into his wheelchair frame here when the seat burned through and gave way. No doubt, he had passed on before this occurred."

"At some point, the small E size aluminum oxygen cylinder mounted on the right rear of his wheelchair exploded, more than likely the first one to do so. It was at this point that Mr. West's lower right arm was no doubt severed and his right leg was also injured. The other E sized cylinders were stored there," he gestured, "in a metal rack that was supplied for them."

"Did they all explode?" He continued to take photos as Hawke explained.

"We didn't find any cylinders that were still intact. It's not unusual for us to see small aluminum medical cylinders exploding in the home fires of older folks. A lot of seniors are using oxygen.

"When our men arrived, the small cylinders were still exploding. The firefighters stayed back and evacuated the surrounding homes. They could not afford to fight the fire unsure if any more full cylinders remained inside. That's when the big one blew. A fireball hurled burning debris in every direction, and soon afterward most of the home collapsed. I found the top of the large cylinder, with the regulator still attached, out in the back yard of the home next door. I checked the valve. It was open."

Hawke walked cautiously back across the burned remains. "Here is where the bottom of the large cylinder was found."

"The large cylinder?"

"During my investigation, I discovered several randomly shaped chunks of thick curved steel scattered throughout the home and some were outside on the front and back lawns of this home and the neighbors. When I moved some of the burned wood from the home's collapsed structure, I found the lower portion of a large compressed gas cylinder. I showed these chunks of steel to the manager at one of the local compressed gas providers where the city does business. He confirmed they were part of a compressed gas cylinder. He said it was a K size oxygen cylinder, which is about five feet tall and nine inches in diameter with around 250 cubic feet of gas under 2200 pounds of pressure."

"Where are these chunks now?"

"I have them in an evidence box for you."

"Great. Thanks."

"I also have for you the remains of what I believe was the ignition device."

"What is it?"

"It's the remains of the inner workings of a cell phone that was found under debris in the living room."

"Really?"

"I can't be sure, but with West's limited mobility, I can't imagine why he would have a cell phone in the living room and not here in his den where, according to his neighbors, he spent most of his time watching TV?"

Norm nodded.

"By the way, I was told by the operations manager at Resi-Med, Mr. West's oxygen provider, that all the oxygen cylinders they'd delivered to Mr. West were E size aluminum small medical cylinders. They said they kept eight to ten in his rack. They were about to switch him to an oxygen concentrator, but hadn't yet made the change. They have no record of his ordering or receiving a larger size cylinder."

"Could he have obtained it somewhere else, from another provider?"

"Possibly," Hawke admitted, "but it's not likely."

"I'll check with all the local suppliers to see if they've delivered a tank that size to this location," Norm said.

"That would help verify what we suspect. However, the most interesting fact I learned at the compressed gas store was, according to the manager, he was confident this cylinder was for *industrial* gas, not medical. The cylinders are normally painted differently when they are rated for medical use. The difference in the oxygen is minimal if any. The issue is traceability and continuity of use."

"Does this mean what I think it means?"

"What do you think?"

"Based upon what you've told me, I believe someone wanted to accelerate Mr. West's demise, and they chose to purchase an oxygen tank that didn't require a doctor's prescription."

"I think you may be right detective," Hawke said. "This cylinder, if it *was* filled with industrial grade oxygen, could have been purchased by just about anyone. I believe its presence was intentional, put here for one reason, and it worked."

Norm nodded. "I wonder if the culprit knew the cylinder was likely to explode?"

"I'd say yes." Hawke looked around at the home's remains. "He likely hoped it would explode in order to help hide the evidence."

Norm took his last photos. "I'm glad you did such a thorough job with your investigation and called this in."

"Me too," Hawke said as he bent to pick up what looked to be a piece of metal that had been melted by the heat. "This fire burned so intensely, fueled by the abundant supply of oxygen, that it did more damage in ten minutes than most do in thirty. In an oxygen rich environment, literally *everything* becomes flammable."

CHAPTER 49

Rome, Italy

Mike and Cris decided to walk the twelve blocks to La Pollarola Ristorante. The restaurant came highly recommended by Lieutenant Petrelli. The streets were crowded with workers on their way home or, like the detectives, on their way to dinner. Mike overheard a number of typically animated Italian conversations as they walked the street. He and Cris shared a smile, both knowing he understood none of what was being said.

Up ahead, Mike saw a crowd which had collected around a couple of street musicians. He knew, based upon advice from several well-traveled friends, this would be a great place to lose your wallet. He patted the hidden money pouch hanging around his neck beneath his shirt.

He spotted an old couple standing together on the fringes of the crowd. With a camera strap around the old fellow's neck, it was obvious they were tourists. They were smiling at each other, clapping their hands. Their heads were bobbing to the Italian music.

He watched a teenaged girl move toward the elderly couple as a young fellow aggressively bumped into the old man knocking him back into the girl who caught him.

"I'm so sorry. Forgive me," the young man said. After he offered his caring comments, he rushed away.

The girl smiled as she moved her hands over the old fellow and acted like she was making sure he didn't fall. The couple assured her they were fine and no harm was done. But, Mike knew better.

"Follow me," Mike said. He was no more than five feet from the old couple when the girl started to walk away. He stepped up and grabbed her by the wrist.

"*Hey, cosa stai facendo?*"

"You're not getting away with that. Give the gentleman his wallet back."

Cris translated his demands as several people turned from the musicians to the new disturbance.

"*Non so quello che stai parlando.*" The girl said. "*Lasciami andare o chiamo la polizia.*"

"She said let her go or she'll call the police," Cris said.

"Call them," he said. "Call the police."

"*Li chiamano,*" Cris told her.

The girl said nothing, but continued without effect to try and wrestle her arm away from Mike.

The people around them were voicing their naïve opinions about Mike restraining the girl until the old man said to his wife, "My wallet; it's gone."

"Give it to him now, or we'll take you to the police station."

Again, Cris translated in Italian.

"*Lasciami andare,*" the girl said. "*Non hai il diritto di tenermi.*"

"She says you have no right to hold her," Cris said.

"Check her jacket pockets," he told Cris. "She didn't have a chance to pass the wallet off to anyone."

Cris reached into the girl's jacket and found two men's wallets.

The crowd voiced their disapproval to the girl.

"That's mine," the old man said and stepped forward.

Cris handed him his wallet, then looked inside the other one for a name.

"*Che e mio,*" a man said in Italian as he approached Cris.

"What's your name?" Cris asked.

"Lazzaro Di Croce."

Cris handed him his wallet.

Mike let go of the girl's arm.

She jerked away. "*Bastardo,*" she yelled as she bolted across the street.

"Thank you so much," the old woman said. "I told him to keep his wallet in his front pocket, but he doesn't listen to me."

"It's a habit," the old guy said as he shrugged, "putting it in my back pocket."

Mike leaned toward the old guy. "This time she's right. The front pocket is good advice while you are traveling."

"You sound like Americans," the old lady said.

"We are."

"Where are you from?"

"Nashville."

"Oh, we love Nashville. We live in Tampa, but we're from New York City originally."

Mike smiled. Keep your valuables safe. These pick pockets like to target the elderly.

"Thank you so much," the old man said.

"Be safe." Mike waved.

They walked a couple of blocks before Cris asked, "How did you know she took his wallet? Did you see her take it?"

"No, but I saw her partner fall into the old fellow and act like he was concerned about his safety, drawing the couple's focus and holding them while she moved in feeling him up for his wallet. That's how it's done."

"So, what are you going to eat tonight, *Cara mia?*"

"What did you call me?"

"Don't you remember? That's what Gomez always said to Morticia whenever she spoke in a foreign language?"

"Who in the hell are Gomez and Morticia?"

"Don't tell me you never watched The Addams Family when you were young?"

"Uh, no. Sorry. When I was a kid in Houston, I was watching Telemundo. We had people named Gomez, but it was their *last* name."

"You didn't answer my question."

"Remind me."

"You're the one with Italian blood, what are you going to have for dinner? Remember, the mayor's picking up the tab."

"Wow, that's right. I think I'll start with an *aperitivo* of cheese and olives served with a crisp *Pinot Grigio*."

"Uh, oh. I did ask."

"For *primo*, I may have *risotto* or *gnocchi*, or *lasagna*."

"I don't know what some of that is, but I'll take lasagna any day."

"For *secondo*, maybe salmon, or steak, or *Zampone* with a nice *Chianti*."

"*Zampone*?"

"It's an Italian sausage."

"Hmm."

"If there's room maybe *insalata* or *Formaggi e Frutta*."

"I know that's salad or some kind of cheese and fruit. Right?"

"*Molto buono, Signore.*"

"I read up on *some* Italian words."

"For dessert …."

"You're going to have room for dessert after all that?"

"Maybe. I may have *tiramisu, cannoli* or my favorite, hazelnut *gelato*."

"Wow. If you eat all that, you won't be able to move for two days."

"That's why I'll probably order a small pizza and a glass of *Chianti*."

Mike laughed.

When dinner was over the detectives were back on the street to walk off some of their carbohydrates.

"We cannot eat like that every day," Mike said. "We'll have to buy new clothes before we go home."

Cris laughed. "It was good, wasn't it?"

"Awesome. Norm's wife, Cheryl makes good *lasagna*. But this dish was *eccellente*."

Cris laughed.

They walked slowly, somewhat because of their meal and partly to enjoy the display windows for the small shops along the street. Cris spotted one of the signs that are pervasive throughout Italian cities. It read: *Gelato*. She had to stop. There was a line of people waiting.

"Go ahead. I'll catch up." Cris smiled.

Mike shook his head. "Where are you going to put it?" He rubbed his belly and walked on.

With her small cup of hazelnut *gelato* and spoon in hand, Cris began her walk toward the hotel. After a few minutes she could see Mike up ahead. She occasionally slowed to inspect a leather shop or sportswear store.

The next time she looked for Mike she noticed a man between

them who was slowing each time Mike stopped or looked in a window. This continued for several minutes. Cris became concerned. She shoveled the last of her gelato into her mouth and tossed the cup and spoon into the trash. She grabbed her cell phone and texted Mike.

"Don't turn around, you're being followed and I don't mean by me—Male, white, thirties, brown leather jacket, black slacks, maybe fifty-sixty feet behind you, same distance in front of me. This guy is no pick pocket. Want me to kick his ass for you?"

Mike texted back. "I'll slow down. You keep coming. Be ready."

Immediately, Cris's adrenaline was up. She thrived on situations like this.

Mike returned his cell phone to his pocket and stopped to look in a store window. He saw the man out of his left side peripheral vision. He was walking slowly. In the distance he could see Cris closing on the man.

Mike gave her a moment and as she approached the man from behind Mike turned to continue his casual walk. Abruptly, he spun to his left and ran at the man. Startled, the stalker turned to run, but Cris had caught up with him and as he turned she grabbed his clothes and pulled him into a sweeping hip throw, depositing him on the street before he could flee. He fell on his back and his breath was jarred from his lungs by the impact. Before he could manage to right himself, Cris rolled him over, and pulled his right arm up behind him. She sat on his lower back forcing his arm as far up between his shoulders as it would go.

She spewed Italian commands at the man who was shouting his own between screams of pain.

Once Cris had the man under control, Mike started laughing.

"What?"

"I'm sorry. It's just that you reminded me of a lady wrestler I once saw on cable."

"Lady wrestler? Gee thanks," Cris said as she forced her entire weight down on the man's lower back. She pushed his head down against the street with her left hand as her right hand held his arm tight against his back.

"She won too. Nice work."

"Glad you enjoyed the show." Cris said with a tone of sarcasm.

Mike called Lieutenant Petrelli, who sent officers to the scene, but the commotion itself brought the Polizia that were already in the area. It took only minutes.

After Mike's explanation and the officer's call to Petrelli for verification, they handcuffed and loaded the man into the back of one of their cars. Mike and Cris, rather than return to their hotel, caught a ride to the police station with one of the officers.

Two of the officers recognized the thug as a local muscleman for hire.

"He has a history of violence. How did you catch him?" the officer asked Mike.

"I didn't; Cris did it all. She didn't need any help."

"Really?"

Mike nodded.

The officers laughed.

"She must be one of those large presents in a small package," one of the officers spoke up. "This man is violent. He has put people in the hospital."

"All these police skills and in such an attractive package," another officer said in accented English as he smiled, obviously flirting with Cris.

The officers all gave Cris high fives and asked her to accompany them after work for a beer. Cris graciously declined stating it had been a long day and she was still suffering from jet lag.

"Maybe tomorrow," she said.

"*Si, domani,*" one officer said.

"The beer, it is on us." Another officer laughed. "*Arrivederci.*"

"I would hate to fight her when she didn't have jet lag." The men joked as they left the station.

Mike smiled at Cris. "Looks like you've found yourself a fan club."

Cris smiled.

"Sergeant," Petrelli said. "I appreciate your interest and willingness to assist with this investigation, but if you wouldn't mind, I'd rather you allow us to interview this man without your presence."

"I'd like to hear what he has to say, but I understand your concern. If I'm not there, he may offer up more information than he would otherwise. I'd likely feel the same way if our roles were reversed."

"Thank you for understanding. If you two can be here in the morning, say nine o'clock, we'll go through everything our detectives have collected since we received the call from America and we'll go from there. Can I get an officer to drive you back to your hotel?"

"Oh, no. It's nice out, and we need to walk. See you in the morning."

"You gave in sort of quickly," Cris said as they stepped out onto the street.

"This is *his* world. He gets to make that call. We'll read the transcript of the interview tomorrow."

"Do you think they'll get anything useful out of the guy?" Cris asked.

"I hope so. Otherwise, we're going to have to follow him when he makes bail."

"Copy that."

CHAPTER 50

Polizia di Stato
Rome, Italy

Lieutenant Petrelli and one of his uniformed officers entered the interview room where Paolo Ciresi was waiting.

"Mr. Ciresi? I am Lieutenant Giancarlo Petrelli. Do you understand why you are here?" Petrelli began his questions in his and Ciresi's native language.

The man hesitated. "No."

"We would like you to tell us why you were following Sergeant Neal tonight."

"Who?"

"Mr. Ciresi, we can spend the night playing games with each other or we can come to the point and resolve this issue like intelligent men. What do you say?"

Ciresi appeared unsure of what he should do.

"If you cooperate and answer my questions, maybe things can be worked out and you may be able sleep in your own bed tonight. How does that sound?"

He continued to stare at the table. "I was not following anyone. I don't know why those people jumped me. I was only looking for a gift for my sister's birthday."

"Ah, your sister's birthday? Mr. Ciresi, what is your sister's name?"

"Her name is ... Arianna."

"When is her birthday?"

"Her birthday is ... coming up ... coming up next week."

"I'm sure it is, Mr. Ciresi. I'm sure it is. Are you aware that it is a crime to threaten or intimidate another person on the streets of our city?"

"No."

"Are you aware it is also a crime to lie to a police officer, such as myself?"

Ciresi looked up at the uniformed officer, who nodded his agreement.

"It is. And, based upon your actions witnessed here tonight by a number of law enforcement officers, you are guilty of both those crimes. After further investigation, we may also find other crimes of which you are also guilty."

"I was not attempting to threaten anyone, and I have not li—."

"Mr. Ciresi," Petrelli interrupted. "Do you have a sister?" Petrelli put his face close to Ciresi's. "Do not lie to me again."

He hesitated. "She is my cousin."

"Mr. Ciresi, perception is reality and Sergeant Neal thought you were attempting to intimidate him, or worse. So, are you prepared to go before a judge and explain your actions and accept the consequences for this crime and any others we will discover?"

"I ... I don't. Wait a minute." He sighed. "I was told to follow him."

"By whom?"

"I don't know."

Petrelli threw his arms in the air. "I thought you weren't going to lie to us?"

"I *don't know*," Ciresi shouted. "He called me. He offered me two hundred thousand Euros if I ... ." Ciresi stopped.

"If you what?"

"If I took care of ... the American."

Petrelli and the officer exchanged glances.

"When did you get this call?"

"Today."

"Did you receive the call on your cell phone?"

"Yes."

"Who do you *think* it was that called you? And, why would he call *you*?"

"I don't know."

"You are lying again."

"He said another man gave him my number."

"Who?"

"I don't know."

"What were you going to do to Sergeant Neal?"

"I was only checking him out."

"Checking him out to see if you could kill him?"

"No."

"What is your cell phone number?" Petrelli asked and then turned to his officer. "Get me his phone."

Petrelli paced the floor. "What time did you get this call?"

"I don't remember; sometime this morning."

The officer returned with Ciresi's phone. Petrelli scrolled to the man's recent calls.

"Mr. Ciresi, until we resolve this and we discover who tried to hire you to kill Sergeant Neal, you're going to be a guest of the Polizia di Stato."

"Look, I received a call asking me if I wanted to make a lot of money. I said 'of course'. The man told me he had a client who wanted a man killed. I told him I did not do that kind of work. He said he knew that I didn't, but wanted me to know there was a large sum of money available for the man who decided he *could* do it."

"Who was this man?"

"I told you. I do not know. He spoke with a German accent. That is all I know."

"How did he get your number?"

"He didn't say."

Petrelli continued to look through Ciresi's phone calls.

"I asked him how much money because I was interested in case I knew someone who was willing to kill someone for money, maybe I could help arrange it and make some money myself on the side without being involved. I do not do this kind of work."

"Without being involved?"

"Yes. I mean no. Not being involved."

"If you arranged a murder, how is it you wouldn't be involved?"

"I wouldn't do it myself."

Petrelli decided not to pursue Ciresi's brand of logic. "What kind of work *do* you do?"

"Enforcement, collections, jobs like that."

"You are an enforcer."

"You make it sound ugly. I'm trying to pay my bills by getting others to do what they've previously agreed to do."

"So he offered you two hundred thousand Euros?"

"Yes. I did not believe him at first, so I decided to act like I would do the job in order to see what a man looked like that was worth that much money."

"Seriously?"

"The man on the phone told me this American would be spending time with the police because he was in Rome to locate the wealthy man who was offering two hundred thousand Euros to have him stopped."

"Did he say anything that could help you to know who he was?"

"Not that I remember."

Petrelli stared across the table at Ciresi.

"Now that you've met Sergeant Neal, what do you think about the price?"

"I think he may be a normal man, but he has a bodyguard who is not normal."

"Oh?"

"She is lethal. I am an experienced man. I am able to take care of myself. It is embarrassing. When I stood and saw how small she was, I could not believe she was able to do that to me."

"Maybe you are not as tough as you thought, if you're getting your ass whipped by a woman who is just over five feet tall. I think *that* may be your issue."

"Maybe he is a man more special than I thought if he can attract powerful women to be his bodyguard. Who is this Neal anyway?"

"That's none of your business."

"You called him Sergeant. Is he an American soldier? A cop? Killing a cop is not worth two hundred thousand Euros. Staying alive and out of prison is worth much more. I wouldn't do something so stupid."

"Oh, no," Petrelli said. "I'm sure you wouldn't."

CHAPTER 51

Hotel Sonya
Rome, Italy

Mike woke in response to a high-pitched car horn on the street below his hotel window. It was now six hours since he'd passed out on the strange bed with the spongy pillows. As soon as he laid down last night he wished for one of his over-sized goose feather pillows back home in Nashville. But, he was much too tired to allow this to interfere with his sleep.

He scanned the small hotel room as consciousness arrived. It took him a few seconds to recall where he was. It didn't take long for him to begin thinking about last night's stalker episode and his search for Barrett Stone.

Mike knew he would not be able to go back to sleep. Once his mind focused on an active case in the morning, he knew he may as well get up. Since he missed his normal cardio last evening and it was still early, he decided he would hit the hotel's gym for a run on their treadmill.

He pulled on his running clothes and followed the hotel's signs to the gym. He pulled open the glass door and was greeted by a hand-made paper sign hanging from a well-worn treadmill. *Fuori Servizio* was printed in large letters and below it in English were the words 'Out of Order'. Mike looked around the room for a substitute machine, but saw nothing that would satisfy his cardio requirements. He knew the only option available to get his heart rate where he needed it, was outside on the streets of Rome.

The temperature was in the high sixties. The humidity was half that. It was perfect. In an attempt to examine his route options, Mike grabbed a map from the concierge and scanned the streets around the hotel.

A uniformed bellman, who looked to be in his late twenties, approached as Mike propped his foot on the edge of a planter full of flowers and bent to double-tie his laces for his run. The man looked to be fit and possibly a runner himself.

"*Buon giorno, signore.*"

"Good morning." Mike stood and read the man's nametag: Fabrizio. He knew what the man said, but was not yet comfortable responding in kind."

"I see you are a runner?" the man said in accented English.

"You can tell?" Mike asked.

"You wear ASICS. Only serious runners spend that kind of money on running shoes."

Mike nodded. "I guess you're right. I have to wear these; I have flat feet. Are you a runner?" Mike finished tying his other shoe.

"Yes, but I cannot afford ASICS, not at the rate I wear out shoes." He smiled at Mike and again admired the shoes.

"Tell me," Mike said, "where is the best place where I can run a few miles, I mean kilometers?"

The bellman smiled at Mike's self-correction. "If you take this street," he pointed east, "one and one half kilometers, you will come to an autostrada where you can run for many kilometers northwest or southeast. Myself, I would go southeast. The road is better, as are the sights."

"You are very kind."

"It is my pleasure, *signore*. Enjoy your run."

"*Grazie*," Mike said, a bit more comfortable with a word he'd practiced in the mirror before his trip.

"*Prego.*" The bellman raised his hand. "*Ciao.*" He smiled as he walked through the hotel's revolving door.

Giovanni Ricci sat slumped in the driver's seat of his Fiat looking out across the bottom edge of the driver's side window. Gio, as he was called, was staked out waiting for a chance to see the American. He strained to hear the exchange between the man in shorts and the bellman. He looked at the photograph given to him by the German and then back at the man. He was confident. This was the same man.

He was motivated not only by the generous compensation he'd been offered, but also by the chance to pay back the American for the arrest of his friend, Ciresi.

Gio knew well the area the bellman had suggested for the American's run. As the American jogged away from the hotel, Gio watched him and then followed, making sure he was not spotted.

Mike jogged across the hotel's cobblestone entrance and onto the narrow street headed east. As he ran, he admired the striking architecture along both sides of the street. The Italians had invested so much more effort into their elaborate designs over the years than many of America's architects. Several of the buildings back home looked to be focused on contemporary function more than style or classic beauty. Most were gray, or beige or gray-beige in color; whatever shades of concrete were chosen.

Gio was driving slowly as he approached the American from behind. He planned to pass him, turn around and position himself to continue his surveillance. As he pulled alongside him Gio looked away so the American could not see his face. He pulled his car into a busy parking lot, made a 360 degree turn behind a building and then pulled back along side the structure so his car was hidden from sight. He got out of his car, lit a cigarette and stood at the corner of the building so he could watch the American as he approached.

Once he had passed, Gio watched to be sure he did not make a turn. He was still following the bellman's advice. When Gio began to have difficulty seeing him, he tossed his cigarette to the ground, returned to his car and pulled forward. He watching out his window as the American ran toward the outskirts of the city.

As Mike drew closer to the autostrada, the buildings became more sparse. Most of the villas appeared to be positioned in the midst of orchards, or vineyards.

Mike could see the highway up ahead going southeast and northwest. With the sun climbing in the sky, he chose to take the bellman's advice.

The countryside was like so many coffee table books he'd seen over the years. However, this morning's views were more vivid, more colorful and much more interesting. He wished he'd brought his digital camera along.

Villas, some quite large, were positioned hundreds of meters off the highway with long roads splitting the property and dividing olive orchards or vineyards as they connected the homes to the highway. Some of the drives leading up to the estates were lined with tall dark green cypress trees creating the beautiful image he'd seen in so many books and movies set in Italy. Mike imagined these homes had been handed down from fathers to sons over dozens, perhaps hundreds of years.

For a moment, he wondered; if it wasn't for Barrett Stone, would he have ever seen this extraordinary country. He tried to take his mind off of Stone, and absorb the impressive scenery. After all, the mayor told him he was on a working vacation.

Once the American reached the autostrada and ran to the southeast, Gio pulled forward to the intersection and turned in the opposite direction. He watched the American in his mirrors until he reached a spot where he could turn the car around and park. Gio continued to watch the man until he moved away from the populated area and out into the countryside.

Gio saw the American was approaching the large olive groves where the homes and potential witnesses were few and much farther apart. He pulled the car into gear and accelerated.

Mike glanced at his wristwatch. He'd been running for forty-five minutes. He wanted to run for hours and take in more of the landscape, but he knew it was nearing time to turn around and get back to the hotel. He and Cris had a meeting with Petrelli at 09:00. Mike didn't want to be forced to admit he was late because he was sight-seeing.

He was admiring a multi-acre hillside vineyard in the distance when he heard from behind him the growing whine of an approaching car. Running so that he faced oncoming traffic, Mike wasn't concerned about the car, but self-preservation and the unfamiliar roadway moved his strides to the outer edge of the pavement.

As the whine of the small engine grew louder, Mike glanced over his shoulder in time to see that the car was now on *his* side of the highway. As he leaped from the pavement he felt the impact of the car's front fender strike his upper calf. The blow rotated his body causing him to land on his side in the thick grass.

Mike's head struck the dirt at the bottom of the ditch, but he never lost consciousness. From the ditch, he could hear the car's engine revving as the driver went through the gears and raced away with no intention of stopping or allowing anyone to identify him or her. Mike was unable to see the driver or the plate. But when he'd turned, he caught a glimpse of the car. It was a small red car, one of several hundred thousand in a country where red cars had always been the favorite.

Mike knew it would be best to lie still in the ditch for a while until he regained his breath and his equilibrium. He moved each of his limbs slowly to be sure nothing was broken. When he moved his hand to the tenderness in his calf he realized he would likely have a painful bruise there and another on his ass from the impact with the ditch. He rolled onto his left side in an effort to stand.

Mike had no trouble convincing himself—this was no accident.

CHAPTER 52

Green Hills
Nashville

Preparing the necessary equipment was easy. Not only did Wade Powell already own the AC manifold gauges, refrigerant tanks and all the necessary hand tools, he also had access to a blue van that could easily become the service van he needed.

He designed two magnetic door signs on the Internet and ordered them. He bought the signs and paid for next day delivery all for less than sixty dollars.

Powell used his hunting binoculars to watch the coming and going of the detective's renters. He discovered that the woman who lived upstairs left for work at about seven o'clock and dropped her son at school on her way. They were gone from home each day until the afternoon. The boy rode the bus home and arrived around three-thirty. His mother was home by five thirty. This span of time during the day would allow Powell more than enough to complete his work.

He'd driven by the house once this morning and was on his second trip acting as if he was looking for an address. The young mother and her son had been gone for over an hour. If they'd forgotten anything they would have been back for it by now. He readied his gear and drove the recently labeled "HENRY'S HVAC" van down the block and a half to the cop's driveway.

He parked in the driveway at the front corner of the house so anyone who saw him could also see the company logo and know he was there servicing the AC system for the coming hot Nashville summer.

With his leather tool bag in one hand and pale green refrigerant tanks in the other, he walked across the front lawn to the opposite end of the house where the central heat and air system was located. He was glad to see that the home's upstairs used a small split system separate from the unit serving the larger square footage downstairs. Powell had no issue with the woman and her son.

He used a cordless nut driver to remove the metal cover of the unit. He began his bogus once-over visual check of the system for anyone who might be watching. He was ready to make the planned alteration when he heard a raspy voice behind him.

"What the hell are you doing?"

Startled somewhat, Powell turned to see an old man with a sagging frown. He was wearing a dingy T-shirt tucked inside his pants. The leather belt to his navy work pants was pulled tight across the top of his pot belly. His thin comb-over failed to cover his baldness, but did successfully top off the *old fart* look.

This guy's got to be in his eighties, Powell thought.

"What's up, old dude?" Powell shouted so the old man could understand him. He knew all people this age were hard of hearing. He picked up a shop towel and began wiping his hands as though they were greasy.

Sergeant Neal's neighbor from next door had shuffled across his lawn and approached Powell from behind without making a sound.

"The sky is up, ya dumb ass. I asked you a question. And stop yelling. I ain't deaf."

Powell was surprised by the old man's moxie. "I'm doin' the annual preventive maintenance on Sergeant Neal's AC unit like he asked me to do before he left town."

Powell watched for any concern in the old guy's face. There were so many wrinkles running in so many directions, he couldn't see any emotional shift.

"Besides slowin' me down, what are *you* doin'?" Powell asked, continuing to shout if only to irritate the old man enough to make him leave.

"None of your damn business, you yahoo." The old man kept his hands in his pockets and each time he spoke, he jingled their contents as if to accent his bold chatter.

Powell laughed out loud at the old man's tough guy routine. "So, is there somethin' I can do for you or are you here to just irritate me? Hey, I'll tell you what. What say I give *your* system a once over and get it ready for the summer like I'm doin' for the Sergeant here?"

"You can leave my system alone," the old guy warned Powell. "That's what you can do, by damn. I don't need your bullshit," he mumbled. "My boy takes care of all that maintenance crap." He rattled the contents of his pockets again.

"I'll tell you what I'm willin' to do," Powell began again. "Since you're such a nice guy, I'll check your central heat and air and since I'm already here, I'll give you a twenty percent discount on the labor *and* for the referral the Sarge doesn't even know about yet, I'll give you and Sergeant Neal both coupons for ten percent off next year's inspections. That way you can both be winners. You can't beat a deal like that. Whadaya say?" *With this much sales pressure, the old guy has to believe I'm for real.*

The old man squinted and waved his hand in the air toward Powell like he was swatting at a fly. "I have a better idea," the old man said as he turned back toward his house. "Why don't you go ..." The old man mumbled some incoherent comment to complete his advice on what Powell should do to himself.

Powell couldn't understand all the old man said, but he was confident of what he'd been told to do.

Mumbling the entire time, the old man limped back across his yard toward his back porch. Using the handrail, little by little he pulled himself up the five steps. He stopped inside the screened-in porch, and looked back at Powell. As he pulled open the rear door, Powell gave him a military salute. The old man frowned again and gave Powell a single-finger salute. Powell laughed out loud, glad the old guy was finally gone.

Powell knew it would be best if he didn't waste any more time. There was no way to be sure if the ornery old man was convinced he was a real HVAC technician.

In his years as a handyman, Powell had seen dozens of heat exchangers with cracks. Some occurred at the welded joints, and others were due to the repeated expansion and contraction of metal. He'd heard horror stories about how undiscovered cracks allowed large volumes of carbon monoxide to enter homes and either injure or kill the home's occupants.

He made sure his body blocked any visibility of his actions from old and prying eyes. He pulled out the small cordless drill and mounted the cobalt bit. He angled the drill so he could make a small hole at the rear of the heat exchanger. He oiled the sight and began to drill. Once the hole was finished, he inserted the brass fitting attached to the hose running from the tank. He opened the valve on the tank and allowed its pressurized contents to move into the enclosed living space on the bottom floor. Powell acted as though he was still checking out the system while the compressed gas in the tank emptied itself. Once the needle on the regulator pointed to empty, he closed the valve, disconnected the hose and attached it to the other full tank. When the second tank was empty, he plugged the hole with super glue and cleaned up his mess.

The pale green tanks hadn't contained refrigerant as labeled. They'd been full of compressed carbon monoxide which was now moving through the ductwork and filling Sergeant Neal's home to a level hundreds of times that of the EPA's maximum exposure level.

As Powell replaced the last of the sheet metal screws on the unit's hood, he collected his tools from the grass and turned for a look at the nosey neighbor's house. The old man was standing in the window watching him. His face was frozen in a frown.

Powell waved his hand holding the gauges, threw back his head and smiled as he said softly to himself, "You're too damn nosey old man. I can't afford to let you live."

CHAPTER 53

Polizia di Stato
Rome, Italy

Mike limped into the conference room moving like a man twice his age.

"What happened to you?" the Lieutenant asked.

"It was one of your Rome Welcome Wagon members, with their warm Italian reception."

"What is a Welcome Wagon?"

"It's an American hospitality institution. I was being sarcastic."

Mike moaned as he eased his uninjured cheek down onto one of the chairs at the conference table.

"I woke up early and decided to go for a run this morning. A friendly bellman outside the hotel entrance started talking about running and I asked him where would be a good place to run. I ran to the area he suggested, enjoying the countryside and the vineyards. It was beautiful until I looked behind me and saw a car about to hit me. Fortunately, I jumped off the road and into the ditch, but not before the car struck my leg."

"What did the car look like?" Petrelli asked. "Did you see the plate number?"

" I gave all the information I had to the Sergeant a little while ago.

He said he would check to see what they can find. I didn't see the driver or the car's license. It was a small red car. I have no idea what make or model." Mike shrugged his shoulders.

"I'm sorry," Petrelli said. "We normally treat our guests better than this."

"I would hope so." Mike smiled.

"I must tell you about our discussion with Ciresi last evening."

"Oh?"

"He confessed that he was offered two hundred thousand Euros —to kill you."

"Really? By whom?"

"He says he doesn't know who it was that called him. He assured us he was only checking you out. He meant you no harm."

"Of course." Mike looked at Cris. "Stone knows we're here."

"How?" Cris asked.

"I don't know. There's a small group that's aware of our trip." Mike looked at his wristwatch. I'll check with the Lieutenant when he comes in and see who's in the loop. Maybe someone's been nosey about why we're not on duty."

"Sergeant, is your leg going to be okay?" Petrelli asked.

"Yes, I'm sure it'll be fine. I've got a good sized bruise on my backside from my landing in the ditch. I'd show you, but I wouldn't want to get Cris excited."

"Oh, yes. By all means," Cris said. "I'm sure I wouldn't be able to contain myself."

Both men laughed.

"Lieutenant Petrelli? Pardon me sir," a young officer said as he entered the conference room speaking in Italian. "We received a call from Detective Gastone. He is interviewing the staff at *San Matteo* Hospital. He says he may have something on the two Americans we are searching for."

Mike looked at Cris for a translation.

Cris leaned toward him and explained what the young man had said.

Mike looked at Petrelli.

The Lieutenant waited for Cris to finish. "Will you be able to walk?"

"For this," Mike said, "I could run."

"*Sinora Contini,*" Detective Gastone spoke to the nurse in Italian, "this is Lieutenant Petrelli and Detectives Vega and Neal from America. Can you please explain again what you told me earlier?"

As she spoke, Cris translated.

"There were two of them, Americans. They were here for facial reconstruction. Dr. Groom, the plastic surgeon was also from America. He booked an operating room for the day and was scheduled to perform the surgeries, but yesterday morning, just before he started to draw the guide lines on the patient's face, the doctor received a call that his wife, back in the United States, had suffered an ischemic stroke. He asked us to explain to Mr. Strong and Mr. Marshall and offer them his apologies."

"That was their names? Strong and Marshall?" Petrelli asked.

"Yes. Mr. Strong insisted his surgery should be first. He had already been given his anesthesia and was asleep when Dr. Groom received the call. Mr. Marshall was still in his room. He had not yet received medication."

"Do you know where the two men are now?" Petrelli asked.

"No, sir. Once Mr. Strong regained his strength, they both left the hospital in a taxi. They did not say where they were going."

"Does the hospital have security cameras?" Mike asked.

"I'm sure they do in some places," Petrelli said. "Let me get the head of security down here and we'll find out."

"When I call Lieutenant Burris, I'll see if he can locate this Dr. Groom."

Petrelli left the group and Mike turned to Cris. "Ask the nurses if they talked with the two men while they were here."

Cris asked them in Italian.

"We talked with Mr. Marshall. He was a nice man. The other man, Mr. Strong was—how do you say it? Ms. *Contini* looked at the other nurse, "*Un cazzo.*"

"*Un stronzo,*" The second nurse added. They both laughed.

"It has to be Stone," Cris said.

"Oh?"

"He's a prick and an asshole here too."

CHAPTER 54

East of Rome, Italy

There were no more than six ounces left in the bottle of Stoli that Barrett had opened this morning. Thanks to the property manager, he still had most of two cases of the premium Russian vodka in the cupboard.

Like always when Barrett drank heavily, Al tried to keep his distance, but it was more difficult now. He couldn't go home.

Barrett was difficult when he was sober. When he was drinking, his mood could turn on an innocent comment from sour to shitty. It didn't take much to get him ranting about whatever insignificant irritation he could conceive.

"C'mon Al, have a drink. I had the real estate woman get you a case of Jack Daniel's. The least you can do is try to empty it. What's the matter? Are you being antisocial?"

"All right. I'll have one," Al agreed in order to appease him like he'd done for years.

Barrett stumbled toward the kitchen counter that had become his personal bar.

"I'll fix it," Al said, hoping to make it mostly Coke.

"No." Barrett held up his hand. "I have it. I've had plenty of practice bartending since this morning."

No shit, Al thought.

Barrett reached into the freezer for a handful of ice cubes. "Here you go, Mr. Marsh—," Barrett burped. "Mr. T. Albert Marshall."

Al grabbed the glass with both his hands as it slipped through Barrett's and started for the floor.

Al took a sip to lower the level of liquid in the glass and prevent any more from splashing on the kitchen floor. The color made the drink *look* like it had some Coke in it, but it tasted like pure Tennessee sour mash. He knew Barrett was trying to help him catch up.

He walked out onto the patio and sat at the table where he parked his 80 proof highball with no intention of touching it again.

"Albert, what are we drinking to today?" Barrett said as he sat. "Wow. Now that's a view." He looked out across the rear of the property at the rolling hills of groves and vineyards separated by long rows of tall Cyprus trees.

Barrett turned and stared at Al. "You're awfully quiet today."

"Yes, I guess I am."

"What's on your mind?"

Al didn't want to get started with Barrett in his current state. But, he'd been in this situation before, and he knew if he didn't participate in the conversation, Barrett would get pissed, then loud and obnoxious. It was easier just to try and talk with him.

"I've been concerned lately, about … you know, all this … all the change. I'm not used to looking at everyone I see and wondering if they're a cop that's looking to lock us up. I worry since we didn't have our surgery, are we now in jeopardy of being discovered? I feel like maybe we need to stay here at the house until you can get Doctor Groom back over here and our surgeries done. Are the Italian police looking for us? Do they have our pictures? How do we know, one way or the other? There's a lot to be apprehensive about. I don't see the Nashville police giving up and dropping the fact that you screwed so many people out of their retirement savings."

"*We* screwed so many."

"Whatever," Al said not willing to argue the point.

Barrett nodded. "I know. I don't want all my planning to be ruined by some ambitious Italian cop. That's what the facial reconstruction was all about." He sucked down another gulp of vodka. "Thanks to that idiot doctor, my plans are stalled."

"*Your* plans, but *we* screwed them," Al said under his breath.

"What was that?"

"So, do you have a backup plan?" Al asked.

"A backup plan? To what? Facial reconstruction?"

"You usually have everything all thought out," Al said, attempting to mask his criticism with a compliment.

"Maybe not this time," Barrett said. His comment was loaded with sarcasm. "I mean, what the hell kind of stupid question is that anyway?" Barrett stood, stumbled and drained his glass. "What kind of *backup plan* would you prefer, Mr. Marshall?"

Al knew better than to say anything.

"You can grow a beard." Barrett said as he walked past Al on his way back to the vodka. "You can let your damned hair grow out. You can do *something, anything* to help make all this happen the way it's supposed to. I don't know. What the hell do you expect from me anyway?" Barrett yelled from the kitchen.

Here we go. I'm glad we're isolated out here or the neighbors would be calling the cops to report a domestic disturbance. Al changed his mind and took a gulp of his whiskey.

Barrett walked back out to the patio with his full glass. He stood quiet for a moment. He leaned against one of the posts supporting the pergola and stared out at the horizon.

"I spent most of my damn life without a family—a real family. You know that. You were there for much of it."

Barrett took another drink. "I remember one night before you came to live with us. I was sitting in my room looking out my open window at a full moon, wondering why I was at home alone with an old housekeeper who didn't give a damn about me, while my father was out carousing with his friends. I couldn't figure what I was doing wrong that made him want to be somewhere else.

"I made myself a promise that night. I swore that when I grew up I would never allow anyone to prevent me from having anything I felt I deserved."

He turned toward Al and stumbled, but caught himself against the post. Out of nowhere he said, "Meredith Bowles—that bitch." Barrett's taut face displayed his anger. "I was in my early twenties. She had plans to lay claim to my father's fortune. She thought all she had to do was throw herself at him, satisfy him physically, and she'd be set for life. But, she failed to factor in one thing." He took in a large breath and gritted his teeth. "Me."

Al was confident his suspicions were about to be confirmed.

"That gold-digging bitch was awakened to the cruel facts just prior to her final nap."

"What do you mean?" Al asked, wanting unequivocal confirmation.

"What? Are you stupid? I shot her between her expensive enhanced breasts and watched the bitch die."

Al was not so much stunned by Barrett's confession as he was with Barrett's casual demeanor. The fact he had admitted to murdering his father's fiancé had no impact on him. But then, he *was* drunk.

"People who get between me and what's mine should be prepared for the worst. You should know that by now, I don't tolerate anyone I can't trust. If I didn't believe I could trust you—you wouldn't be here either." He stared at Al. "You wouldn't be anywhere."

"So, is that it? If you get in the way of Barrett Stone and his money, you'd best beware?"

"More—or less."

Al nodded. "You're a power whore. Any method allowing you to control other people becomes your drug. And, the worst of it is, you're not satisfied without a frequent fix. During your childhood life wasn't kind, but you need to understand, we've all faced obstacles. My dad didn't spend time with me either. But that's because he was *dead*." Al paused. "Then, my mom died. Sometimes life really sucks. But, it doesn't give us *Carte Blanche* to dump it all on others in spades. It doesn't work that way."

"What the hell do you know, you little shit?"

Al was opening a topic he'd intentionally avoided for a long time, but he knew liquor sometimes worked like truth serum, and he wanted to hear the facts. He wanted to hear this from Barrett while his lips were loose and he was talking bold.

"Is that what happened to Tyler?"

Barrett's face reddened more than it had in response to the liquor. The veins in his neck bulged and he staggered toward Al.

"Let me tell you something about your so-called *friend*. That son of a bitch was flat broke due to his own incompetence. He was strapped. I offered him a way out, a way around bankruptcy. He agreed to it, not readily, but he did agree to it. After he went home and became intimidated by his puritanical conscience, he changed his mind. He came back to me and offered me an alternative that I, in my benevolence, accepted. He was going to introduce me to someone who could do for me what he decided he could not. But, over the next forty-eight hours and after more deliberation with his mis-guided scruples, he decided the right thing to do was go to the police and expose my intentions, so he could feel good about himself. That kind of thinking can get you shot."

"You bastard." *You did kill him.*

"I told you—getting between me and what's mine is not a safe place to be."

Barrett's comfort with what he'd done infuriated Al as much as the act of killing Tyler. Al wished he could so easily place his morals on hold and give Barrett back what *he* deserved.

"I cannot sit back and allow people to destroy what is rightfully mine."

"You can't just kill people who get in your way."

"The hell I can't." Barrett turned and entered the kitchen. "They're all getting what they deserve."

Al drew in several anger induced breaths. In the middle of his flood of tears, he ran at Barrett. Even though Barrett was drunk, he was able to sidestep Al's charge. Al was no fighter. He pushed Al and caused him to fall into the kitchen counter.

Al climbed to his feet, grabbed his bottle of Jack Daniel's whiskey from the counter and threw it at Barrett, who dodged it and watched it break on the floor next to his feet. Barrett took a drink of his vodka and walked back outside as though nothing had happened.

Al stomped off to his bedroom, grabbed his car keys and went out the front door.

"You son of a bitch. You haven't yet seen what's rightfully yours. But it's coming."

CHAPTER 55

Rome, Italy

His satellite phone announced an incoming call.

"Mike Neal."

"Hey Mike, it's me," Norm said. "You got a minute?"

"What's up, partner. I thought you might be the mayor calling for a status report."

"The mayor? Is he wearing you out?"

"Not really. He's only concerned about us bringing Stone back. What's up?"

"Remember my case where the house was burned and the arson investigator told me he thought it may have been a homicide rather than an accident? I checked it out and it looks like the arson guy was pretty sharp. The evidence says it's a homicide that looks like an accident because it was staged. The arson investigator found the remains of a large oxygen cylinder that wasn't supposed to be there."

"Interesting."

"I talked with the old guy's neighbors and one of them said he was a retired child psychologist of all things. He had a practice here in Nashville for years. I searched for anything I could find on the old man's name, Clayton West. I saw on the Internet where he was not only a member of the American Academy of Clinical Psychology, but he was a partner in a counseling group in the Vanderbilt area for over twenty-six years."

"Did you check for his client list?"

"Did I check for his client list? I'm insulted. I've been a detective longer than you, country boy." Norm laughed.

Mike smiled. "What did you find?"

"I called his old office and paid them a visit. They weren't too excited about giving out West's old client list. I explained this was a murder investigation and if they preferred, I could get a warrant for West's files and for any other files the judge feels could be pertinent to our investigation.

"I love that phrase you taught me, *and any others the judge feels could be pertinent to our investigation*", Norm said in a deepened voice. "It really works."

"Thank you. And, you found *what*?"

"I scanned the list for names that looked familiar. Whose name pops up? Barrett Stone II."

"Stone's father?"

"Yes, he would have been the client since your guy was a minor at the time. Have you found Stone?"

"Not yet."

"If you do and we find out he's the one who killed West, I owe you a huge steak."

"That works. By the way, did the Lieutenant hand off any of my active cases to you?"

"Yes. I was given the Cynthia Gaston and Charles Briggs books."

"Listen, if you need anything on those, call me. Cynthia Gaston's husband was devastated and I hated to leave him like I did. I hope he understood."

"I talked with him for quite a while. I told him you and I used to be partners and you hated to have to hand off his wife's case, but you were glad it was given to me. He said he understood."

"He's a good kid. I met his mom and dad that night. He comes from good stock. Thanks for taking care of him."

"This is the main reason I called you. You'll be glad to know your old partner caught some luck on Cynthia's case already. I was showing snapshots from the video to some of their neighbors who knew the Gastons. I was hoping someone might recognize the suspect. One of the neighbor men said he thought the man in the video looked like one of the landscaping crew that mowed the grass at the complex, but he couldn't be sure. I paid a visit to the landscaper's office and showed the owner the video. He confirmed the suspect was his employee. He gave us the man's information and he was picked up today."

"That's great. I'd love to see that one cleared quickly for Bobby's sake."

"It looks as though it could be a slam dunk," Norm said. "I'm on my way to interview the suspect now. With the video, I'm counting on a confession."

"Do it, partner."

"I'll keep you posted."

"Thanks, Norm and good luck."

CHAPTER 56

Rome, Italy

When he narrowly avoided a head-on collision with an approaching tour bus, Al quickly became aware he was driving too fast on Italy's narrow roads. He wiped his tears, slowed to a safer speed and shifted most of his consciousness from his anger to his driving.

All these people were not your enemies, you moron. I'm sick of all this, and I'm sick of you. It's over. It's time for you to crash and burn.

Al pulled the small car into the public parking lot. The *Caffé Collegare* was only two blocks away. He checked his pocket for the flash drive as he exited and locked the car.

"*Buongiorno, signore.*" The hostess greeted Al as he settled in front of one of the rental PCs.

"*Buongiorno. Cappuccino, per favore?*"

"*Si, signore. Un momento.*"

Al wasted no time signing on and logging into his email account.

He looked at his wristwatch to check the time in Nashville. It was early. His Internet service provider's header announced one unread email.

Al:
Hope you are well and things are progressing. We need a status report back here in Nashville.
Best,
T

Al typed his response.

T:
It is time.
I'm out, and I'll be on my way within the hour. I need you to send the current data file <u>immediately</u>. I'll be waiting for it.
Thanks,
Al

While Al waited for the response, he began his letter to Sergeant Neal.

Sergeant Neal,

The purpose of this letter is to notify you of how you can collect the murderer and thief Barrett Stone and return him to Nashville for the prosecution and imprisonment he deserves.

I have been a witness to many of his financial crimes and he has today confessed to the murders of Mrs. Meredith Bowles and my friend Tyler McKinnon.

While it's true I have ridden his coattails for years, it has not been without regret or purpose. I am not the greedy man that is Barrett Stone, but I am also not the fool he thinks I am. His plan to steal the hard earned savings of several good and decent folks has fueled my plan to stop him. Watching Barrett Stone herd these innocent old folks into his lair and suck their life's savings from them was difficult.

I learned of his plan almost a year ago, long after he had begun his fraud. Since that time I have remained close to him in an effort to stay aware of his moves and to be prepared at the proper time, to block his vindictive efforts.

I will admit that it appears I have allowed myself to become a party to his perverted greed, but the truth will soon be made clear. I ask that you do your part and bring Barrett Stone to justice.

You may feel you should also pursue me for his crimes. I understand that perspective, but I cannot allow it to happen. I assure you, I have not taken, nor do I plan to take, any of his ill-gotten gains.

If you will follow the map I have included and arrive at the time I have specified, you will find Barrett focused on his computer and oblivious to his surroundings. He is a deceitful, but methodical man.

I wish you the best in your efforts to bring Barrett Stone to justice for his sordid crimes and assure you by the time you read this message I will sadly be gone from this beautiful city, and soon afterward, the country. Good luck.

Sincerely,

Al Ricks

Al printed the letter and as he folded the paper with the map and inserted it into an envelope, he looked again at his watch and then for the response to his email.

A:
I'm glad I woke up early and checked on you. Glad you're safe.

The latest data file is attached. Please notify us when you arrive at your destination.
Take care.
T

Al clicked on the icon to open it. He smiled as he paged through the file and located the data he needed.

Tracey, you're an angel.

He pulled the flash drive from his pocket, pushed it into the USB port and went to work. Al had been on the computer for a little more than an hour when he pocketed his flash drive and logged off. He stood and waved to signal the café hostess he was leaving. "Caio."

"Grazie, signore. Caio."

Al wished he could have seen the look on the girl's face when she found the two hundred Euro note beneath his saucer.

He returned to his rental car with a tranquil feeling and drove to the Hotel Sonya, where according to Sarah Stone, Sergeant Neal was staying. He parked at the main entrance as if about to register. He pulled on his baseball cap and sunglasses, and marched to the front desk. He handed the desk agent the envelope addressed: *Sergeant Mike Neal, Guest – Confidential.*

"Can you see that your guest Sergeant Mike Neal gets this please? It's quite important."

"Si, signore."

Al slid the desk clerk a folded fifty euro note.

"I will take care of it personally, sir."

Al tipped his cap. He turned and began his exit from the beautiful city of Rome and his final departure from his subservient past.

CHAPTER 57

Verona Porta Nuova
Verona, Italy

Al looked at his wristwatch. He knew Mary Ellen hated it when the phone rang early in the morning. She always feared it would be bad news. This time, it would be the opposite.

"Hello?" She spoke the greeting as if it was an anxious question.

The sound of her voice made him smile. "Hello, sweetheart."

"Oh, my God." She gasped. "I love you." She started crying.

"I love you more." Al smiled, enjoying her tear-filled response to his call.

"I've missed you so much." Her voice cracked. "You have no idea."

"I've missed you too babe," Al said. "I wondered if you would answer the phone."

"I was afraid not to at this hour. Where are you?"

"It's best if I don't say."

"Are you okay?"

"I'm fine," Al said.

"Any news I need to know about?"

"It's all done. It's over."

"Oh, thank goodness. I've been so stressed out."

"It's so great to talk with you. Are you packed?"

"Not completely. How much time do I have?"

"Your flight is tomorrow afternoon."

"Oh, Al. I have so much to do. I'm not sure I can ..."

"Babe. Hey. Don't worry about it. Pack what you can, and I'll buy you everything else you need here. It's no problem. Did you send the quitclaim deed on the house to your sister?"

"Yes. She said with the shortage of jobs in Detroit, this was a God send. They're so excited about living in Nashville."

"That's great. I'm sure she'll be glad to use whatever things you leave behind. Be sure to explain to her why you can't tell her where we'll be. She will very likely be questioned by the police. Let her know you will check in with her later."

"I understand. Where am I flying to?"

"Your electronic ticket will be in your email later today. Be watching for it and print it. The ticket will tell you your destination."

"I'm still uneasy about things. That detective came to the house. He made me so nervous. I tried to cry the whole time so it would distract him, and I wouldn't have to talk so much."

"How did it go?"

"Just like you said it would. I did okay, I guess. I'm no actress, but I didn't hear from the police again."

"That's great. It'll all be over soon, honey. Listen. It's important during your trip to conceal your identity like I explained before I left. There is a chance you could be followed."

"Okay. I need to call Sarah right away. She's all set with my transportation, just waiting for the final word."

"Good."

"I want to see your face. Did you get the new—?"

"No." Al interrupted. "The doctor had an emergency back home."

"Oh, I'm so glad. I'll still get to kiss my favorite face."

Al laughed. "We need to get off the line. I love you so much."

"I love you too."

"I'll see you the day after tomorrow. Be safe and don't forget to watch for the *Cubbies*." He hung up the phone.

Al knew if the police wanted to trace his call, they could do so in much less time than he and Mary Ellen were on the line, but discovering he'd called her from a bank of fifteen phones in the Verona, Italy train station would do little good in their attempt to locate him.

He threw his back pack over his shoulder, pulled his blue Chicago Cubs baseball cap down on his forehead and approached the train platform.

CHAPTER 58

East of Rome, Italy

Slumped into a fetal position in a chaise lounge on the villa's patio, Barrett woke with a jackhammer headache and major case of cotton mouth. The sun broke over the vineyard-covered hills and warmed his face.

"Oh, shit." He squinted as he rolled over to avoid the intense light. He inspected his surroundings through thin slits between his eye lids and decided he was still in Italy. He was sure he was lying perfectly still, but for some reason, everything was moving.

He thought about shouting for Al, but between head throbs he recalled what took place last evening. His confident superiority caused him to feel that some of last night's aggressive banter needed to be said, but Barrett knew he may have gone a bit too far. Al's car was still gone.

"Screw him."

As Barrett continued to awaken, he recalled his confession of responsibility for the deaths of Meredith Bowles and Tyler McKinnon.

Tyler. That one set him off. He altered his position and squeezed his eyes closed.

Barrett was confident he'd made the right decision. He stopped short of admitting to smothering Al's mother in her sick-bed with a pillow—his first attempt to protect his inheritance was made at the age of twelve.

Barrett began to wonder if Al might be brave enough to retaliate for Tyler's death. The more he considered it, the less chance he thought there would be. Al was not the type to seek revenge. He was more likely to accept his fate, absorb his disdain, and try to move on. Barrett had never seen him do otherwise.

"He'll be back. He needs me, and he knows it." Barrett grunted as he rolled himself into a seated position.

"Son of a bitch. Good vodka should not do this to you."

He sat with his head in his hands attempting to contain the incessant pounding. He needed to get inside for some water. He was having trouble swallowing. He tried to stand, but his instability altered his immediate plan and he sat back down.

"Whoa." *Let's try that again.*

Barrett managed to stand, but this time without releasing his hold on the back of the chair. Erect now, he held his ground until his equilibrium caught up with him. He moved hand over hand along the wall navigating through the kitchen until he arrived at the refrigerator. He grabbed the door handle and paused. He saw the clock hanging on the wall above the refrigerator. He had time to shower and dress before it was time for his account transfers.

As Barrett finished dressing and returned to the dining area, he had second thoughts about his step-brother's reluctance to retaliate for the murder of his best friend. He went back to the bedroom, took the pistol from beneath his pillow and placed it on the dining table next to his laptop PC.

No sense taking chances.

Barrett poured a fresh cup of dark roast coffee, and sat at the dining table. As his laptop booted up, he sipped his coffee and began to rethink his plans in case Al was now out of the picture. Other than relocating soon to a spot known only to him, he saw no reason to alter his plans. He decided to contact the real estate lady when he was finished to have her look for an alternative villa, maybe a smaller one, but it had to have a view that was at least as good as or better than this one.

His computer's desktop was now up and ready. He pushed in his air card, gave the PC time to acknowledge it and signed on to his Internet portal. He selected the access point for his largest and favorite private banking account in The Cayman Islands, GRC

Wealth Management. He entered his user name, password and account number. His impatience was rewarded with the rotating and annoying hourglass, signifying the incomplete account search. Finally, the header for his account came up and at the bottom right corner displayed his current balance: $00.00.

Barrett froze. "What the ...?"

Maybe this is the one I drew down to zero and moved the balance to the Belize account. I don't recall doing that, but....

He logged out and began again.

Too much on my mind.

This time he pulled up First Bank of Belize and clicked the login button. When his account page filled the screen, he looked at the bottom line. $00.00.

"Son of a bitch!" Barrett shouted. "Now what?"

He pulled up his electronic contact list and placed a call to The First Bank of Grand Bahama.

"You have reached The First Bank of Grand Bahama, Freeport."

This was his only other Caribbean bank. The rest were in Europe.

"Damn it!" Barrett checked his wristwatch and calculated the time in the Carribean.

"Our banking hours are eight o'clock until four o'clock," the recorded voice said. "If you know your party's extension, enter it now."

"I don't know his damned extension."

"If not, press one to access the voicemail registry and search by last name."

"He's from Nassau. I have no idea how to spell his damn name. Son of a bitch!"

Barrett's frustration dominated his senses and he failed to hear the popping of the gravel beneath the tires of the approaching sedans until they were just outside the villa. He ran to the front window.

"Damn it." He turned back to the dining table, picked up his pistol and shoved it under his belt. He ran through the open patio doors.

Outside, he sprinted down the hill and into the old olive grove. He heard a man's voice shouting in English behind him.

"Stone. Stop. You're making things worse."

Screw you. Screw all of you.

Mike and Cris left the car at the same time. Mike saw where Stone entered the grove and took the same row.

"You take this row." He gestured to the one that was two rows to the right. Cris disappeared behind the trees.

The ground was not level, nor was it remotely suitable for running.

"Be careful," Mike yelled. "Don't step in one of these holes and twist an ankle."

"Copy that." Cris's legs were no where near the length of Mike's, but she was almost as fast.

Mike could hear the uniformed officers shouting in shortened breaths at each other in Italian as they ran the rows outside where he and Cris were running.

Mike stopped when he heard the report of a pistol. "Don't shoot him. I want him alive."

Cris shouted her translation of Mike's words to the officers.

"Lui e quello di ripresa," the Italian officer shouted.

"He said Stone was the one who fired the shot," Cris shouted.

"Great. The crazy son of a bitch has a gun. Make sure everyone knows he's armed." Mike pulled his Beretta and crossed the grove rows toward the sound of the shot.

Mike heard an exchange of shouts, all in Italian, from the same direction as the gunshot. He moved toward them.

"Smettere! Smettere!"

Mike continued to move in the direction of the shouts. Cris was nowhere in sight.

There was another shot.

"Shit." Mike said to himself as he ran. He lost track of which row Cris was in. "Cris," he shouted.

Mike stopped to listen for her response. "Cris," he shouted again.

He heard male voices in Italian, but had no idea what was said or who said it; then after a moment of quiet, he heard Stone's voice.

"Neal. You need to put your gun down and come this way. Follow my voice."

Mike didn't like the confident tone Stone was using. He moved through the rows toward Stone's voice.

"Neal." Stone shouted again.

Mike stepped between olive trees to see Stone with his left arm around Cris's neck and a pistol in his right hand, pointed at her head.

The Italian officers had their pistols aimed at Stone.

"Damn it," Mike whispered as he moved slowly toward Stone. He looked down the iron sights of his Beretta at what he could see of Stone's head. The five foot ten Stone was turning back and forth putting Cris between him and the three Berettas pointed at him. He was doing his best to hide behind Cris. Her five feet and five inches was making it difficult.

"Sergeant Neal, it's nice of you to finally show up." Stone smiled.

Mike continued to move slowly toward Stone as he kept his aim tight on what he could see of him protruding from behind Cris. In his peripheral vision, Mike could tell the two officers were watching him as much as they were watching Stone.

"Stop right there, all of you. You need to drop your guns and kick them over here to me."

Mike paused his advance, but kept his aim. He glanced at the two officers who were watching to see what he did. Mike nodded to them to put down their weapons.

"If you want her to live through this Neal, you'll do what I'm telling you."

The two officers laid down their pistols, half-heartedly kicked them toward Stone and then stepped back.

"Mike's eyes were focused on Stone, but he didn't see Barrett Stone and Detective Cris Vega. He was looking at Connie Neal, his seventeen year old sister in the grasp of her killer, a smiling Manuel Avila. A distressing vision—now almost twenty years old.

"Put the gun down, or she dies."

Mike continued to stare down the pistol's beaded sights watching for a shot.

Cris cleared her throat and said, "You're choking me." Her words pulled Mike back from his emotional past.

"That's the idea bitch," Stone said. "Tell Neal to drop his gun or you're going to die."

Mike watched as Cris put her hands on Barrett's forearm to try and loosen his hold.

She raised her eyebrows and said, "Mike, put your gun down. Code ten eighty-five." Ten eighty-five code was Prisoner Escape.

"What the hell's ten eighty-five? If you don't drop—"

Cris clamped down onto Stone's forearm with her hands and pulled her legs up to meet her abdomen. Stone wasn't ready for the added weight. He loosened his hold. Her weight pulled him forward and down exposing his upper body. Mike fired.

The bullet struck Stone in the right shoulder shattering his scapula. He screamed. The pistol fell from his grip to the dirt. Cris maintained her hold on his left arm and, using a shoulder throw, hurled him to the ground. Stone screamed louder as his injured shoulder struck the ground. Cris grabbed his pistol.

She smiled as she looked at Mike for approval. Her face and most of her body were covered in dust.

"You're a mess," Mike said, "in more ways than one."

"Thanks. Nice shooting."

"It's all those hours we put in on the range," Mike said. "You okay?"

"I'm great," she said, still breathing hard, but smiling.

Mike laughed. "You're an adrenaline junkie."

"Guilty, your honor."

"How'd he get hold of you anyway?"

"I ran between the trees. He was waiting on me. He tripped me and then jumped me, the bastard."

"Chiamato l'ambulanza," the Italian officer said.

"Grazie."

"He said he called for an ambulance." She took a huge breath and laughed as she blew it and much of her stress out. She looked at Stone writhing on the ground in pain. "Let's go asshole." She hooked her hand under his left shoulder.

"Let me look at that wound first," Mike said. "No sense letting him bleed to death before the ambulance gets here."

Mike asked Cris to have one of the officers apply pressure to Stone's shoulder wound. To Cris's pleasure, this caused Stone to scream again.

Cris walked to where Mike was standing, "So, what do you think about that Beretta?"

"One more reason to love Italy," Mike smiled.

"Si signore." Cris laughed.

CHAPTER 59

Northern Italy

Thomas Albert Marshall gave his passport and a confident smile to the Verona train station agent. Without issue, he boarded the train and settled in ready to enjoy his tour through the Italian Alps on his way to the southern Austrian border just north of Brunnero, Italy. Within hours, the train would arrive in the beautiful valley city of Innsbruck, surrounded by the snow-capped Austrian Alps.

Al was in awe of the way their plan had worked so well. Barrett's assumption that he was so much smarter than everyone else permitted the mechanics of the plan to progress without a hiccup. Barrett convinced himself everyone around him was an idiot and at the mercy of *his* guidance.

Once Barrett confirmed to Al his plan to abandon everything and leave the United States, Al called Sarah Stone. They established their common desire not just to stop Barrett, but to reimburse the massive losses incurred by the trusting clients of Stone Asset Management. Many of these investors, Al discovered, were also friends of the Ballengers, Sarah's parents. Throughout the ordeal, Al remained confident he could trust her.

Al smiled as he thought about the idea to use the keylogger software in order to obtain Barrett's private banking data. It was genius on the part of Sarah's computer savvy friend Tracey and it performed exactly as planned.

On the night they left Nashville, Al copied the client worksheet data into the special Excel file Tracey gave him. He sent the file to Barrett's email much like he did other data on a daily basis. The attached software was poised waiting for Barrett to open the worksheet. When the attachment was opened on their first day in Rome, the keylogger went to work covertly expanding and loading itself onto Barrett's laptop. Once installed, the software collected each of Barrett's keystrokes and saved them to a data file. Each time Barrett logged onto the Internet regardless of his location, the keylogger not only continued to collect all his keystrokes, his account numbers and his passwords, but it also sent the collected data files including screenshots and URLs from previous sessions to an email account back in America which was established for that purpose.

Al had been concerned something could happen to him in Italy and all would be lost if no one else had access to the data, so he suggested they have the keylogger transmit the captured data files to a new email account and stored on Sarah's PC back in Nashville for safe keeping until needed. This way, if anything happened, Sarah could execute their plan herself.

Al's insistence that they wait to purge the accounts allowed him time to confirm Barrett's guilt in Tyler's death.

During his stop at the Internet café in Rome, Al completed the transfer of all Barrett's assets. He sent an electronic message, which Tracey had provided him, to Barrett's email. When Barrett opened his email next, the uninstall program was initiated and it removed the keylogger leaving his laptop as if the software was never there.

Al was glad the nightmare was over and that his Swiss bank was sending the monies back to the investors. He was proud of what they'd accomplished.

The hotel Al had chosen for his reunion with Mary Ellen was The Grand Hotel Europa. It was a five star hotel located in the heart of Innsbruck. Its proximity to the railway station would make it convenient for all the trips throughout Europe he had planned for the two of them in the coming weeks.

He laid his head back against the seat and slept the balance of the trip.

Al's train arrived at the Innsbruck station on time and he decided to walk the block and a half to the hotel.

"She's going to love this place," Al said out loud as he scanned the hotel's façade.

"*Guten Tag,*" the doorman said.

"Hello." *That's right, they speak German.*

"*Willkommen.*"

"*Danke,*" Al said laughing at his feeble attempt at the language.

He entered the lobby and turned a three-sixty as he examined the stunning architecture. The place was awesome. He couldn't wait for Mary Ellen to see it.

He checked in, showered and prepared to grab some much needed sleep.

CHAPTER 60

Rome, Italy

Mike stood at the foot of the hospital bed staring at Barrett Stone, who was currently drugged up and asleep. Lieutenant Petrelli had placed an armed officer on either side of the door to his hospital room until he was released or relocated to the state police holding cell.

Stone's left wrist was hand-cuffed to the bed rail and his right arm lay useless, immobilized in a sling and taped tight against his side.

Mike asked the two officers if he could get them coffee or anything else while he was out. Both thanked him and confirmed a hot expresso would be appreciated. Mike left the room and stepped outside the hospital wing to make a satellite phone call.

"Mayor? Mike Neal."

"Hello, Mike. Do you have good news for me?"

"We have Stone, sir."

"Say that again, please."

"We have Barrett Stone in custody, sir."

"Thank God. Is he in jail?"

"Not exactly."

"What do you mean?" The mayor snapped.

"He's in the hospital, sir."

"Why the hospital?"

"I shot him."

"Really?" The mayor sounded as though he liked the fact Stone had been shot.

"Yes, sir. He resisted arrest and was threatening the life of an officer."

"Not Cris, I hope?"

"Yes, sir. It was Cris, but she's fine. She wasn't hurt. I shot him in the shoulder."

"You should have killed the son of a bitch."

Mike wasn't expecting that from the mayor. "I'm happy just to have him in custody, sir. I'll have to let the courts decide his fate."

"You're right. I'm ... angry."

"I understand, sir."

"I know you do. You've been there."

"Yes, sir."

"When did the Doctor say Stone could travel?"

"He said if nothing changes, we may be able to fly home tomorrow."

"Good."

"Sir, I want you to know that Al Ricks assisted us with Stone's capture."

"Why would he do that?"

"Ricks sent a letter to the hotel instructing us where we could find Stone and how best to take him."

"Wrote you a letter? How did he know you were there, much less how to find you?"

"My guess is, he and Sarah Stone were in contact with each other. She's the only person, outside the MNPD, who knew where we would be staying."

"This gets more complicated by the minute. Do we need to consider action against her?"

"No sir, I don't think so. Ricks stated in his letter that Stone confessed to him during a quarrel that he'd killed not only Tyler McKinnon, but also your sister."

"Bastard—lousy *bastard*. I knew it. I knew he did it."

"Ricks said he wanted the truth to come out, and assured me he had not taken any of their clients' monies, nor did he intend to."

"Do you believe him?"

"Actually, I do. But, I can't explain why. Gut feeling, I guess."

"Your gut instincts have a pretty good track record."

"Thank you, sir."

"The DA has issued a murder warrant for Stone in the death of Tyler McKinnon and, in case Norm Wallace hasn't told you yet, he's filing another charge of conspiracy to commit the murder of Clayton West. Dr. West was Stone's childhood therapist as well as another of Stone's hoodwinked investors. As soon as I can, I'll call the DA's office and we'll add the warrant for Meredith's murder. What do you feel we should do about Ricks?"

"I think we should delay any efforts to locate him," Mike said. "I wouldn't have a clue where to start anyway. I'm not sure it's worth the expense."

"Do we have any reason to believe he killed anyone or assisted Stone with any of the murders?"

"No sir, no evidence of it."

"*I'd* say forget about Ricks for the murders, but that's a call for the DA to make," Mayor Rowe said. "Oh. I forgot to tell you; my daughter Samantha received a check this morning from a bank in Zurich. It was for the full amount she gave Stone to invest. Any ideas?"

"Yes sir. I have reason to believe she may not be the only Stone investor in Nashville to see their investments returned to them."

"Ricks?"

"Yes, sir."

"For now, by being an active partner in Stone Asset Management, he has to remain a party to the fraud warrants."

"Yes, sir. I haven't discussed it with Brent Spangler in our Fraud Division, but if the investors are fully remunerated like Samantha, where's the fraud? They *gave* their money to Stone of their own free will. If they get it back. No fraud exists, right?"

"It may fall to intent, so legally Sergeant you may be off base, but morally I agree with you. Let's allow some time for this to unfold. I'll talk to the D.A." Mayor Rowe paused. "Ricks could have kept it all, you know."

"Yes, sir. That's what I was thinking. He explained his position in the letter. I'll let you read it when I get back."

"Hmm. People never cease to amaze me," Rowe said.

"At least this time the amazement comes from a strangely positive act."

"Yes. I know Samantha is happy about it."

"Actually, I'm guessing Ricks is too, sir. It appears that stopping

Stone and returning all the investors' funds was *his* plan all along."

"That's great, Mike. Listen, come see me when you get back. I want to shake your hand. Samantha told me she wants to take you to dinner at The Palm for saving her inheritance and lessening her embarrassment in front of her friends and her family."

"Really?" Mike grimaced. "I'll call you when we know for sure when we're leaving."

"Great work, Sergeant."

"Thank you, Mr. Mayor. We'll talk soon." Mike ended the call.

Mike remembered Samantha's photo on the mayor's credenza when he visited his office. *One more beautiful woman to spend time with might not be such a bad thing unless of course her father had the power to fire you on a whim. That's ... living dangerously.*

He thought about his social calendar. *Spend time? What time?*

Mike entered the hospital cafeteria searching for coffee for the guards, but instead he found Cris and Sergeant Barone rubbing knees under a small bistro table, speaking Italian and laughing like teenagers. Each was staring and smiling, blinded by the other.

"So this is where you went."

"Hi, Mike." Cris escaped her trance. "How's Stone?"

"He's in my favorite condition for a felony prisoner, unconscious."

"He deserves it. So, what's up?"

"I'm getting coffee for the guys upstairs. You two gonna be here long?"

Cris shrugged. "I don't know. Do *you* have any plans for this evening?"

"Yes. I'm going back to the hotel and crash right after I put some notes together on today's ordeal."

"Nico asked me to go dancing. We were discussing the possibilities."

"Nico?" Mike acted like he didn't know who she was referring to.

"Sergeant Barone." Cris tossed her head in the Italian detective's direction.

Mike looked at the sergeant, who smiled. The man looked like a hungry wolf that had spotted a limping rabbit.

Mike nodded. "Whatever." He turned, approached the coffee bar and rolled his eyes.

CHAPTER 61

Rome, Italy

"The doctor plans to check on Stone's condition at noon and let us know if he can travel," Petrelli said. "He asked that you, Cris and I be there for the update."

"We'll be there." Mike ended the call.

The hospital administrator had contacted both Stone's doctor and Petrelli's office yesterday asking that the guarded patient be released or relocated as soon as possible. His presence was disruptive, causing both the patients and the hospital staff considerable anxiety.

The doctor was semi-pleased with Stone's progress, but Mike knew the continued presence of armed Polizia di Stato in the hospital hallways was not conducive to the relaxed recovery of the hospital's other patients.

The doctor arrived on time, shadowed by two nurses. He checked Stone's wound and replaced the old dressing. He reluctantly declared the patient could fly back to the United States under conditions which he rattled off to Mike and Cris before his swift departure. The nurses remained in the room to assist Stone with the clothes they'd brought him. The detectives stepped outside the room with Petrelli.

"Is there anything I can do to assist you further?" Petrelli asked.

"We could use a ride to Fiumicino," Mike said as he offered his hand.

Petrelli smiled. "Absolutely, and I will loan you a set of quality Italian handcuffs and key for your flight."

Cris took the cuffs and said, "You can pick these up at the Criminal Justice Center in Nashville when you and Detective Barone come to Music City for a visit."

"That sounds tempting, detective. I will try to arrange for one of our criminals to run away to Tennessee, so we can expense it."

They all laughed.

"I don't guess these will make it through customs," Mike said as he removed his holstered Beretta and extra magazine.

"Oh, yeah." Cris handed her pistol, magazine and cell phone to the officer standing guard outside the room.

"I'm going to have to leave now," Petrelli said. "I wish you both good luck with your prisoner. I'm glad we were able to help you locate him. Have a safe trip home."

"Thank you very much," Mike said as he shook Petrelli's hand. "We couldn't have done this without your help."

"I agree," Cris said, offering her hand to the lieutenant.

"It was our pleasure. Come back and visit when you can. *Caio.*" Petrelli smiled as he turned and walked toward the exit.

"*Caio,*" Cris said and then turned to Mike. "Great guy."

"Where's Barone?"

"He had to work today, why do you ask?"

"Just curious," Mike said. "That's a shame. I thought he would be here to see you off."

"You're not going to let this go are you?"

Mike smiled. "I don't know what you're talking about."

"Oh, no. You have *no* idea."

Mike chuckled, and then turned back toward the room as a nurse opened the door.

"He is ready."

"Grazie," Mike said proudly.

"Prego." The nurse smiled at Mike's Italian.

"That's all he knows," Cris said.

"Mi scusi?" Mike said using his best Italian accent.

The nurse laughed.

Cris just shook her head.

CHAPTER 62

Bellevue
West Nashville

Paulina Jankowski was devastated when she lost her husband Marek. Together with their four adult children, they'd dreamed about and planned their fiftieth wedding anniversary celebration, complete with a six piece polka band. Five weeks short of that memorable day, Marek developed a brain aneurism and died.

Paulina had not been away from her beloved Marek for more than a few days in over fifty years. The time following his passing was heartbreaking. Paulina received support from all her children, but her eldest daughter Marie lived nearby in Nashville with her orthodontist husband and two young children. Marie was always there for her mom. They saw each other frequently.

"Was that the doorbell?" Paulina asked.

"Yes, mom. I'll get it." Marie was visiting today in order to give her elderly mother's home its monthly cleaning.

Marie scanned the porch outside the front door, but could not see anyone. Then she saw a large white truck pass in front of the house.

"It may have been Fed-Ex. Let me look." She opened the door and found a Fed-Ex envelope lying across the door's threshold.

"It's an envelope from ...." Marie looked again. "It's from Switzerland?"

"What? From where?"

Paulina had become hard of hearing in recent years. Marie came closer to talk with her mom. "It says it is from a bank in Zurich, Switzerland. It's addressed to you and dad."

"Hmm. Open it, honey."

"Do you know anyone in Switzerland?" Marie asked as she pulled the strip to open the envelope.

"Not that I know of, but your father knew a lot of people in Europe, especially from the old country."

Marie pulled apart the cardboard sides and found a business size envelope at the bottom.

"Looks like a letter." She turned it over. "There's no return address or name." Marie tapped the contents to the end of the envelope and carefully tore off a narrow strip at the other end. She blew on the opening and removed the paper from inside. As she unfolded the letter, another piece of paper dropped into her lap.

Marie laughed as she saw what was written in the letter, "It's one of those international scams."

"A what?"

"A scam. You know, a con. They send you a letter to convince you to give them your social security number or your bank account number and then they steal your identity and your money."

"That is so cruel. How can people do that to each other?"

"Mom, there are a lot of evil people in the world. You have to be careful about what you share. Always make sure you ask me about things like this before you get involved."

Marie re-read the letter. She picked up the paper from her lap and looked it over. As she did, her brow furrowed. "Mom, do you know a man named Barrett Stone III?"

"Oh, yes. He's the one who stole our life savings. Is that another one of his tricks?"

"I'm not sure. This letter is saying the enclosed check is real. How much did he take from you and dad?"

"Marek knew Barrett's father and was comfortable investing a large portion of our savings with him. If I remember correctly, it was over two hundred thousand dollars. Your father sold some CD's in order to take advantage of the opportunity. We thought it was a good investment that we could use to take care of us in our later years. Sadly, we were wrong."

Marie held up the check. "This is a cashier's check for two hundred and twelve thousand dollars."

"Is it fake?"

"Based on this letter, it's real. It says it's repayment of your entire investment with Stone Asset Management. The sender is not named. It says it's from a friend. Whoever it is, they apologized for what Stone did to your investment portfolio."

"Let me see it."

Paulina inspected the check. She looked up at Marie. Her face began to tighten and her cheeks flushed. Tears ran down both her cheeks.

Marie put her arm around her mom's shoulders and hugged her.

Paulina cried. "Oh, Marek."

CHAPTER 63

Fiumicino Airport
Rome, Italy

Mike had notified the airline that he and Cris would be escorting a prisoner back to Nashville. The airline's concern was diminished when Mike explained that Stone's right arm was incapacitated by the wound's binding and his free hand would be handcuffed to one of them while he was seated between them throughout the flight.

The three of them waited in a small room which the airline had provided in order to keep the sight of Stone's handcuffs from disturbing the traveling public. Stone was cuffed to Mike's chair.

Mike's phone vibrated. It seemed odd because he always kept his phone in his right jacket pocket. This vibration was coming from his left pocket. As he fished it out he remembered he put Stone's cell phone in his left pocket. He'd confiscated it when Stone was taken into custody. Mike looked at the phone's screen and then held it in front of Stone.

The text message read: "I found her. It's definitely her. Elena Triano. What do you want to do now? Call me." Stone's eyes closed and his head went backward. He began to bang it against the back of his seat.

"Damn it! Damn it!" Stone said out loud.

Mike wasn't sure what the message or the unsettling response meant, nor was he curious enough to ask. He returned the phone to his pocket, glanced over at Cris and shrugged. Mike could tell she was fighting to contain her laughter.

Stone faced forward with a hypnotic stare. Out of nowhere he said, "Women," and then shook his head.

If this was supposed to elicit Mike's curiosity, it failed. Mike kept his attention on his magazine.

This declaration by Stone, simple as it was, didn't go unnoticed, nor would it go unchallenged, by the only female in the vicinity. Being a strong and opinionated woman, the comment captured Cris's interest.

"Do you have a problem with women, Stone?"

Don't get involved. Stay out of it. Mike said to himself. He wondered if he should say the same to Cris.

"It's like this." Barrett forced out a large breath. "I've only cared for one woman in my life—one." He held up his index finger as far as his cuffed wrist would allow. "There was an age difference, but we were working that out when she left seventeen years ago."

"Wait a minute," Cris said as she brought her hand up. "Seventeen years ago you were what, sixteen?"

"Seventeen. Almost."

"Oh. That's different." Cris looked at Mike and shrugged.

"I came to Italy to find her. I hired a private investigator. He was helping me locate her. The message on my phone was from him—telling me he'd found her."

"Wow. That's a real tear jerker, Stone. By the way ... your timing sucks. I didn't think you were the sensitive kind of guy," Cris said. "You seem more the 'my way or the highway' type. You sure you're able to deal with the sensitivities and opinions of a woman? By the way, I thought you were married?"

"Don't remind me."

Cris glared at him. "I get the impression sharing isn't one of your relationship strengths?"

"It's a long story." Stone said, signifying his disgust. "From day one, my marriage has been a relationship built around *forced sharing*."

"Ahh, you're referring to the pre-nup Sergeant Neal told me about. I thought those came about as the result of *bi-lateral negotiations*."

"This one came about more as the result of bribery and a healthy dose of fraud. Rules were broken. Advantage was taken."

"Oh?"

"Yeah. She learned more from me than I'd intended."

"I hate it when that happens." Cris picked up her paperback novel as a signal to Stone that she'd heard all of his self-absorbed rhetoric she could handle.

"She's going to hate what just happened as much as I do."

"What do you mean?" Mike asked as he lowered his magazine.

"I mean she isn't going to get a penny for her daddy's multi-page pre-nuptial agreement."

"What about all the money you made from your own investments?"

Barrett forced a disgusted laugh. Mike and Cris looked at each other.

"You want to let us in on the humor?"

"Before you and the cavalry arrived at the villa, I was attempting to reposition my investments—a habit of mine. However, the first four accounts that I checked were empty. I assume that somehow the rest suffered the same fate. Someone got their hands on my personal information and drained my assets. So, since there's none for me, there's not any for the bitch either."

Mike forced a cough and pulled his magazine closer.

Mike looked over Stone's head to check out Cris's response. She closed her eyes and shook her head.

The door opened and they all watched a well-dressed young man in a pilot's uniform approach.

"Sergeant Neal?"

"I'm Mike Neal."

"We're ready to board you folks. We're going to allow you to board ahead of our other guests."

"Thanks."

The trio stood. Mike unlocked the handcuff from the chair and hooked it over his wrist. He turned him so that they were face to face.

"There's something you need to know. The sooner you know the better."

"What?" Stone asked, offering him a puzzled look.

"Whoever cleaned out your accounts is sending your investors' money back to them."

His eyes widened and his nostrils flared. "Damned Ricks. I knew it. Son of a bitch. I oughta—"

"Timeout," Mike interrupted. "I think you've done enough damage. Get all this shit out of your system now, before we board the plane. After we're on board, I don't want to hear it. Not a word. You got it?"

Stone finally nodded. "How do you know this?"

"I talked with the mayor yesterday. Samantha Rowe received a cashier's check for her entire investment."

Stone clinched his lips together as he looked at Mike, his face reddened by the revelation.

"When you're through with your tantrum, put a cork in it and we'll go."

Stone hung his head and breathed deeply. He continued to stare at the floor.

As casually as they could, the trio strolled out onto the busy concourse, through their gate and onto the large jet, bound for home.

CHAPTER 64

Kranebitten Airport
Innsbruck, Austria

The Innsbruck morning was brisk. The sound of church bells caused Al to think about how grateful he was that his ordeal was almost over. He knew he'd been blessed and he said a brief prayer of thanks for what he'd been able to do for all of Barrett's victims.

According to the flight status board for arrivals, Mary Ellen's flight from London was on time. Al decided the best place to wait for her was in baggage claim. If he knew Mary Ellen, she would have every one of her suitcases packed and maybe some boxes. He found a bench with a good view of the escalator. He was so excited to see his wife, he couldn't sit still.

Her flight number was posted on the digital marquee in front of him. People were exiting the escalator and gathering in the area around the carousel. The red light started flashing and the carousel began to move. After a few moments, bags entering from outside began to travel the U-shaped track. Most were snatched off promptly by anxious travelers.

A couple of times bags passed by that looked familiar to Al, but there was no Mary Ellen to claim them. He stood and walked around to be sure he wasn't missing anyone. He came back to his bench, adjusted his Cubs baseball cap and scanned the area. What could have happened? He was getting nervous.

Al craned his neck to see around a group of folks who had stopped in front of him to greet arriving passengers. He was about to stand in order to see around them when an old lady walked in front of him and rolled a huge suitcase over his toe.

"Ouch," Al stood.

"Oh, I'm so sorry. Are you hurt young man?"

The old lady's large hat struck him in the face and knocked his cap askew. There was no way Al would admit it even if he was hurt.

"No ma'am. Are you okay?"

"Oh, yes. I'm fine. Are you an American?" She asked with a shaky senior voice.

"Yes ma'am, I am," Al said.

"I thought so. I knew you were a good man when I first spotted you," the old woman tilted her head back and gave him a big smile, "eight years ago."

Al's eyes bulged and filled with tears. He wrapped his arms around his wife and whispered in her ear, "If you're going to look this hot when we get old ... I can't wait. I love you so much."

Both of them laughed and kissed like mother and son to maintain appearances.

Al pulled her oversized bag behind him, as they walked to the carousel to claim her other luggage. It took both of them to get the bags out the sliding doors to Al's waiting limousine.

Once inside the car, Al removed Mary Ellen's hat and gave her a huge hug and kiss.

They sat staring, smiling and holding hands.

"I have missed you so much," she said.

"Me too, babe. Me too."

Al kissed her again.

Mary Ellen held his cheeks in her hands and looked into his eyes.

"You're going to love the hotel," Al said.

"I'm going to love *you*," she gave a sly smile.

Al laughed. "Before I forget to tell you, our appointments are at eight o'clock day after tomorrow morning with Dr. Groom at the Center for Reconstructive Surgery. Have you decided anything on your new look?"

"I haven't had time to think about that or much of anything else," she said.

"I believe we should go for the Faith Hill and Tim McGraw look. What do you say?" Al laughed.

"I'm happy getting to look at *this* beautiful face again."

He kissed her. "I'm afraid if we look like our photographs, this new life of ours could be cut short by the authorities."

"Al, I'm ready for any life with *any* look, as long as I get to spend it with you."

"Honey, that wish has already been granted."

Al handed the bellman a ten dollar bill and locked their hotel room door behind him.

"So," Mary Ellen said, "I don't mean to break the mood, but you never told me how much Barrett took from all those people."

"In total, it was over forty-five million dollars."

"Oh my word. I had no idea it could be that much."

Al nodded. "I'm afraid so, but it all went back where it came from—every penny. Some of the checks were sent out Friday afternoon. The last was to be sent yesterday. All of them shipped Fed-Ex International Priority so they would arrive as soon as possible."

"I'm so proud of you."

Al smiled. "By the way, that forty-five million didn't include Barrett's *personal* assets, only those from the investors. Barrett had over nineteen million of his own money in one of the Zurich accounts and in one of the Caribbean accounts." Al smiled again. "I took that, too. He can't use it where he's going."

"What are you going to do with *that* money?"

"It's gone too. I transferred fifteen million into Sarah's account. That was the amount of her pre-nuptial agreement. I sent Allison McKinnon a cashier's check for three million, and I sent Shannon a check for one million. She'll flip out." Al laughed.

"She's earned it, putting up with him," Mary Ellen said. "Is there much left?"

"We still have all the money that I made over the years with *our* investments."

"How much is that?" Mary Ellen cringed, then smiled.

"Four million, six hundred thousand." He smiled and gave her a hug.

"Wow," she said with a huge grin.

"I'm going to consider the two facial reconstructions as wedding gifts from Mr. Bradford Strong to Mr. and Mrs. Albert Marshall since he already paid for them weeks ago."

"Who? Oh, Marshall." She laughed. "That's us."

Al dropped to one knee as he pulled from his pocket a burgundy velvet covered ring box.

"Mary Ellen gasped, and then laughed."

When they married, Al was not able to afford a nice ring. They settled for modest matching gold bands.

Al smiled as he slowly opened the box toward her.

"Oh, my. It's gorgeous, Al. You shouldn't." Mary Ellen stared at the three carat white diamond ring in a yellow gold tiffany setting.

"I'm glad you like it." Al hoped this one showed her how much he loved and appreciated her. He removed it from the box and took her hand. He pushed the ring onto her finger with the gold band.

"Why Mr. Marshall," she said in a heavy southern accent as she brought the ring up for a closer look. "This is awfully forward of you. She turned away, still looking at the ring. After all, we just met. I do believe I deserve to be properly courted before we do anything ... brash."

Al smiled, more than ready to play along.

"Why don't you stop by my place this evening," she said, "and maybe we'll discuss your intentions over dinner."

"I'd be honored to have you join me for dinner. What time should I call for you?"

Mary Ellen began to unbutton her blouse as she watched Al's eyes enlarge and his mouth drop open. She stepped toward him and switched to unbuttoning *his* shirt. He helped with hers.

"Mr. Marshall, you can call on me right after I make you glad you fell in love with me."

"Oh, yes ma'am." Al kissed her as he continued unbuttoning her blouse.

CHAPTER 65

Green Hills
Nashville

Jennifer Holliman and her fourteen year old son Mason were not just Mike's tenants in the upstairs apartment, they were also his friends. They weren't used to him being gone for more than a day. They were anxious to have him back home and to hear about his trip.

Mason and his Jack Russell Terrier, Tag were in the back yard behind Mike's patio playing ball when Tag started barking. He bolted for the driveway.

"Mom," Mason shouted when he saw Mike's car.

Jennifer heard both Tag's and Mason's excitement. She knew Mike was home.

"Hi, buddy." Mike climbed out of his car and Mason wrapped his arms around him.

"Boy, am I glad you're back," Mason said.

Mike hugged him tight. "Me too."

Mike was the closest thing to a father Mason had known since he was four years old. Mike spent as much time with Mason as his work allowed.

"Hello stranger," Jennifer said as she came down the black metal stairs from their apartment.

She had a huge smile on her face. Her blonde hair was pulled back in a pony tail that bounced with each stair step. The pony tail and tight blue jeans made her look younger than her mid-thirties. Mike enjoyed watching her move down the stairs.

"Hi," Mike said as he opened his arms. "How are you?"

"I'm fine *now*." Jennifer wrapped her arms around Mike, laid her head on his firm chest and squeezed him hard. "I missed you," she whispered as she looked up at him. She stretched onto her tiptoes and kissed him on the lips. She'd never done that before.

Mike smiled at her and her warm greeting.

"How was Italy?" she asked as she licked her lips.

"It was beautiful." He looked into her eyes and thought about the kiss. "It looks like all the great photographs, only better."

Mike started pulling his bags from the trunk.

"Hey Mike," Mason said, "you missed all the excitement last night."

"What do you mean?"

"The cops were here around midnight."

Mike jerked his head back toward Jennifer for validation. She nodded.

"Mr. Hinkle next door had a home invasion," Mason said.

"Is he okay?" Mike asked Jennifer, but she only smiled and looked back at her son. She wanted Mason to explain what happened.

"Oh, *he's* fine. The sergeant said when the guy broke in, Mr. Hinkle was sitting in the dark in his living room. The guy either didn't see him or thought Mr. Hinkle was asleep until he shot the man with that Taser you got him."

Mike smiled. "Seriously?"

"Yeah. The sergeant said when they got there, Mr. Hinkle was leaned back in his lounge chair watching TV with the remote in one hand and the Taser in the other. The probes were still attached to the guy's chest and Mr. Hinkle was zapping him with twelve hundred volts every time he tried to get up."

Mike laughed. "Good for him."

"The EMTs hauled the guy to the hospital. I watched them from my window. He was really out of it. They said Mr. Hinkle hit him with the electricity six times."

"He bought that pain when he decided to break in." Mike pulled out the extended handle on his large suitcase, picked up his briefcase and started for the patio door.

"So, tell us about Rome," Jennifer said. "Did you see the Coliseum or the Vatican, or the Trevi fountain?

"Mike smiled. I didn't have much time for sight-seeing, but what I saw was nice and very old." He searched his pocket for his house key.

"Did you see anything really cool?" Mason asked.

"I saw cops driving around in Alfa Romeos and even one in a Lamborghini. That was pretty awesome. We should get some of those for the detectives." Mike smiled. "I took pictures. We'll look at them later." Mike unlocked the door, and Tag rushed inside the house.

"Tag," Jennifer shouted without effect. She shook her head.

"What else did you see?"

"Mason. Let Mike get his bags in the house."

"What's the matter with *him*?" Mason looked at Tag lying on the kitchen floor. "Tag." Mason pushed the door back and stepped into Mike's kitchen. Tag was lying on his side in the middle of the kitchen floor with his mouth open and his tongue hanging out.

Mason knelt down over Tag to see what was wrong. Mason began to sway. He collapsed next to the dog.

"Mason!" Jennifer screamed.

"Stay back," Mike said. He stepped into the kitchen and immediately noticed the difficulty he had breathing. He coughed. He held his breath, grabbed Mason and managed to drag him outside onto the patio and away from the door.

"Oh, my God!" Jennifer came over to her son. "Mason?"

Mike coughed. He took a couple of deep breaths of outside air, held his breath and went back in for Tag. He grabbed the dog and closed the door behind him. Mike continued coughing as he laid the dog on the grass.

He came back to Mason and started CPR. "Close Tag's mouth and cup your hands around his snout. Blow steadily into his nose two breaths and then do five chest compressions. Be careful of his ribs."

"What's wrong?" Jennifer asked.

"I'm not sure." Mike continued CPR on Mason. "Right now, we need to get them both some fresh air."

Mason started coughing in between gasps.

"Mason?"

"Oh man," Mason put both hands on his head. "My head is

killing me."

"Are you feeling sick?" Mike asked.

"Yeah, a little."

Mike grabbed his cell, keyed 911 and put it on speaker while he coached Mason with his breathing.

Mike identified himself, requested an ambulance and the Hazardous Materials Team from the Police Department. "There's something in the house that's reduced or displaced the oxygen level. Okay."

He closed his phone. "They're on their way."

"Swap with me," he said to Jennifer when he realized Mason was okay.

Jennifer came to Mason and held him. His consciousness comforted her, but he was still coughing occasionally.

Mike began to work on Tag. He alternated chest compressions and blowing into his nose. The dog finally began to respond, but he was lethargic. He hacked several times and then threw up in the grass.

Mike picked him up and placed him next to Mason who petted him and scratched behind his ears. He was certain both were going to be fine, but the EMTs needed to verify there was no permanent damage.

By the time the Haz-Mat Team arrived the EMTs had both Mason and Tag on oxygen and were monitoring the oxygen levels in their systems. Mike took some oxygen from the tank, but he told the EMTs he wasn't exposed as much as Mason and Tag.

While one of the Haz-Mat techs suited up, the other, Officer Bobby Pruett talked with Mike.

"How old is your furnace?"

"I replaced it when I remodeled the place a few years ago, why? Are you thinking the heat exchanger has cracks?"

"Sounds like it."

"Think again. I turned my system down before I left. My guess is it hasn't come on in over a week. The unit for the upstairs apartment is separate from mine. Thank goodness."

"Hmm. I'm at a loss then until Tim goes inside."

"I'm ready," Tim Rawls said, before he pulled down the mask to his air tank.

Officer Rawls stepped into Mike's kitchen and closed the door. In less than two minutes Rawls came back outside, closed the door and announced, "It's carbon monoxide. It's the only thing that's reading high. I'm going to walk the house to be sure and then I'll pull an air sample."

"10-4." Pruett turned to Mike. "I'm going to check your central unit anyway." He picked up his toolbox and walked toward the end of the house.

"Haven't we had enough excitement lately?" Mr. Hinkle asked as he limped toward Mike. "What the hell is going on now?"

Mike explained to Hinkle what had happened.

"That reminds me." Mr. Hinkle began to shake the contents of his pockets as he spoke. "You know the SOB that broke into my house last night? He's your air conditioner man. But, he didn't get to rob me. No sir, what he got was a shocking experience, by damn. I zapped his ass with that Taser gun you got me."

"Mr. Hinkle. What did you say about an air conditioner man?"

Pruett stopped and also listened to Hinkle.

"He's your air conditioner man." Hinkle jerked up his pockets again. "Yep, he's the same jackass that was out here servicing your unit the other day. Don't you pay those guys enough so they don't have to burglarize the neighborhood to make ends meet?"

"How do you know he was my air conditioner man?"

"Because he had your unit laid out all over the lawn. I asked him what the hell he was doing and he said you asked him to service the unit while you were out of town."

"Mr. Hinkle. Did he tell you I was out of town or did you tell him?"

"I ... I don't remember. But I zapped his ass. You should have heard the moaning and groaning." Hinkle laughed.

"Did you tell the officers you saw him here working on my unit?"

"Yeah, but they said Powell was no HVAC technician."

"Who?"

"Powell. The cops said his name was Powell. Don't you know your own air conditioner man?"

Mike connected the remaining dots.

"Let me see what I can find," Pruett said.

Mike pushed the speed dial for Lieutenant Burris's cell phone.

"Burris."

"Lieutenant. I need your help. This is important."

"Where are you?"

"I'm at my house in Green Hills. Listen. I need to be sure the Sheriff's Department still has Wade Powell in custody. He was arrested last night following a home invasion at my neighbor's house. He's guilty of much more than a home invasion. He's already served five years for manslaughter. This breaking and entering alone will send him back, but right now I need to be sure he's still locked up."

"I'm sure they have him, but hang on." Burris put Mike on hold.

It took no more than five minutes for Pruett to remove the unit's panels and follow the tool marks to the patched hole behind the heat exchanger near the ductwork.

"Here it is," he said to Mike. "He had to do this with a small drill, maybe a Dremel. The space is tight."

"I'll call my *real* HVAC guys and get it repaired tomorrow. I'll leave the unit off until then."

Pruett began to reattach the unit's cover. "I'm glad you guys didn't get hurt any worse than you did."

"I'm glad I had the extra insulation installed between the first and second floors when I decided to rent out the upstairs. Otherwise ..." Mike looked at Mason and Jennifer. "I don't want to think about it. Anyway, thanks for all your help."

"You got it, Mike."

Burris came back on the line. "Mike."

"Yes?"

"They have him."

"Great. I have strong evidence of an attempted murder."

"Whose murder?"

"Mine."

"What?"

"I'll explain later. Make sure they keep him locked up. Thanks."

Mike walked back to the patio where Jennifer and Tim Rawls were talking with Mason who was smiling and petting Tag.

"How are you feeling?" Mike asked.

"I'm good." Mason said, still looking affected by the nerve-racking ordeal, but he was breathing without issue.

"Do you need to take some more oxygen?"

"I'm fine."

"You need to be sure, because I don't want to hear any excuses tomorrow when I kick your scrawny butt in a round ball one-on-one, first man to twenty-one."

"You wished *old man*," Mason said.

"Old man?" Mike faked a frown and grabbed his gut. "That hurt."

Jennifer and Mason both laughed.

"Now, I'm really gonna have to beat you like a drum."

Mike grabbed Mason around the torso and started tickling him.

"No. No." Mason screamed and giggled as he tried to grab Mike's hands.

Jennifer laughed. She thanked God for both her blessings.

CHAPTER 66

Green Hills
Nashville

By the time the Hazardous Materials Unit packed up their fans and cleared the house for occupancy, Mike was dying for a hot shower in *his* shower, not some tiny phone booth shower like the ones he'd suffered with in Italy.

Mike was shaving when his cell phone rang. He put the call on the speaker.

"Mike Neal."

"Are you ready?" Carol asked.

"Not yet." He continued to shave.

"Why not? You said earlier you'd be ready by now."

"I thought I would, but I had some issues that caused me to get a little behind."

"Mmm, I *love* your little behind."

"You are a *crazy* woman." Mike laughed.

"And you like it, don't you?"

"You got me there." Mike toweled off the remaining shave cream. "So, are you still picking me up?"

"Yep. I'm the dedicated chauffeur tonight. Everything is my treat—until we get back. Then it's your treat."

FACE THE MUSIC

"You sure know how to push the buttons."

Carol laughed. "You bet I do."

Mike looked at the phone to check the time. "I should be ready in ... about a half hour."

"I'll try to be patient," she said. "You can be the doctor."

Mike laughed out loud. "See you soon." He ended the call.

Mike was ready earlier than expected and decided to make a quick call to Allison McKinnon to give her an update.

"Hello."

"Allison, it's Mike."

"Hi. Are you back?"

"Yes. I got back earlier today. I wanted to let you know we were able to locate Barrett Stone and he's now in jail downtown."

"Good. I'm glad to hear it."

"Al Ricks told me Stone confessed to Tyler's murder, but of course that's not admissible since it's hearsay."

"You talked with Al?"

"Not exactly. He sent me a letter."

"A letter?"

"Yes. He helped us catch Stone, before he disappeared himself."

"Where is he?"

"No idea."

"What's going to happen to Stone?"

"He's facing charges of securities, investment, wire and mail fraud as well as one count of first degree murder for Tyler's death. Fortunately, our lab techs were able to pull one of his thumb prints from a wrapper on some of the money in Tyler's safe. That, along with proof that Stone's home computer was used to manufacture false evidence against Tyler convinced the judge to sign the indictment."

"Good."

"The DA is working on a conspiracy to commit murder charge in the death of Clayton West. West was Stone's childhood therapist as well as one of his many deceived investors. We expect the murderer will plead on this and take Stone down with him. The DA is also attempting to strengthen a second rather cold first degree murder charge against Stone. He hopes to be able to firm up both of these counts soon."

"It sounds like he's going to be away for awhile."

"I'd say so."

"Do you plan to pursue Al?"

"Not at the moment. We don't have any idea where he went, or for that matter what he's guilty of. One of our detectives has been trying to speak with his wife again, but she's not answering the phone or the door. We're going to focus our efforts on Stone."

"I received a letter from Al today. It came with a check for three million dollars."

"Wow, that's a lot of money."

"He explained some things about Tyler and about Stone. He said the money was from Stone's investment portfolio and not a part of the investors' funds."

"Good."

Carol knocked twice on the back door and stepped into the kitchen. Mike's mouth fell open and although Allison continued to speak, he heard nothing. He wasn't sure if it was because he hadn't seen Carol in a while or if she just looked that good. Her perfume was hypnotic. He watched as she strolled across the kitchen intentionally trying to arouse him. She smiled, confident of her sensual distraction.

"That ... should ... come in handy and help get you started on a new life. I'm happy for you."

He looked at Carol and smiled. She pulled out a chair and sat across the kitchen table from him. She winked and leaned forward displaying her assets on the table.

"Thank you." Allison hesitated. "Mike, I've been thinking."

There it was. It pulled part of his attention away from Carol. It was one of the top dreaded expressions on the female phrase list. 'I've been thinking'. This was never followed by anything that made a man comfortable. The only idiom more unsettling was 'We need to talk'.

Mike saw Carol check her watch. He nodded and held up a hand as a request for a little more time. He forced himself to look away in order to momentarily focus on Allison.

"I know you and I had a good thing going back at UT," Allison said, "but you weren't ready for a serious relationship. I understand that. We were young then, too young."

Mike was trying hard not to look back at Carol. He needed to concentrate as he listened to Allison so as not to sound distracted and hurt her feelings.

"It was so good to see you again. I was wondering, do you have any interest in maybe giving *us* another chance?"

"*Oh, hell. How am I supposed to answer a question like this with*

Carol trying to seduce me from three feet away?

"Uh ... I don't know." He rubbed his forehead. "With all the turmoil lately and the trip to Italy, I haven't been able to give anything else much thought."

"You don't have to answer right now. Just consider it. That's all I'm suggesting. Consider it."

"Sure. I'll think about it," Mike said as he searched for a good way to end the call before it became even more uncomfortable for him. "I wanted to give you an update and check to see how you were doing."

"I'm glad you called. You have my number."

"Yes, I do. We'll talk again soon. Tell your mom I said hello."

"I will. Thanks for calling."

"See ya." Mike ended the call and struggled to mask his large inhale and exhale.

"Who was that?" Carol asked.

"Allison McKinnon, the widow of the victim in my last homicide before I left for Italy." There was no way Mike was going to tell Carol about Allison and UT. No way. Not now. Not later. Not ever.

"What is it you're supposed to think about?"

I knew it. I knew this was not going to turn out well. I should have waited to call Allison.

Mike assured himself, telling the truth at this point would only make things worse.

"She wanted me to suggest where she should invest the money she received from Al Ricks. He sent her three million dollars from the account of her husband's murderer."

"Wow. A rich widow."

"I guess."

"So, you're doing financial consulting on the side now?" Carol laughed.

"Trying to help out the survivors, like always."

"Are you ready now?"

"Yes ma'am. I'm hungry." Mike gave Carol a kiss worthy of the time they'd spent apart.

"Mmmm," Carol moaned and gave him a long hug.

"Let's go."

Mike fastened his seatbelt before they left the driveway. He looked over at his beautiful chauffeur. It felt funny with Carol driving, but he was determined to enjoy it.

"Where are we going?"

Before Carol could answer, Mike's cell phone started ringing.

"Sorry." Mike apologized.

"Mike Neal."

"Mike, this is Samantha Rowe. How are you?"

"I'm fine Samantha. How are you?"

Mike cringed as he realized too late he'd said her name—out loud. He slowly looked over at Carol to check her expression. She did not look happy.

"Mike, when are you going to let me take you out to dinner?"

"Uh, I don't know." Mike was choosing his words more carefully than before. "Do you have a suggestion?"

"What about tonight?"

With his elbow on the door's armrest, Mike put his head in his hand. "Uh, that's not good."

"Tomorrow?"

"I recently returned from a trip out of the country."

"I know," Samantha reminded him.

"Oh, yeah."

"I'm really busy right now. What say I call you in a few days after I get caught up?"

Mike looked back at Carol. He pulled the phone away from his ear and mouthed the words, "I'm sorry."

Just then, Samantha said, loud enough for Carol to hear, "remember, I owe you a good time for saving my ass."

"What did she say about a good time and her ass?"

"Samantha, I have to go now. I'll call you later. Okay? Bye." Mike silenced his phone.

"That was not what it sounded like."

"Oh, really?"

"That was Mayor Rowe's daughter, Samantha."

"Oh? When did you meet her? Better yet, when did you earn a *good time* by *saving her ass*?"

"I haven't met her yet."

"Yet?"

Mike exhaled forcefully. "Carol, listen."

"Oh, I'm listening."

"What you just heard was risk management."

"Risk?"

"Yes, if I don't handle ... wait a minute, let me use another word. If I don't coddle ... hang on."

Carol turned her head toward her side mirror and stifled a laugh as she backed out of Mike's driveway.

"If I don't treat this girl properly, yes I said girl, I could be putting my future at risk. I have no interest in her other than having her tell her father I was gracious, professional and a gentleman."

"I'd say," Carol began, "if she can't give daddy that same report, you're gonna have more than the mayor to worry about." She offered a sly smile.

"See? That's what I like about you. No bullshit. Cut to the chase. State the facts. Clears everything up." Mike turned his head and looked through his reflection in the passenger side window out into the night. "Just the facts, ma'am. Just the facts." He smiled to himself.

Carol laughed out loud.

"What's so funny?" Mike asked, faking his annoyance and smiling at Carol.

Carol pulled her car to the intersection stop sign, stopped and pushed the shifter into park. She turned to face Mike and said, "You are—and I have missed you so, so much." She leaned across the console and gave Mike a long deep kiss.

"And I've missed you too," Mike whispered.

"Remember this next time you're looking for a traveling companion." Carol smiled.

"Are you sure you want to go to dinner right now?" Mike pulled her into another kiss and they ignored the drivers behind them honking their horns.

ACKNOWLEDGMENTS

For their unending support and exceptional contributions, whether by counsel, critique or encouragement, all have been fuel for my passion. I must thank Dew Wayne Burris, Steve Teer, Beth Teer, Ken Howell, Derek Pacifico, Nancy Sartor and Deb Simpson.

To the members of The Sisters (and Misters) in Crime, where I found a welcoming family of authors and genre enthusiasts, encouragement, and lots of fun. Thank you.

To my wife Sandra, for thirty-seven happy years, for your undying support, and especially for patiently believing in me. Thank you, always.

AUTHOR BIO

Ken Vanderpool is a life-long fan of Crime Suspense and Thriller fiction who began to write his own in 2006 following an eye-opening medical procedure and an intimate encounter with his mortality.

Ken is a graduate of Middle Tennessee State University with his degree in Psychology and Sociology with a concentration on Criminology. He has also graduated from the Metropolitan Nashville Citizen Police Academy and twice graduated from the Writer's Police Academy in Greensboro, North Carolina.

His first novel in the Music City Murders series, *When the Music Dies*, was published in 2012. He is currently at work on the third in the suspense series, *Stop the Music*.

Ken has spent his entire life in Middle Tennessee and proudly professes, "There is no better place on earth." Ken currently lives in Murfreesboro, Tennessee with his wife Sandra and their Cairn Terrier-ist, Molly.

www.kenvanderpool.com

Made in the USA
Charleston, SC
16 June 2015